Also by Linda Lael Miller

NEVER LOOK BACK

Linda Lael Miller

DOUBLEDAY LARGE PRINT HOME LIBRARY EDITION

ATRIA BOOKS
New York   London   Toronto   Sydney

This Large Print Edition, prepared especially for Doubleday Large Print Home Library, contains the complete, unabridged text of the original Publisher's Edition.

ATRIA BOOKS
1230 Avenue of the Americas
New York, NY 10020

Copyright © 2004 by Linda Lael Miller

ISBN 0-7394-4741-6

ATRIA BOOKS is a trademark of Simon & Schuster, Inc.

Manufactured in the United States of America

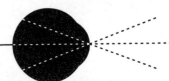

This Large Print Book carries the☐
Seal of Approval of N.A.V.H.

For Nancy Berland,
wonderworker

ONE

If there's a maniac or an ax murderer within a hundred-mile radius, he—or she—will come straight to me, Clare Westbrook, hapless attorney at law, like steel filings to a magnet.

Guaranteed.

Take Peter Bailey. Please—take Peter Bailey.

The very day I opened my new storefront office, in one of Phoenix's less sought-after neighborhoods, he wandered over from the mental health clinic next door and peered at me through the glass door, hands cupped around his face. It was a childlike stance, reminiscent of a little boy yearning after puppies gamboling in a pet store window.

Of course I didn't know his name yet.

Nor did I know he was under psychiatric care, though it wouldn't have taken a nuclear physicist to figure it out. He had that look—eyeballs spiraling in two directions, lean body seeming to hum with that frenetic energy peculiar to those whose brain chemistries are seriously out of whack.

I remember that I sighed philosophically and reminded myself that I'd chosen my office because it was smack in the middle of Dysfunction Junction. I'd recently inherited twenty-odd million from the father I never knew, and after weighing my suddenly expanded options, I'd taken the high road. Since bringing in a paycheck was no longer a matter of desperate compunction, I had decided to use my law degree and my hard-ass reputation to strike a few blows for the underprivileged. The ones who needed my expertise but were unable to write a retainer check—at least, one that would clear the bank.

The man staring through my door probably qualified.

I crossed the mostly unfurnished room, turned the lock, and let in a rush of hot desert air. October, and the temperature was still high enough to roast a lizard on a rock.

"May I help you?" I asked.

He recoiled as though I'd thrust something sharp at him, and for a moment I thought he was going to bolt.

"You're Clare Westbrook," he said, shifting from foot to foot. "I've seen you on TV. Lots of times."

Thanks to my recent involvement in some very high profile cases, just about *everybody* had seen me on TV, or in the newspapers. He looked me over, and his mouth quivered a little. Drool gathered at one corner, and he wiped it away with a feverish motion of one hand.

"You're prettier in person," he added earnestly.

I'm used to comments about my looks—shoulder-length dark hair, fairly good body, brown eyes, and high cheekbones. When I look in a mirror, I don't see those things. I just see *me*, a complicated bundle of faults, foibles, and contradictions. I'm smart as hell, for instance, but common sense often eludes me.

"Thanks," I said. "Was there something you wanted?"

"My friend, Angela—I think she's in trouble. A *lot* of trouble."

Now we were getting somewhere. I stepped back so he could pass. "Come in."

He hesitated, wringing his hands a little, then ducked back to the middle of the sidewalk to look both ways and then up. That, like his eyes, should have been a clue to his mental state, but I was trying to set up a pro bono practice, and for that, I needed clients. Just then, I wasn't too picky.

"This isn't a good place, you know," he observed, edging nervously over the threshold, sweeping the room with his gaze. "The bad people know you're here. They might try to hurt you."

A spark of uneasiness flashed in the pit of my stomach.

"Tell me about Angela," I said carefully, indicating the client chair facing my newly purchased desk. I hurried to move a box of file folders so he could sit down. "What kind of trouble is she in?"

He didn't sit. He seemed too agitated for that. "I shouldn't have come here," he said. "I'm supposed to be next door. I have an appointment with Dr. Thomlinson. Do you know Dr. Thomlinson?"

Ah, I thought. Yes. The doctor had introduced himself earlier that morning, warned me that one or two of his patients might stray my way. Many of them were paranoid schizophrenics, he'd said. No need to be alarmed—they were mostly harmless. Pick up the phone, and he'd send someone to round them up.

"I know him," I affirmed pleasantly, edging a little closer to the telephone on my cluttered desk. "If you're late for your appointment, I'll certainly understand if you have to rush."

He shook a finger at me, already backing toward the door. "You need to be very careful. The dolls. You have to look out for the dolls."

"Right," I said. "I'll be careful."

With that, he was gone.

I sagged into my chair, hoping that interview wasn't going to set the tone for the rest of my career.

After a few minutes I was over it. I got back to work, and since nothing out of the ordinary happened that day, or the next, I figured I was home free. I was destined to save the downtrodden.

Three nights later, feeling industrious

and—okay—avoiding some things that were going on in my personal life, I decided to paint my office.

My on-again, off-again lover, Detective Anthony Sonterra, and I were in the "off" phase again, leaving a serious gap in my social calendar. So there I was, at ten-thirty, with only my niece Emma's dog for company. Perched on the top rung of a folding ladder, I glanced with pride at the legend newly scripted on the barred window. My name, my degree.

It still did something for me, seeing them so prominently displayed. I'd earned my sheepskin the hard way, waiting tables at a Tucson bar by the ridiculous name of Nipples, hitting the books on every break, sleeping a maximum of four hours a night. After graduation, I put in five years of indentured servitude with Harvey Kredd—a.k.a. "Krudd," in police circles. Harvey specialized in setting the guilty free, and he was the shyster's shyster.

Believe me, I paid my dues.

Beneath my name, in smaller letters, was the proviso: Qualified Clients Defended at No Charge.

By "qualified," I meant innocent—as I

defined the word. Much to Sonterra's annoyance, not to mention that of the prosecutor's office, I see shades of gray, and I make allowances for extenuating circumstances. In the three days since I'd signed the lease on the storefront—a former lawnmower-repair shop—wedged between Dr. Thomlinson's clinic and a thrift store, I'd already turned away half a dozen prospective clients, and I wasn't even open for business yet. I'd accepted two others: Barbara Jenkins, a woman accused of conking her abusive husband over the head and rolling him into the fishpond in their backyard, where he subsequently drowned, and a slightly nerdy and very overweight young man named David Valardi. David was a computer whiz, allegedly the creator of the insidious Barabbas virus.

Now, paint-smudged, tired, and ravenously hungry, I was ready to call it a night. I stepped down a rung, and in one seemingly eternal moment, my front window splintered with a horrendous crash. A barrage of bullets slammed into the wall, inches above my head.

I dived for the floor and scrambled under the desk, where the dog, a Yorkshire terrier called Bernice, had pressed herself into a corner, whimpering and shivering. I groped for her, checked her for wounds, then gave myself a hasty once-over. Fortunately, neither of us had sprung a leak.

It's the neighborhood, I thought, with that odd detachment that comes of abject fear, remembering Sonterra's admonition. "Counselor," he'd said, just before our last big fight, "in Phoenix, nobody in their right mind sets up shop on a street named after a president."

I waited, braced for another round of artillery fire. My heart was beating so hard that for a few moments I couldn't hear anything but the blood roaring in my ears, and I was definitely hyperventilating. Clutching the dog to my chest with one arm, I used my free hand to ferret through the bottom drawer of the desk for my purse, and the .38 and cell phone inside.

I had barely connected with the 911 operator when I heard the sound of sirens and screeching tires in the near distance.

I gave the dispatcher my location.

"Officers are en route," she told me calmly. "Are you injured? Is the assailant on the premises?"

I closed my eyes, breathing deeply and slowly, trying to regain my equilibrium. "I have no idea where the assailant is," I answered after a few more desperate slurps of oxygen. "I don't think I'm hurt, but I'm scared." *Shitless*, clarified the voice in my mind, which always wants to put in its two cents.

More squealing of tires. A hard rap on the street door, apparently still intact. A shout of "Police!"

Still holding the dog, which had just peed down the front of my T-shirt, a violation I could well identify with, given the circumstances, I crawled to the side of the desk and looked around the far edge. After all, anybody can lay rubber, knock on a door, and say they're the law.

There, where the inside and outside light met in a blurry pool, I saw two cops, guns drawn. One was scanning the street, the other squinting between the bars on the door.

"That was fast," I told the dispatcher.

"Let them in," she prompted.

Duh, I thought. "Now there's an idea," I replied aloud, getting to my feet, dog, soggy T-shirt, and all. "Thanks."

The dispatcher chuckled good-naturedly, and I imagined what she was thinking. *Shots fired? All in a night's work, and not uncommon here in Presidentsville.* "Stay on the line, please. I need to confirm a few things with the officers. By the way, what's your name?"

"Clare Westbrook," I answered shakily. I was on a cell phone, rather than a landline, which meant the pertinent information wouldn't necessarily pop up on her computer screen.

My legs were like noodles. I swayed on my feet, took a firmer grip on the dog, and braced the cell between my ear and shoulder. Somehow, I got across the room, worked the dead bolts, and admitted the cops.

"Are you all right, ma'am?" asked the one on the left, who had been covering the street. His gaze dropped to the dog.

"Yes," I answered, surprised at the steadiness in my voice, and introduced myself. My internal organs had turned to jelly, but I'm resilient by nature. In a crisis, I slip into my inner phone booth and become Super-Lawyer, saving the hysteria for later.

"The dispatcher wants to speak with one of you."

The other officer accepted the cell phone, thrust at him by me, while his partner took me lightly by the arm and squired me to the nearest chair.

"What happened?" he asked, words that could be carved on my tombstone, I've heard them so often. Crouching in front of me, with a creak of his leather service belt, he took one of my hands and simultaneously patted Bernice's furry little head.

While I explained, as coherently as I could, the other guy finished his conversation with the 911 operator. I watched, out of the corner of one eye, as he took out his own cell phone, dialed a number, muttered a few words, then grabbed a bottle of water from the miniature refrigerator on a nearby wall and brought it to me, politely twisting off the lid first.

I narrowed my gaze, even as I accepted the water with a nod of thanks. I'd seen this guy before, I realized, in the group photo of Sonterra's softball team. I guessed, accurately, it turned out, that he'd just called his good buddy and given him an update on the adventures of Clare.

Without a trace of chagrin, Cop Number Two gave a slight, crooked grin, confirming my suspicions.

"Anybody out to get you?" the crouching cop asked. His name tag read "Atienzo," and I decided I liked him. His manner was gentle, nonconfrontational.

The dog began to squirm, and I set her down on the floor, stalling while I weighed the question. Two months before, I'd had some problems, but that was over. It didn't even occur to me to mention Peter Bailey; I'd written him off as local color.

"Not that I know of," I answered between restorative sips of ice cold water. In Arizona, it's important to stay hydrated, particularly in times of stress. I get those a lot.

"It was probably a drive-by," the standing cop said with weary resignation. "This isn't the best part of town."

Shades of Sonterra. Okay, so there are a lot of pawnshops, seedy dives offering "adult entertainment," and boarded-up businesses around my office. There are also some decent restaurants, well-stocked supermarkets, churches, and community centers. Should the good guys bail out, and leave the place to the scumbags?

I held the wet part of the T-shirt away from my stomach. "No," I said carefully, "it's *not* the best neighborhood. All the more reason for me to be here. I like feeling needed."

The guy rolled his eyes, and I could guess what was going through his mind. If he and Sonterra were pals, then he'd most likely been filled in on my history, my stubbornness (to which I readily admit, by the way) and probably my inherited millions, too. I guess he couldn't be blamed for wondering why I didn't just paint my toenails, lounge by a swimming pool somewhere, champagne flute in hand, and watch the dividend checks roll in. On the other hand, it was none of his damn business if I cut each and every dollar bill into little pieces and flushed them down the john. It was, after all, *my* money.

"According to what's left of the window," Atienzo observed, rising to his feet with another symphony of leather and jingling handcuffs, "you defend people for free."

"If I think they're innocent," I specified.

"Innocent," murmured the second cop, as though nobody had ever been accused of something they hadn't done, in the

checkered history of American jurispru-
dence.

I sighed. A lot of cops take a dim view of
human nature, and it isn't hard to see why.
In Phoenix, or any other major city, they run
across so much blood, insanity, and flat-out
meanness, they come to expect it. They are
outgunned, underfunded, and mostly unap-
preciated. You couldn't pay me enough to
do what they do, so I try to keep perspective.

"Some people, Officer"—I squinted to
read his name tag—"Culver, are simply in
the wrong place at the wrong time."

Culver gave a grunt. He was obviously
unconvinced. Oh, well.

Just then, through the shattered window,
I saw Sonterra's SUV whip up to the curb.
He'd made good time, I thought ruefully. He
must have been close by. Homicides were
common in that section of the city, and
even though Sonterra's official beat was
Scottsdale, he often worked in conjunction
with the Phoenix PD. When he wanted to
get somewhere quickly, all he had to do was
snap his handy-dandy cop light onto the
roof of his car and put the pedal to the
metal.

Atienzo busied himself checking out the arc of bullet holes in the wall, making notes for the inevitable report.

Sonterra boiled into the office like a dust devil, and slammed the door so hard that the last tiny fragments of glass tinkled from the front window.

"Fancy meeting you here," I said. We'd had our most recent disagreement two weeks before, when I insisted on moving into the modest house I'd bought in Scottsdale, instead of taking up permanent residence at his place, and we'd been at an impasse ever since. I operate on a need-to-know basis; if I'd cussed and moaned and even shed a few tears over the estrangement, well, Sonterra didn't need to know.

"Jesus," he said, taking in the shambles with a sweep of those chocolate brown, miss-nothing eyes, "this place looks like a back street in Baghdad."

"Of course I'm okay," I said pointedly.

His jawline tightened. Sonterra is a specimen of true genetic excellence, with his dark hair, smoldering eyes, and *GQ* body, but his personality could use a little work. The concept of winning friends and influencing people is beyond him.

"Is the dog all right?" he asked. Bernice scrabbled at his shin with her front feet; he bent to scoop her up, and even let her lick his face. She was in one piece, and there was no blood, so I didn't bother answering. I merely folded my arms and willed him to leave.

He eyed my yellow-stained T-shirt, allowed himself a shadow of a grin. No doubt it cheered him up to know I'd been peed on. "Get your purse, Counselor," he said. "I'm taking you home."

Half an hour alone with Sonterra, with him lecturing me on my poor career choices—just what I didn't need. I looked to Officer Atienzo for some sign of support, since I knew Culver would take Sonterra's side.

"You'll need to give a statement," Atienzo said.

"Tomorrow," Sonterra said flatly. I thought Atienzo looked mildly bent out of shape—detectives outrank uniforms in the cop hierarchy, and sometimes that rubs the guys and gals on the beat the wrong way—but in the end, Officer Friendly merely shrugged.

Sonterra, still holding the dog, fixed me with a glower. "Your car is in the alley, I take it, since I didn't see it out front?" The subtext was, *I've told you a million times: park in well-lighted areas. Are you trying to get mugged, raped, or murdered?*

"Right as always," I said brightly. "Good thing I didn't follow your sage advice. If I'd left my car on the street, it would look like Swiss cheese right about now."

Sonterra lowered his eyebrows and frowned, but I wasn't intimidated and I let him know it with a level look. That always pissed him off, and it prompted me to wonder what he saw in me, since he obviously preferred the acquiescent type. "Perhaps one of these good officers will do us the favor of driving it home for you," he intoned.

"I'll do it," Culver said, like a Boy Scout going for a badge. What a suck-up.

"I'm perfectly capable of driving," I submitted.

Sonterra opened my purse, helped himself to the keys, and tossed them to Culver. "Thanks," he told the other man without breaking his visual headlock on me. "Fifteen Twenty-two Cactus Creek Road. Just leave it in the driveway."

Culver jingled the keys. "Where should I put these?"

It was all I could do not to tell him *exactly* where to put them.

"Lock them in the vehicle," Sonterra said. "There's a duplicate set."

I took the dog back, but gently. It wasn't Bernice's fault that Sonterra suffered from an excess of testosterone.

"Done," Culver replied. He found the back door on his own and went out.

Atienzo paused beside me and laid a hand on my shoulder. "You're all right with this?" he asked, ignoring Sonterra's eyeball scorch. Atienzo had guts. I like that in a person. Plus, he was cute, with brown hair and green eyes and a very nice butt.

"Yes," I said. One of the things you learn while treading the hallowed halls of justice is to choose your battles. Sonterra being on authority overload, I was sure to lose this round, so I decided to conserve my personal resources for the next one. "I'll stop by the station tomorrow to sign the reports."

"Good," Atienzo said mildly. He ruffled Bernice's floppy ears, leveled a look at Sonterra, and strolled out to the waiting squad car.

Sonterra and I just stood there for a long moment, trying to stare each other down. I swear, if the sex hadn't been so good, I wouldn't have given him the time of day, let alone a big chunk of my life.

I watched as Atienzo got behind the wheel, switched off the blue-and-red flashing lights, and drove away. I inclined my head toward the street. "Is he married?" I asked sweetly.

Sonterra isn't the only one who knows how to get under somebody's skin.

Two

Sonterra pushed his shoulders back. "I have no idea," he said coldly, "whether Officer Atienzo is married or not."

I sagged a little as reality caught up to me. My office was a wreck, and the front window was in pieces. Locking the place wouldn't make sense, even with the bars still in place, but I didn't like the idea of leaving my computer, espresso machine, fancy phone system, and Bose radio behind for the looters.

Suddenly, I wanted to cry, and Sonterra must have picked up on that, because he softened a little. "Come on, Clare," he said. "Let's get out of here. There's nothing more you can do tonight."

"My stuff," I lamented, dropping into the

ergonomic chair I'd bought at Costco just a few days before, along with the desk. The few other things I had came from my home office, in the Cave Creek condo I'd moved out of when I bought the house on Cactus Creek Road. I didn't miss the old place much—I had my reasons for reticence—but I *did* miss having my neighbor, Mrs. Kravinsky, close at hand. Eccentric though she was, she had been a good friend.

Sonterra sighed. "Sit down before you *fall* down," he said. "I'll unhook your computer and load it in the car. What else do you want to take with you?"

I told him, and he got to work. That's the thing about Sonterra; he can tick me off with the quirk of an eyebrow, but when the chips are down, he's handy to have around.

Half an hour later, we were in his rig, rolling north on the 101. A CD, Latin and sultry, provided a stirring score, and Bernice lay curled up in my lap, snoring a little.

"Do you have a mole in every squad car?" I asked, partly to counter the romantic effects of the music. "You got there pretty fast tonight."

He looked pleased with himself. "The eyes of Sonterra are upon you," he said.

"You hungry? I don't think there's anything to eat at my place."

My stomach betrayed me with an audible growl. "We're not going to your place."

"Yeah, we are."

I stiffened. "Why?" As if I didn't know.

"Because I'm driving. And because you need a little TLC right now."

"I can do without your particular brand of TLC."

He grinned. "Can you?"

"I'm not in the mood, Sonterra."

"Fine. You've just been shot at. So you might just have to unbend a little and let somebody take care of you."

I was pretty undone. God, I hated it when Sonterra was right.

Fortunately, it didn't happen all that often.

"I repeat, Counselor," he said, switching lanes for the Shea Boulevard exit, "are you hungry?" He knew I was, but he liked making me admit things.

I guess getting shot at would ruin most people's appetites, but mine was in overdrive. "I could eat," I allowed, but grudgingly.

He took the off-ramp and turned into the parking lot of a major shopping center.

Finding a parking space in front of Fry's, a supermarket, Sonterra got out, locking the doors automatically. Bernice and I waited forlornly in the passenger seat, and I got the jitters again, reliving the elemental terror of being a target. My purse was on the floor, and I pressed the side of one foot against it until I felt the hard shape of the .38 stuffed into the side flap. It was small comfort.

Mercifully, Sonterra returned, with a bag of groceries in the curve of one well-muscled arm, before I suffered a panic attack.

"Steaks," he explained, after tucking the bag in the backseat. "I even got one for the ankle-biter." He nodded toward Bernice, who gave a little whimper-growl of acknowledgment. "Heard anything from Emma lately?"

I was grateful that he wasn't going to grill me about the gunfight at my own personal OK Corral. "Postcard from Munich," I answered. "'Having a great time. Send money.'" My niece was studying abroad; one of the perks of attending a private school, Scottsdale style, traveling with a group of twenty-two other girls, closely chaperoned by teachers and volunteer parents. Though I had had my reservations about letting her out of my sight for three months, Sonterra, Mrs. Kravinsky, whom I generally refer to as "Mrs. K," and my best friend, Loretta Matthews, had all lined up squarely behind Emma, working on me until I finally gave in.

Sonterra laughed. "She's a great kid." He glanced at me, and his eyes were soft and serious in the dim glow of the streetlights. "You did the right thing, Clare. I know it was hard, letting go, but think what a trip like that means to a thirteen-year-old."

"I can't even imagine," I answered. When I was thirteen, I was living with my grandmother and my sister, Tracy, in a trailer in Tucson. It was the happiest part of my classically difficult childhood, but visiting places like Munich wasn't even on the dream radar. Back then, we were into survival; we lived on various government handouts, along with my grandmother's Social Security checks and sporadic bingo winnings. "I miss Emma a lot, even with the puberty thing."

Sonterra didn't say anything, he simply reached over and patted me on the thigh. It was probably intended as a comforting gesture; instead, it melted my bones and sent fire shooting through my muscles. I knew it for sure, then: after the steaks, and maybe a little red wine, he was going to put the moves on me.

Because there were so many unresolved issues between us, I didn't want to wind up in Sonterra's bed. Trouble was, I didn't trust myself not to give in, thus stirring up already muddy emotional waters. He's not the most resistible guy on the planet.

Reaching his driveway, we waited while the garage door slid up. Sonterra pushed a button on his sun visor, and the inside lights came on. I can admit it: there was a certain solace in the familiarity of it all. Golf bag in the usual corner, cans of leftover paint neatly arranged on a shelf, the freezer whirring away against the opposite wall.

Sonterra carried in the groceries, leaving my computer, radio, and coffeemaker in the back of the SUV, and I followed with the dog and my purse.

"Take a shower," Sonterra said, setting the bag on the counter and rooting through it for provisions.

"Good idea," I agreed, looking down at the front of my T-shirt. I put Bernice on the floor, and she immediately trundled over to the dog bed under the windows and went to sleep. Like me, she felt safe at Sonterra's, and why not? It was her second home; the bed had been purchased especially for her, and Sonterra kept kibble on hand, and even a few toys. I could draw a few parallels here, but I won't.

When I came back downstairs, twenty minutes later, wearing the extra jeans and underwear I kept in the bottom drawer of Sonterra's bureau, along with one of his shirts, the steaks were sizzling on the stove-top grill and the wine was poured.

"What would you do without me?" Sonterra asked wickedly.

"Probably date Atienzo," I said.

He shook his head, still smug. "He couldn't do it for you," he replied, turning the steaks. Steam rose in the air, and it wasn't all from dinner.

I perched on a stool on the opposite side of the island and reached for one of the wineglasses. "What makes you think you're such a red-hot lover?"

"Past history," he answered smugly. His gaze slid, smoldering, from my lips to my throat to my breasts.

My nipples hardened. "How do you know I wasn't faking it?"

He didn't miss a beat. "Maybe it was the begging."

I blushed.

"Or the sweating."

"Shut up, Sonterra."

"Or the scratches on my back. I get a lot of heat for that in the locker room at the gym."

I took a gulp of wine. If I'd tried to pretend I was sipping, Sonterra would have known. "You love it," I said.

He laughed. "Yeah," he replied. "I do." He studied me for a long time, and his expression turned somber. "Did I tell you Eddie and his wife are separated? She's in love with some dweeb she met at work. An insurance agent."

Eddie Columbia was Sonterra's partner. I knew him fairly well, though his wife was essentially a stranger. I'd met her at a couple of picnics and softball games, and she'd seemed nice enough. "No," I said moderately, and refrained from pointing out that he and I hadn't been speaking lately, let alone catching each other up on the joys and sorrows of our friends. "I'm really sorry to hear that. Don't they have a couple of kids?"

Sonterra gazed off into the distance, and I couldn't help wondering if he was thinking about his own divorce. It hadn't been particularly acrimonious, as far as I knew, but giving up his stepson, Ryan, had done some major damage. He still missed the boy, and there was the usual guilt.

"Two little girls," he muttered. "They're caught in the middle. That really sucks."

I resisted an urge to go to him, slip my arms around his waist, offer what comfort I could. I knew what would happen if I opened myself up to that kind of intimacy, so I stayed put. No sense in adding to the confusion.

"Yeah," I said. "It does."

"I would have said they were the perfect couple." He let out a huff of breath, full of self-deprecation. "Just goes to show what I know," he said.

I took another sip of my wine. Not the time to offer amateur analysis.

Sonterra's parting from his ex-wife might have seemed easy, on the surface, but in his close-knit, Irish-Hispanic family, wedding vows were a lifetime commitment. For better or for worse, you made it work, no sniveling allowed.

Down deep, he probably felt like a failure, and even though I knew he'd worked through most of that, it seemed that the end of Eddie's marriage had set him back, maybe to square one.

"I don't get it," he said, still distracted. "My dad was happy with my mother. She died, and he grieved for a long time, and now he's happy with my stepmother. How hard is that?"

I figured it was safe to voice an opinion. "It can be *very* hard."

He sighed. "They're even fighting over who gets custody of the dog," he said, meaning, I supposed, Eddie and his soon-to-be-former wife.

"And you think it's got to be that way with everybody?" I asked carefully. I was on perilous ground. "You just told me that your dad is happy. Your brother and his wife seem to be getting along. And look at Loretta and Kip—they're so in love, it's a little disgusting."

He grinned at the mention of my best friend and her husband, but then the lights went out in his eyes, and he neatly dispensed with my theory. "Dad's from another generation. My brother would lose the family landscaping business if he stepped out of line, and he knows it. And Loretta and Kip are freaks of nature."

I shook my head. "It's sad, Sonterra. You're starting to sound just like me."

He didn't answer.

Together, we cleaned up the kitchen.

Then we went upstairs and collapsed into his bed.

He didn't touch me that night, and I was very careful to keep to my own side of the mattress.

THREE

When I awakened the next morning, I was alone in Sonterra's bed and somebody was licking my ear. I was disappointed to realize it was Bernice. I sat up, trying to gather the sleep-scattered parts of my busy brain, and noticed a cup on the bedside table. An oversize yellow sticky note was attached.

Gone to work, Sonterra had scrawled. *Another day, another murder. Eddie picked up your car—it's downstairs, in the garage. All your stuff in back. Recommend you stay put, but you probably won't.* "You got it," I murmured. If Sonterra had his way, I'd still be lying in bed, ready for a little belated love, when he finished his shift. Me, macho homicide cop, you woman.

I crumpled the note and curved a hand

around the coffee cup. Cold, of course. I wondered briefly how long Sonterra had been gone, decided it didn't matter, in the vast scheme of things, and gave Bernice a cursory cuddle before tossing aside the covers and getting out of bed.

My knees were weak. Go figure. I hoped I wasn't coming down with the flu.

After taking a shower, I raided my stash in Sonterra's bureau drawer again and came up with the necessary garb. While the caffeine was brewing, Bernice and I paid a visit to the backyard.

The phone was ringing when we got back inside, and I snatched up the receiver automatically as I poured myself a mug of coffee.

"Sonterra residence."

There was a short silence on the other end of the line, followed by a woman's slightly petulant, "Who is this?"

I stiffened. Who, indeed? "Just a friend," I answered, hoping I sounded casual. Sonterra and I were in a rocky patch, and we weren't having sex, so technically, he was free to pursue other avenues. It shook me, how much I hated that idea.

Another silence, breathy and faintly moist. "Tell him Leanne called, will you?"

Will I ever. "Sure," I said lightly.

Leanne, whoever she was, didn't bother with a good-bye.

Before the phone call, I'd planned to make myself an omelet. Now, my legendary appetite was stalled. I poured some kibble for Bernice and wrote two words on a sticky note, in block letters, pressing hard. LEANNE CALLED.

I finished my coffee, then loaded Bernice into the Escalade and backed out of Sonterra's garage with a slight screech of tires. Luckily, I'd opened the door first.

All the way to the police station, which is downtown, and not far from my office, I gnawed on my lower lip. I was keeping Sonterra at a distance. Maybe he was taking up the slack with somebody else.

Reaching the station, I parked, removed the .38 from my purse, sticking it under the seat, scooped up Bernice, and headed for the main entrance. The guys manning the security setup looked askance at the Yorkie.

"Seeing-eye dog," I said.

One of them grinned. Who says cops don't have a sense of humor? The other one checked every item in my purse, right down to my packet of birth control pills, which I swear he counted.

Bernice and I were finally allowed to pass, and I headed for the reception desk, where I filled out and signed a report relating to the incident at my office the night before.

"So that was you," commented the female officer on duty, reading it over.

I refrained from comment. Okay, so I'm well-known around the cop shops in two counties. I get into situations more often than most people, but it isn't like I do it to make a pest of myself. I just seem to attract trouble, effort on my part not required.

"We'll be in touch," the gatekeeper said, after a long wait.

Less than ten minutes later, I pulled up in front of my office. In the stark light of an Arizona day, I had to admit Sonterra hadn't been far off in his assessment the night before. The place *did* look like something out of a CNN report from Iraq.

With a sigh, I climbed out of the Escalade, taking Bernice with me, unlocked the front door, and went in. First order of business, call the window-repair people. I used my cell phone, since my equipment was still in the car.

They promised to send somebody over right away.

Taking them at their word, I settled Bernice in the desk chair with a dog biscuit and got busy unloading my stuff. I was down on the floor, hooking up my computer, when I heard the bell over the door jingle. Bernice growled, sniffed the air, and went back to her biscuit.

A chill went through me, and when I lifted my head to greet whoever was there, I half expected to get it blown off.

A young black girl stood just over the threshold, looking around with an expression of horror. The cutest child I've ever seen perched on her left hip, dark eyes round and luminous, hair in tidy little corn-rows tied with pink ribbons.

"May I help you?" I asked.

"I hope so," the girl answered. She was tall, with high cheekbones, and her hair, like the child's, was intricately braided, though with beads for accent, rather than ribbons. She frowned, taking in my casual clothes. "Are you Clare Westbrook?"

"Yes," I answered, rising to my feet.

"I'm Shanda Rawlings," she said, looking as though she wanted to sprint in the opposite direction. "I heard you take clients who can't pay."

"Under certain conditions," I replied, indicating the chair facing my desk. "Have a seat."

She sat, but gingerly, her gaze fixed dolefully on the pattern of bullet holes gracing the wall above the coffeemaker. She was visibly tense, and I didn't blame her, given the fact that the place obviously doubled as a target range.

"Can I get you some water or a cup of coffee?" I asked, while we sized each other up. I wondered what she'd been accused of, and if she'd done it or not.

She shook her head, bit her lower lip. "No, thanks."

I snagged a bottle of water for myself and sat on the edge of my desk. Bernice jumped down from the chair and trundled around to sniff at the baby's foot, and the little girl giggled and strained to touch her.

"That dog bite?" Shanda wanted to know.

I shook my head, and Shanda set the child on the floor, where she and Bernice checked each other out.

"I'm in trouble," Shanda said, watching her baby watch the dog, and tears gleamed in her eyes. "I wrote a couple of bad checks a few months ago. My probation officer says I'll probably go to jail, and that means Pretty Baby will have to go to a foster home, because Mama can't take care of her and work, too."

I stifled a sigh and sat back in my chair. "So this isn't your first run-in with the law," I said, venturing the obvious, based on the reference to her probation officer, and resisting the urge to ask if Pretty Baby was the child's real name. It certainly suited her, but it would be a hard sell on the playground.

Shanda met my gaze, and shook her head. "I used to have a small spending problem," she said.

I took a long draw on my bottle of water. "'Used to'?"

She made a huffy sound and threw back her shoulders. "I have changed my ways," she said, measuring out the words and firing them at me like missiles. "If you don't believe me, just ask Father Mike, down at the Community Center."

"It doesn't matter much whether I believe

you or not, Ms. Rawlings," I pointed out. "In this instance, the judge will be calling the shots. Do you have a public defender?"

"He's a doofus," Shanda said, with spirit.

"What's his name?" I pressed.

"Ted Adams."

I had to agree with her assessment. While most public defenders are bright, eager types, underpaid but dedicated, Adams was indeed a doofus.

"You admit you wrote the checks?" I asked.

She nodded miserably. "I did it all right."

"Why?" Rhetorical question. I knew the answer.

"I needed diapers and stuff, for the baby." She shook her head, watching as the little girl reached out a tentative hand to stroke Bernice. Fresh tears pooled in Shanda's eyes. "I don't want to lose my little girl."

"How old are you, Ms. Rawlings?"

She looked at me steadily. "Shanda," she corrected. " 'Ms. Rawlings' is my mama. And I'm almost eighteen. I had my baby when I was sixteen, since you're probably wondering, and no, her daddy is not a part of my life. Me and Maya, we're mostly on our own."

"I see," I said, feeling a pinch in the back of my heart. I set the water bottle down and folded my hands. "Well, Shanda, I do represent people on a pro bono basis, but generally, they're innocent."

"I wasn't innocent *then*," Shanda said directly, "but I am now."

I might have smiled, if the situation hadn't been so serious. Instead, I raised an eyebrow and waited.

"I know that sounds crazy," she went on, with another sigh. "I've decided some stuff, since I got honest. Father Mike said I needed to set some goals. I want to get a job and a car, and go to school nights. That way, me and Maya can have our own place sometime."

I wondered if she'd named the child after Maya Angelou, and if she had, whether it was because she read or simply because she'd caught one of the poet's appearances on *Oprah*. It might seem like a minor point, but I was interested just the same.

"Have you finished high school, Shanda?"

"I got my GED," she said, and those eyes of hers flashed with a combination of pride and defiance. "Took some computer classes, too, at the Community Center. Are you going to accept my case or not?"

"I might," I said. "I want to do some checking first. Starting with Father Mike. If I get so much as a hint that you're messing up, you're out of here."

She smiled bravely; no sign of the slyness I'd trained myself to watch for. "I've got his number right here in my bag," she said. "He wrote me a letter of reference."

I held out my hand.

The letter all but glowed with heavenly light. Despite the recent scandals, there are a lot of good priests out there, quietly doing their jobs, and this guy was plainly one of them. I copied down the phone number and handed the letter back to Shanda. "I'll be in touch this afternoon," I said. "What's your number?"

Her face fell. "Our phone isn't working."

As in, disconnected. I felt another pang of sympathy, for Shanda, for little Maya, and for the no-doubt hardworking Mama, who probably had all she could do to keep food on the table and a whole pack of wolves from the door.

"Maybe you could stop by again later," I suggested quietly.

Shanda was on the edge of her chair. "I have to take the bus," she said. "It's hard with Maya, and it costs money. So if you're just going to tell me no when I get back here, well, don't do me any favors, okay?"

I tried to see myself from Shanda's point of view. White woman, with an Escalade parked outside and a law degree on the wall. She had no way of knowing how similar our backgrounds probably were. For those reasons, and because I instinctively liked her, I was willing to overlook a little attitude, at least for the time being. "Maybe I could leave a message with one of your neighbors, or a friend—?"

Her face hardened, softened again as she lifted Maya off the floor and stood up to leave. "There's a pay phone at the convenience store on the corner," Shanda said. "I'll call you from there. What time?"

I consulted my watch. Assuming I was able to get in touch with Father Mike right away, an hour ought to do. I decided to give myself two, so I'd have a while to mull things over. Experience had taught me that the old adage was true; act in haste, repent at leisure. Not that I always heeded my better angels. "Noon."

Shanda glanced at the bullet holes again. "Funny," she said. "I'm trying my best to get out of this neighborhood, and you're here on purpose."

Before I could comment, the office door swung open and Peter Bailey rushed inside.

"They're after me!" he shouted, and dived behind the file cabinets.

FOUR

"What's the matter with him?" Shanda asked reasonably, frowning as Bailey crouched and peered around the edge of the file cabinet. She shifted her body, putting herself between Maya and my visitor.

"He's harmless," I said, hoping it was true, and put in a call to Dr. Thomlinson, who came to fetch his patient less than a minute after we hung up.

The doctor echoed this sentiment. I wondered why I wasn't reassured.

Once Bailey had been dragged out, and Shanda had gone, I got down to business.

Father Michael Dennehy was a hard man to catch, and the window repair crew showed up just as I was leaving my second message with his secretary. While the guys were measuring for the new plate glass and murmuring about women going into business in the middle of a slum, I picked up the phone and called Shanda's public defender.

By some miracle, he was in.

"This is Clare Westbrook," I told him. "I'm—"

Long-suffering sigh on his end. "I know who you are," he said. "Anyway, you've been getting a lot of media time lately. Lucky for you that Harvey Kredd got blasted, wasn't it? You might still be chasing ambulances if he hadn't. And how about that inheritance?" He whistled. "If I were you, I'd be on a beach in France right now."

I closed my eyes and, temporarily, my mouth. Maybe I hadn't liked my late boss very much, but I didn't consider his murder a career break, and I could have done without the attention from the newshounds. I especially did not appreciate their splashing my new financial status all over the media.

"You still there?" Ted Adams asked.

"I'm considering representing one of your clients. Her name is Shanda Rawlings." I pictured the files on his desk; the average public defender's caseload is formidable. "If you wouldn't mind looking her up—"

Adams's response was clipped. "No need of that. The kid's a chronic paperhanger. She's got two convictions behind her—slap on the wrist both times. Third time's the charm."

I bristled. "She says she's changed."

He laughed. "That's what they all say, Counselor. Or have you forgotten?"

"You sound more like a prosecutor than a defense attorney, Mr. Adams," I said stiffly.

"'Mr. Adams'? Gee, I was 'Ted' at the last legal-eagle banquet. I'm wounded, Clare."

Prick, I thought. "Thanks, *Ted*," I answered. "You've been no help at all." I hung up. The phone rang again before I could pull back my hand. "Clare Westbrook," I answered, ready to take Adams's head off if he'd called back to get in the last word.

The voice was friendly. "This is Father Mike. I have a note here that you called. How can I help you, Ms. Westbrook?"

Relieved, I explained that I was a lawyer and asked about Shanda.

"She's a good girl," Father Mike said with quiet conviction. "Best student in my computer class."

"You're aware that she's in a lot of trouble?"

"Yes." Father Mike sighed, and I could imagine him running a hand through his hair—if he had any. I can often guess people's ages by their voices, but in this case, I had no clue. "Like many underprivileged children, Shanda has made some poor choices in her life, but she's a very bright young lady, and she takes excellent care of her daughter. She attends quite a few activities at our center."

I had noticed that Maya looked healthy, happy, and well-fed. Her cotton dress, though most likely a hand-me-down, had been clean, every ruffle carefully pressed. "Is Shanda one of your parishioners, Father?"

A chuckle. "No. Shanda is not Catholic. She has issues about organized religion. But she's been participating in our youth program since she was fourteen. She's quite delightful, if a little on the prickly side sometimes. On occasion, she's been— well—*physical* with some of the other young people."

I knew all about being prickly, not to mention "physical." I'd bloodied a few noses myself, when I was a kid in Tucson, defending my alcoholic mother when she became the topic of interest during recess. "Maybe she just needs a chance," I mused. I might have been talking about Shanda, but I was thinking of my younger self, full of bruised pride.

"She's worth the effort," Father Mike said quietly. "If you take her case, you won't be sorry."

"I'll hold you to that," I replied, with a smile.

"Shanda won't be able to pay you, you know."

"Yes," I answered. "I know. This is pro bono."

"Ah," he said. "Well, if I can do anything to help, give me a call."

"You would be willing to testify on Shanda's behalf, if necessary?"

"Indeed I would," Father Mike said. There was a pause. "I heard about the—er—incident at your office. The shooting, I mean. There are gangs in that area, Ms. Westbrook. Be careful."

I promised to exercise caution, then we exchanged goodbyes, both of us busy people, and hung up.

The window guys were outside, unloading a sizable piece of glass from their van. I watched, wincing a little, as they carried it across the sidewalk and leaned it against the outside wall.

The telephone rang at twelve o'clock straight up. The new window was in, the crew had taken their check and gone, and I was considering painting my name on the pane myself. After lunch, anyway.

"Well?" Shanda demanded, the moment I answered.

"You've got yourself a lawyer," I said.

Shanda burst into tears.

I waited. I'm not good with tears, my own or somebody else's.

"Thank you, Ms. Westbrook."

"Clare," I said. I glanced at my computer, sitting idle, and my coffeemaker, which was empty, and gave in to impulse. "Shanda, how would you like a job?"

She was silent for a long moment. "Where?" she finally asked, in a whisper.

I laughed. "Here," I said. My gaze strayed to the bullet holes, next on the repair list. "If you're not afraid of getting shot, I mean."

"You mean, work for you? Clare, that would be *awesome*."

"There will have to be a trial period, of course."

"I'm really good with computers."

"No shenanigans, Shanda. Not even so much as a parking ticket. I mean that."

She giggled. "I don't have a car, remember? It would be tough to get a parking ticket."

I stifled a smile. "Be here at nine tomorrow morning."

Another pause. "I'll have to bring Maya. Until I get my first paycheck, I mean. Mama's working days, so there's nobody to take care of the baby."

"I'll advance you the money for day care," I replied. It wasn't that I didn't want a child in the office. It was the possibility of another drive-by bullet bath. I took a breath. "Shanda, you understand that just being here might be dangerous, don't you?"

She laughed. "Yeah, I figured that out when I saw the glass on the sidewalk and the chunks somebody shot out of your wall. That nutcase from next door didn't bother me, though." She paused for a breath. "First thing we're going to do is, we're going to move the desk out of the line of fire."

"You," I said, "are my kind of secretary."

"Assistant," Shanda said. "I don't care what you pay me, but I want to be called your assistant."

I should have known, right then, what I was getting into.

FIVE

After Shanda and I got off the phone, I called in an order for Chinese food. The window lettering and the plasterer could wait.

I was sitting at my desk, snarfing up sesame chicken and fried rice and sharing the odd tidbit with Bernice, when Sonterra showed up. My stomach jumped. Most likely, he hadn't been home to see the note about Leanne's call, which meant I would have to broach the subject. I was dying to know who she was, and I knew Sonterra wouldn't lie if I asked him. Maybe that was why I felt so nervous.

"Don't you ever work?" I asked, when he walked in. I pushed my sesame chicken aside.

"Hello to you, too," Sonterra replied, turning to assess the new window.

"Who's Leanne?" I blurted.

Sonterra faced me. Raised an eyebrow. "Somebody I met through work," he answered. He didn't move.

I felt a lump forming in my throat. "Well, she called."

"Here?"

I shook my head. Consciously relaxed my jaw. "Your place."

A light went on behind his eyes. He grinned. "You're jealous."

"I'm not," I lied.

"Yes, you are." The grin broadened. "Damn. This is great."

I felt my face heat up. "Are you sleeping with her?"

Sonterra crossed the room, leaned toward me, his hands braced against the edge of the desk. "No," he said.

"She wants you."

His eyes twinkled. "A lot of women want me. You, for instance."

What I *wanted* was to slap him—almost as much as I wanted to throw my arms around his neck and kiss his face off out of sheer relief. "Cocky bastard."

He laughed. I could feel his breath on my face, and all my nerves seemed to rush to the surface, thrumming in time with my heartbeat.

I swallowed hard. "If you're seeing this Leanne person, just tell me," I insisted. "Because if I find out you're lying, Sonterra, I'll tear your liver out."

"That's an extreme reaction, don't you think—given that we're at a standoff?"

I blushed again. "She wants you," I repeated.

"She'll get over it," he said.

"Do you want her?"

"I want *you,* for all the good it does."

"What are you doing here?" I reiterated, when I could trust myself to speak without bursting into inexplicable tears.

Sonterra plucked a piece of sesame chicken from the takeout carton and popped it into his mouth, savoring it as he considered his answer. I trembled, and a smile of understanding lit his eyes. He licked his lips. "I was in the neighborhood," he said huskily.

"Bull," I answered.

"We've had some very good times, Clare. Why can't we get back to that?"

I sat back in the chair, to put a little space between us, and tried to look cool. "You mean sleeping together whenever we felt like it, with no commitment on either side?"

"Was that so bad?"

"No," I admitted.

"Move in with me. Let's see if we can get it right."

I closed my eyes. Opened them again, quickly. Just the night before, he'd been telling me how disillusioned he was when it came to love and marriage. "No possible way." *Not without a wedding ring.*

He selected another piece of chicken, touched it lightly against my mouth, smiled when I opened for him. His index finger brushed my lower lip, lingering there just long enough to send a shudder through me.

"Why not?" His voice was a rumble, sleepy and deep.

"Because I'm not ready. Because *you're* not ready. Last night, you as much as told me that marriage was hopeless."

He frowned, looking puzzled. "Who said anything about marriage?"

"Who, indeed?" I shot back. "Damn it, Sonterra, I'm not shacking up with you just so you can have sex whenever you want!"

"You want to get married?" He sounded mystified.

I was pretty confused myself. I *didn't* want to get married—did I? "How do I know? We never get past the topic of sex. We never actually talk."

"Have you been watching Dr. Phil?" he asked.

I was mortified. "Go to hell, Sonterra."

"Listen," Sonterra said. "I've got next weekend off. Let's go up to my cabin. If you want to talk, we'll talk. We'll walk in the woods, watch a few DVDs, try to figure this thing out."

All of a sudden, I was scared, though I couldn't have said precisely why. "We'll strip each other naked and make love like monkeys as soon as we step over the threshold," I joked, but it was lame, and both Sonterra and I knew it.

He shrugged. "Maybe. But once we get that out of the way, maybe we can settle a few things."

"Like what?" He was turning the tables on me. I was confused.

"Like where this is going. You're right— we don't really connect, except in bed. I think it's time we either came to terms or called it off and went our separate ways, don't you?"

I wondered if Leanne had anything to do with this sudden change in the weather, and I couldn't say a word. I just sat there, with my mouth open. I closed it before Sonterra could feed me another piece of chicken. That little trick had already wreaked havoc with my senses.

"What's your answer, Clare? Are we spending the weekend together, and hammering this thing out once and for all, or not?"

Six

Spend the weekend at Sonterra's cabin, and maybe get dumped.

Spend the weekend in my new but empty house, bouncing off the walls.

Choices, choices.

I wished I could call Loretta for advice, but Sonterra was still looming over my desk, and I knew he wasn't going anywhere until he got an answer—read, the one he wanted. No way was I going to call my best friend and yammer about my wishy-washy inner child with him there, taking in every word.

"All right," I said glumly.

Sonterra pretended to flinch at my obvious reluctance, but that infamous grin was still playing at the corner of his mouth. "A little enthusiasm would be nice."

"Take it or leave it, Sonterra."

"Consider it taken."

His cell phone chirped. He popped it out of the case on his belt, flipped it open, and snapped, "Sonterra."

I tried to pretend I wasn't listening.

He frowned. That's the trouble with being a homicide detective; the news is rarely good. "Where?" he demanded. There was a long pause, then Sonterra barked, "I want the scene secured—now. Call Eddie and have him meet me there. And tell the uniforms to keep the reporters away. Last time, they showed up five minutes before we did and tracked blood all over the premises."

I winced at that last image, but my ears were wide open.

Sonterra hung up with a jabbing motion of his thumb, and no good-bye. But then, he didn't usually bother with "hello," either.

"Big case?" I ventured.

He was already on the way to the door. "A judge just turned up in an alley with a knife in her jugular," he said. "Film at eleven."

With that, he was gone. He could at least have told me the judge's name.

"Holy shit," I told Bernice, and reached for the remains of my sesame chicken. Call it morbid curiosity, call it ambulance-chasing, but given a choice, I would have gone with Sonterra if I'd thought for one minute that he'd let me. Ducking past crime-scene tape was his prerogative, not mine. Rats.

After sitting there stewing for a while, I finally managed to shift my attention back to the tasks at hand and called the sign painter, then the drywall guy. Stalwartly, I resigned myself to a dull afternoon.

I should have been so lucky.

I was just about to close up early and head for home when a familiar personage ducked in from the street, wild-eyed, too thin, and sweaty. Today, I reflected, Peter Bailey looked as if he'd built his personal philosophy around an intricate web of government-conspiracy theories. He wore heavy jeans and a turtleneck, even though it was a hundred degrees outside.

"Stay away from my file cabinet," I said, as he glanced back over one shoulder. Did he think he was being followed? Probably, and there was no telling by whom. I wondered if he was taking his medication.

Suddenly, he didn't seem all that harmless.

I eyed the nearest blunt object, my stapler, and casually drew it closer. *Oh, right,* mocked the pesky little voice in my head, which never gives me credit for brain one. *If he comes at you, you can staple his eyelids to his cheekbones.*

"Mr. Bailey—"

"Not today," he said. "I'm not Mr. Bailey today." His mouth opened and closed oddly, reminding me of a fish in dry dock. "I know who shot up your office. They wanted to scare you away. Next time, they'll kill you."

Now he *really* had my attention. I leaned forward, fondling the stapler. "Who shot up my office, Mr. Bailey?"

"Bad people. The kind who fly around in black helicopters, watching honest citizens. It's got to do with your boyfriend."

Before I could come up with an answer, or even another question, the door opened and Dr. Thomlinson stepped into the office. He was dressed in chinos and an oversize sweatshirt. "Peter," he said mildly. "You're late for your appointment." He gave me an apologetic look. "Hello, Clare."

Bailey's agitation increased, and his sweat glands worked overtime. An odd, sour smell wafted from his clothing. "You have to *leave* here," he said in a hoarse whisper. "They're everywhere. The people in the black helicopters."

"Peter suffers from delusions," Thomlinson reminded me in a mild tone. "Severe ones, I'm afraid," he went on, with a weary sigh. "Come along, Peter. We need to discuss your medication, among other things."

"Dolls," Peter sputtered. "Dolls, everywhere. They're evil. They're like an army. They're going to take over the world."

"Hush, Peter," Dr. Thomlinson said gently. "You need your medicine—"

"I don't want any more pills," Bailey said. "They make me crazy."

Can't have that, I thought, with an unsettling twinge of pity.

Under the desk, Bernice whimpered and tried to wrap herself around my left foot. I was going to have to look into doggy day care; the stress of coming to the office was obviously too much for her. And then there was the deadly peril factor.

Dr. Thomlinson drew nearer. "Peter," he

repeated, more insistently this time. "Come with me."

Bailey gripped the edge of my desk, as though to anchor himself in a typhoon, and his knuckles bulged, dead white. Words tumbled out of his mouth in a spitty, staccato rush. "They're after me, too!"

The black helicopter folks, no doubt. Or the doll army. Along with the FBI, commandos from the eleventh dimension, and the secretarial staff of the *Jerry Springer Show,* I supposed, though of course I kept this observation to myself.

Thomlinson took his arm. "That's *enough,* Peter," he said, and tow-boated the man toward the door.

I let out my breath. Bad people, dolls, plotting an uprising, black helicopters on the prowl. I hate it when that happens.

"I'm sorry, Ms. Westbrook," the doctor said, after giving Bailey a subtle shove out onto the sidewalk. "This won't happen again."

Bailey, meanwhile, flattened himself against the new window, steaming it up with his nostrils, smudging it with his sweaty palms, which were pressed to the glass. He was doing that fish thing again, with his mouth.

The sesame chicken curdled in my stomach.

I stroked Bernice's tiny, silken back, calming her, calming myself. "That's enough excitement for one day," I decided aloud.

Thus resolved, I locked the front door from the inside, made sure the coffeemaker was off, and snatched up my purse. The Escalade was parked in the alleyway behind the storefront, contrary to Sonterra's instructions, and believe me, I looked both ways and under the car before I made a dash for the driver's side, just in case Bailey had managed to give his doctor the slip.

SEVEN

The traffic was intense, and forty-five minutes had gone by when I pulled into the garage at my place.

As soon as we'd stepped inside the kitchen door, Bernice squatted and peed on the slate tile. Sighing but sympathetic, I mopped up the mess with paper towels while she progressed to her dish and sniffed at yesterday's kibble.

The house, the only major purchase I'd made after the windfall from my father's estate, besides the Escalade, was not huge—three bedrooms, three baths, with a postage-stamp yard and a pool the size of the average hot tub—but that evening, it seemed as vast and echoing as a medieval cathedral. Maybe it was because I hadn't gotten around to buying furniture, but just then, I figured it had more to do with my recent, and definitely eerie, encounter with Peter Bailey. Emma's absence was an element, too, and as obnoxious as Sonterra could be, I wouldn't have minded if he'd been around.

I picked up the remote, turned on the kitchen TV, and thumbed my way to a news report. I waited through three commercials, a piece on light treatment for acne, and five minutes of good-natured bantering between the local coanchors, which usually signals a slow news day. Finally, though, Sonterra appeared on-screen, looking exasperated, intense, and incredibly hot as he shouldered his way out of some alley, through a crowd of curiosity seekers and members of the press. Some hapless reporter shoved a microphone in his face and for one second, I thought Sonterra was going to jam it up the guy's nose.

"When we know something, we'll tell you," Sonterra snapped, and kept going.

A yellow banner, reminiscent of crime-scene tape, ran across the bottom of the screen, proclaiming, Celebrity Judge Murdered in Scottsdale.

The reporter carried on gamely. "Well, Benecia," he said, apparently addressing the female coanchor, back at the studio, "as you can see, the police aren't giving out much information in this case. All we can really say for certain at this point is that Superior Court Judge Henrietta Simpson has been savagely murdered."

"Terrible news, for the entire valley," Benecia lamented, as the cameras kicked in again on her end.

"Not to mention Judge Simpson," I added, just as the phone rang.

I snatched up the receiver, hoping for Sonterra, and details on the case-of-the-hour. Next, Santa Claus would beep in on call-waiting. "Hello?"

There was a short silence, during which I braced myself for anything from a sales call to a death threat, but then Emma came on the line. "Hi, Clare. It's me."

Good feelings rushed through me, pushing everything else aside. "Hello, Emma," I said, thumbing off the TV and sinking into a chair at the kitchen table. Small muscles tightened in my throat. "Are you okay?"

"Sure," she said, with affectionate disdain. "I'm awesome."

"Still in Munich?"

"Nope. We're in a hostelry in Florence—got here two days ago. Thanks for putting that money in my bank account—my ATM card is working again, finally."

I laughed, glad she couldn't see that there were tears in my eyes. "Don't mention it," I said. Emma was a force of nature in her own right, and all I had left of my only sister, Tracy, who had died seven years before.

"Somebody shot up your office," Emma said, cutting to the chase.

I closed my eyes. Damn the internet. Either Emma had seen the news on the *Arizona Republic*'s website, or someone had emailed the grim details from home. "That's true," I admitted, "but I'm okay."

I heard a quiver of fear in Emma's voice. "Who did it? Clare, is somebody trying to kill you again?"

"It was probably a random act of violence," I said, slipping into the all-too-common vernacular of our modern reality. "Please don't worry about it. I want you to enjoy your time in Europe—"

"Don't *worry* about it?" Emma broke in, sounding a little shrill. "I thought this was over. You need to close that stupid office,

Clare. Stop being such a do-gooder. You're rich now, you can—"

"Emma," I said gently but firmly, "stop."

She started to cry. "What if something happens to you?"

"Sweetheart, nothing is going to happen to me." In my head, I heard the sounds of glass exploding and bullets thunking into my office wall. I saw Peter Bailey's face in my mind, heard him raving. Maybe humor would work. "I have a great guard dog."

Emma made a sound that was part giggle, part sob. "How is my very favorite dog in the whole world? I really miss Bernice. Loretta and Kip, too, and Mrs. K, and Tony—"

The poor kid. Her real dad had been a career criminal, and I knew she cherished a not-so-secret fantasy that Sonterra and I would get married and live happily ever after. Although she had a close relationship with Loretta's husband, Kip, Sonterra was the odds-on favorite.

In my more unrealistic moments, late at night, mostly, when the rest of the world was asleep, I had a similar dream. "Everybody is fine," I said. "I'm thinking of putting Bernice in doggy day care, though.

It's hard on her, going to the office with me every day, and I don't have the heart to leave her home alone."

"Just make sure there aren't any bigger dogs there. They might be mean to her."

"I'll see that she's safe," I promised gently. Emma had inherited Bernice from my late boss, Harvey Kredd, after his untimely death, and she loved the animal even more than I did. "Tell me about Florence," I encouraged. I wanted her take on Italy. I also wanted to steer her away from the subject of people trying to kill me.

"Art overload," Emma said, making me laugh again, through my tears. "If I see one more crumbling statue, one more fresco in a grotto—"

"Poor baby," I teased.

Another silence. "I'm pretty homesick."

"That's okay. This is your first big trip. You're growing up so fast, Emma."

"Sometimes I don't feel very grown-up," she confessed.

I can relate, I thought, wiping my face with the back of one hand. "You're the oldest thirteen-year-old I know."

"If this gets to be too hard, can I come home?"

"Yes," I said, "but I think you'll regret it if you do. All your life, this will be the thing you didn't finish."

Her sigh bounced off some satellite and touched down softly in my ear. "Do you ever get tired of being right?"

"I'll let you know if I do," I answered, with another laugh.

"Are you seeing Tony?"

"Yes and no."

"What is that supposed to mean?"

"It means we're on speaking terms."

Emma spoke to someone on her side, then came back to me. "Got to go," she said. "More frescoes coming up."

I smiled. "Have fun, sweetie."

"Think about closing down that office, okay?"

"Okay," I agreed, though I already knew what my decision would be, and, most likely, so did Emma. She was a very smart kid.

I don't give up, even when it might mean saving my own life.

EIGHT

After the conversation with Emma, I took a diet dinner from the freezer and nuked it, but five minutes later, I couldn't have said what I ate. I wandered aimlessly through the house for a while, Bernice toddling at my heels, shaking my head at the couch, which looked forlorn in the new setting, being a holdover from the old place.

I checked my email on the computer in the den, another grossly under-furnished room, and counted it a plus that there were no predictions of my imminent demise. I shuddered, recalling the lurid images I'd received on that same screen only a few months before. One had been a photograph of Tracy, decidedly dead. The other had been of me, creatively doctored to show me with blue skin, a gaping mouth, and empty, staring eyes—remarkably realistic, missing only the bugs and animal bites.

I went upstairs to my barren bedroom, and into the adjoining bathroom. There, I took a short, lukewarm shower, keeping one eye open for stray psychos, dried off, and put on a pair of white terrycloth shorts and a T-shirt. I hadn't shopped for furniture, and I hadn't shopped for clothes, either. In fact, I was still wearing things I'd bought in law school.

I told myself inheriting millions would be a major adjustment for anybody. It wasn't that I was afraid to spend money; I just wanted to make good decisions. I'd set aside a trust fund for Emma, and paid cash for the house and car, against my tax attorney's advice, but I hadn't gotten much further than that. All I knew for sure was that I didn't want the figures in my bank account to define me as a person, and I'd felt the same way when I was poor.

I tried not to listen for the phone, though the truth was, I still hoped Sonterra would call and fill me in on Judge Henrietta "Henry" Simpson's sad fate. Judge Henry had been a television and radio star, in addition to her judicial talents, and her motto was Let 'Em Fry. She'd been big with the far right. I wondered if, somewhere out there, there was a liberal with blood on his hands.

I went downstairs to brew a cup of herbal tea, and I was taking my first steamy sip when the doorbell rang. Sonterra, with an update. I was sure of it.

I barefooted it to the front door and flung open the door without looking through the peephole first.

Major mistake. Peter Bailey stood on the step, wearing the same smelly clothes, clutching a fat manila envelope to his chest.

I tried to close the door, but he blocked it with one foot.

"Please," he said. "Don't be scared." He sounded coherent. I might have been marginally reassured, if his eyeballs had been pointing in the same direction. As usual, they weren't.

"Go *away*," I told him. Bernice growled uncertainly from somewhere around my right ankle.

"Today—I'm sorry . . . it was the medicine—"

I pushed on the door as hard as I could, but to no avail.

"Just take this," Bailey said, offering the envelope. "Look at what's inside. I'm not going to hurt you, I promise."

I frowned. Curiosity often gets the better of my better judgment. "What is it?"

Bailey's throat worked. Over his right shoulder, I saw Melanie Witherspoon, my neighbor, walking her one-eyed golden retriever, Waldo. She smiled, a little uncertainly, and waved. Maybe she was picking up vibes from Peter, maybe she was just being friendly.

"Proof," Bailey said, at last, shoving the envelope at me.

I took it. Melanie and Waldo started across the street, headed toward us.

"Hi, Clare," she said, with a note of cheerful determination.

Bailey stiffened, whirled, and bolted.

Melanie, Waldo, and I watched as Bailey disappeared around the corner at a lope.

"What a strange man," Melanie said. "I hope I didn't interrupt anything, but something about him made me—well—nervous." She was in her early thirties, like me, and sold antique jewelry over the internet as an avocation. I'd met her and her husband, Jack, who looked about fifty, when I moved in. Along with Loretta and Kip, they'd helped carry boxes, and afterward, we'd all sat around on the floor in my living room, drinking wine and eating pizza.

I let out my breath. "I'm okay," I said. Bailey's envelope felt oddly warm in my hand, as though he'd somehow charged it with his personal energy.

Melanie's blue gaze dropped to the packet. Her hair was a pretty auburn color, cut in a bob, and she had the body I want in my next life. "Really?"

I nodded. "Would you like to come in?" I asked, as an afterthought. I liked Melanie, and I certainly appreciated her concern, but the last thing I wanted was a neighborly chat. I was tired, my nerves were frayed, and there was that envelope. Even though it repelled me, I could hardly wait to look inside.

"I'd better get back to Jack," she said, with a shake of her head and a little smile. "Since his heart attack, I don't like to leave him alone for too long."

Jack was a psychiatrist and, since his illness, he'd been practicing out of his home.

"Sure," I said, hoping I didn't sound relieved. "Thanks for being so willing to come to my rescue, Melanie."

"I'm not sure Waldo and I would have been much help," she said with a laugh. We exchanged good nights, and she and the retriever headed back across the street.

I shut the door, locked it, and then just stood there for a long time, staring at the envelope Bailey had brought. He'd said it was "proof," but proof of what? His insanity?

Did I even want to see what it contained?

Damn straight, I did.

I went back to the kitchen, sat down at the table, my cup of herbal tea, now cold, at my elbow.

I considered calling Sonterra, and immediately discarded the idea. I was a big girl. I didn't need police protection to open an envelope.

Slowly, I lifted the flap. No explosion. No white, powdery cloud of anthrax spores.

I peeked inside.

Pictures. Black-and-white eight-by-tens.

A sick feeling jiggled in the pit of my stomach. *It's got to do with your boyfriend.* Peter Bailey's words rang in my ears, and I thought of the mysterious woman who'd called Sonterra's place that morning. He'd said she was just someone he'd met at work, and I'd believed him, but I'm only human, and I've watched my share of two-hour TV movies. I tried to prepare myself for the possibility that Peter Bailey had somehow managed to photograph an explicit encounter between Sonterra and Leanne.

I drew a deep breath and pulled the pictures out. There were at least a dozen, printed on thick, cheap paper.

I forced myself to focus. At first, I couldn't register what I was seeing. When I did, I was at once relieved and horrified.

The pictures were beyond bizarre.

Dolls. Naked dolls. Dolls with splintered china heads. Dolls with their hands and feet bound with narrow strips of what looked like duct tape. As disturbing as all the images were, one stood out from the others. It showed a group, all staring blankly into the camera, and incredibly lifelike.

Dolls, everywhere, Peter had raved. *They're evil. They're like an army. They're going to take over the world.*

I shuddered. Indeed, the dolls resembled, if not an army, then a small, macabre mob, about to advance upon the viewer.

"Sweet God," I whispered, my nape tingling. My insides churned. "What the hell does this mean?"

No answers came.

I called Loretta at home, and Rosa, the maid, told me she was out. I dialed her cell number. I needed moral support.

She answered in two rings. "Hello, Clare." Loretta always checks caller ID.

"I want you to see something," I said.

"See what?" Loretta asked reasonably.

"Pictures. I met this crazy guy at the office last week, and tonight he brought me this packet of pictures. He's trying to tell me something, but I'll be damned if I can figure out what."

"Shit," Loretta muttered. "You've attracted another maniac. What is it with you?"

"It's a gift. Are you going to look at these and give me some input—not to mention sane company—or not?"

"I'll be there in ten minutes—I'm just leaving Divas." Divas was the circuit gym Loretta had joined after she got tired of Pilates and yoga. With Loretta, variety is the spice of exercise. "What kind of pictures are these, anyway? If they're dead bodies, like before, I'm not sure I want to see them."

"They're dolls," I said distractedly, still studying the black-and-whites. They were really quite good, composition-wise. Possibly downloaded from some website with an address like Sicko.com.

"Dolls," Loretta repeated.

"You have to see them to get the full effect."

"I'll just bet. Did you call Tony?"

"And tell him what? That I want to report a doll atrocity?"

Loretta let out an audible breath. "I have to start hanging out with a better class of people," she said.

"Yeah," I agreed dryly. "First dinner at the White House, and now this. If you don't watch out, you'll have no reputation left."

Loretta laughed. "Bitch," she said.

"I love you, too," I replied.

Fifteen minutes later, her Lexus whipped into my driveway, and I was there to meet her. Even after a workout, Loretta managed to look chic. Her outfit was probably in the same price range as a Picasso print, and that was without counting her jewelry.

I had the pictures, thirteen in all, spread

out on the kitchen table, and I poured coffee for both of us while Loretta perused. She kept grimacing, and she flipped each sheet over, just as I had done before her arrival, looking for a name, a number, anything. Finding zip.

"This is seriously peculiar. You got these from the nutcase *du jour?*"

"Peter Bailey," I said, and gave her a brief rundown on the three encounters with my favorite mental patient. "It's a message, obviously, but the meaning eludes me."

"Me, too," Loretta admitted. "I still think you should show them to Tony."

"Maybe," I said, but reluctantly. He was up to his eyeballs in the Judge Henry murder investigation, after all. He didn't need me tugging at his sleeve.

"Clare, I don't like this. Whoever took these is a very sick puppy."

I folded my arms. "Gee," I said, in a wry tone. "What an insight."

Loretta skewered me with an impatient glance, went back to studying the pictures. "Obviously, it's some kind of threat, or warning. You're in danger, Clare."

A frisson of fear skittered down my spine. Bailey had scared me a little, but except for putting his foot in the way when I tried to close the door, he hadn't actually been aggressive. He'd seemed earnest, desperately so, but not really hostile.

"Thank God Emma is in Europe," I said.

"You've got to report this to somebody," Loretta insisted. "If you don't call Tony, I will."

"Oh, you're a big help."

"Have you got a better idea?"

"Yes," I said, brightening. "I think I do."

NINE

Like me, Dr. Thomlinson liked to get to work early. At seven-forty-five the next morning, seated across from him at one of the long tables in the free clinic's waiting area, I laid the pictures out for him to see. Bernice was next door, in my office, holding down the fort.

"Peter gave you these," he said reflectively.

Since I'd already told him that, I figured the remark was rhetorical, and didn't say anything.

Thomlinson shook his head, looking aggrieved. "He's been in a halfway house for the last six months, but I think it may be time to send him back to the hospital."

I'm not sure why, but I felt a pang of sympathy for Bailey. "Clearly he has some kind of fixation with me," I said quietly. "Perhaps he's said something in a session—?"

Dr. Thomlinson gave me an indulgent look. "You're an attorney, Ms. Westbrook. You understand about doctor-patient confidentiality."

"My life might be at stake," I said, feeling slightly less neighborly than before.

"Peter is quite harmless," the doctor told me, picking up the photos again, examining them one by one. Frowning all the while. "Still, these are very distressing images."

"Yes," I said moderately.

"He must have gotten them off the internet. Peter is quite good with computers."

"Does he have some kind of thing about dolls?"

A rueful smile. "Not that I know of. His specialty is conspiracy theories. As I've told you, Peter is a paranoid schizophrenic, Ms. Westbrook."

I held out my hand for the pictures. So much for getting a professional opinion. "Perhaps the police will be able to help."

Dr. Thomlinson surrendered the evidence, but reluctantly. "I hope you won't contact them—at least, not before I've had a chance to discuss this with Peter. Given his specific delusions, with regard to authority figures, especially ones in uniform, he might suffer a serious setback."

I stood. "I'm not unsympathetic," I said, somewhat stiffly, "but, for obvious reasons, I'm concerned. The man is turning into a stalker."

"Peter has never been violent, to my knowledge. And I assure you, he is normally well-supervised."

"Is he? Then what was he doing running around loose last night?"

I had him there, and a couple of beats passed before he answered. "No system is perfect, Ms. Westbrook," he said, spreading his hands. He got to his feet. "Even in the best facilities, patients sometimes slip through the cracks."

I looked at my watch. Shanda would be arriving any minute, closely followed by my client, Barbara Jenkins. Her trial was set to begin in a month, and if we were going to convince a jury that she hadn't drowned her husband in the fishpond out behind the house—or, at the least, hadn't meant to— we had some planning to do.

"I can give you until five o'clock," I said.

"If you haven't cleared things up with Mr. Bailey by then, I'll have to call the police."

Thomlinson's inscrutable face hardened. "Five o'clock, then," he said.

Shanda was making coffee when I arrived next door.

"Bad news," she said.

"Oh, great," I replied. "What?"

"You shouldn't write your password on sticky notes," she told me, pointing to the offending slip of yellow paper affixed to my computer monitor. With a few keystrokes, she brought up a picture. I stared at the screen, my mouth open. A doll, like the ones in Peter Bailey's photos, buried to its neck in a wooded area, with a tiny tombstone behind it. I squinted at the words etched into the marker.

I warned you.

I shouldered Shanda aside and sat down at the desk, looking for the sender's information.

"You want me to call the police?" Shanda asked.

Bernice leaped into my lap, scaring me halfway into my next incarnation. I shook my head. "Get Dr. Thomlinson from next door."

She nodded and left. A couple of minutes later, she returned with the shrink.

"Still think Bailey is harmless?" I asked.

Thomlinson looked at the screen and paled. "Oh, dear," he breathed.

"I want to talk to him myself, Dr. Thomlinson," I said. "Now."

The doctor seemed stricken. "I called the halfway house," he told me, still staring at the doll grave. "Peter's gone."

I tensed. Of course Peter was gone. He'd been out in the woods, burying dolls and taking pictures. After that, he'd probably made his way to some internet café, where he'd sent the email in question.

Something Dr. Thomlinson had said earlier came back to me. *Peter is quite good with computers.* Good enough, quite possibly, to trip through cyberspace without leaving a trail.

Wide-eyed, Shanda pulled out her own chair and shoved it toward the doctor. He sat down, looking a little shaky. "Immediately after we spoke," he said, "I telephoned to arrange an appointment for Peter. The director of his residential facility told me he wasn't there for bed-check this morning."

Shanda handed him a bottle of water, already opened. He drank.

I reached for the telephone. Dialed the nonemergency number for the Phoenix Police Department. The dispatcher listened patiently to my tale of woe, and it must have sounded pretty routine to her. She was polite, however, and promised to send an officer at the earliest opportunity.

Surprise. I got Sonterra.

I was in conference with Barbara Jenkins when he arrived; I looked up, and our gazes locked for a moment. Bernice ran to him like a long-lost friend, fickle dog, and he hoisted her into his arms. He and Shanda engaged in a muffled conversation, and I did my best to concentrate on the business at hand.

My client turned in her chair, saw Sonterra, and gasped.

"You," she said, her face bloodless.

"Hello, Mrs. Jenkins," Sonterra replied, with an affable smile.

I closed my eyes for a moment, mentally scanning the arrest report. If Sonterra's name had been in it, I would have noticed. "You two have met?"

"Over a body," Sonterra said. His manner was easy, but his eyes were watchful. Oh, I knew that look. *Damn.* He'd been in on the initial investigation. How had I overlooked an important detail like that? "Your husband's, I believe?"

Mrs. Jenkins spun in her swivel chair, glaring at me. "You know this man?"

"Sort of," I admitted.

"To say the least," Sonterra put in.

Shanda was clearly intrigued, but she had the good sense not to say anything.

"You weren't the arresting officer," I told Sonterra. "I would have noticed."

"I was there in an advisory capacity," Sonterra replied. "It was a reciprocal thing. Phoenix was short-handed, and one of their guys called me."

"Isn't this a conflict of interest?" Mrs. Jenkins asked.

"No," I said.

Mrs. Jenkins clutched her purse to her chest. "I don't think—maybe I should get another lawyer—"

"Mrs. Jenkins—" I began, but she was dashing for the door.

"Thanks," I said to Sonterra, when she was gone. "You just cost me a client."

Sonterra was unruffled, as usual. "She did it," he said dismissively.

I let that pass. "Why are you here?"

"Something about a dead doll?"

"I didn't call Scottsdale PD. I called Phoenix."

Sonterra opened his mouth.

"And don't tell me they're short-handed," I said, shaking a finger at him.

He grinned. "Okay, I won't."

"Wait till you see this," Shanda told him, and marched right over to my desk. In a heartbeat, she had the picture up on the computer screen again.

Sonterra followed, and I watched as his grin faded and the skin over his cheekbones drew taut. "Son of a bitch," he breathed.

"There's more," Shanda said, and produced the packet of doll photographs. If she noticed my look of displeasure, she ignored it.

Sonterra set Bernice down, then checked out the photographic evidence. His expression was grim. "What the hell?"

"A man named Peter Bailey brought them to my house last night."

"*Last night?*"

"Uh-oh," Shanda said, ducking her head and sidestepping out of range.

Sonterra slapped the pictures down on

the desk and leaned into my face. "Why didn't you call me?" Each word was clearly differentiated from the others, like a verbal telegram.

I bristled. "Why would I? Are you the head of Doll Homicide these days?"

Sonterra nudged me out of the chair and took my place, then entered a series of swift commands. "Nothing," he said, about two minutes later.

I stood next to him, arms folded.

"Tell me about this Bailey dweeb."

I gave another account, beginning with Peter's visit to the office, finishing with Dr. Thomlinson's discovery that his patient had skipped out of the halfway house.

Sonterra snapped open his cell phone, pressed a button, and gave someone a slew of orders. As quickly as that, there was an all-points bulletin out on Peter Bailey.

I felt a little better, though I was still in hot water with Sonterra. Nothing new about that.

He went next door, ostensibly to harangue Dr. Thomlinson, and returned with Bailey's mother's address, phone number, and other pertinent information.

"How did you do that?" I demanded. "He wouldn't tell me anything!"

"Come on," Sonterra said, neatly dodging my question. "We're going to pay Mrs. Bailey a visit."

I was stunned. "I get to come with you?"

"You'd probably follow me anyway."

We left Bernice in Shanda's care, went outside, and got into Sonterra's SUV.

"You think Peter will be there?" I asked, as we sped through the streets. "At his mother's, I mean?"

"According to the doc, she's his only living relative. It's as good a place to start as any."

"I didn't want to bother you with this," I said. It was the best I could do, in the olive-branch department.

A muscle twitched in Sonterra's jaw. "Don't look now, Counselor," he bit out, "but somebody wants to kill you. *Again.*"

I tried for a joke. "Besides you?"

He gave me a scathing look. "What else has been going on that you haven't told me about?"

"Nothing," I said, after a few moments of thought. My life is so eventful that sometimes it's hard to keep track.

His knuckles tightened on the steering wheel. "You're sure?"

"Relatively," I answered.

He swore.

Peter Bailey's mother lived in a modest brick ranch-style house, in an old but well-maintained part of Phoenix. The way Sonterra slammed on the brakes, leaped out of the car, and stormed up the front walk, it was a wonder she answered the door.

She was small, with gray hair and glasses that made her eyes look three sizes bigger. She wore a cotton housedress and an apron, and she didn't smile, or unlock the screen door.

"Yes?"

Sonterra showed his badge, introduced himself.

Mrs. Bailey peered at the ID, her nose nearly touching the screen. I wondered if she was stalling, maybe giving Peter a chance to slip out the back door, but then she worked the latch and let us in.

"We'd like to speak to your son, Peter, if he's around," I said.

The living room reminded me of my grandmother's trailer. There were crocheted throws on all the chairs, and every table was crowded with cheap figurines.

No dolls in plain sight, but that didn't mean there weren't any. I imagined them crowded into closets, with their little china or vinyl ears pressed to the door, and shuddered.

"Peter is living in a halfway house," Mrs. Bailey said, and if she was lying, she was flat good at it. "I haven't seen him since my birthday, last June. He's not allowed to go out very often, and it's hard for me to manage the bus, so I seldom visit him."

Sonterra wanted to tear the place apart, I could tell by the way he stood, and by the waves of Latin-Irish intensity rolling off him. "This is Clare Westbrook," he said, in a commendably moderate tone, inclining his head in my direction. "She's had several visits from your son, yesterday morning at her office, for instance, and last night, at her home."

Mrs. Bailey's eyes widened. She put a hand to her bosom and sank into an overstuffed chair. She assessed me with dazed concern. "He didn't hurt you, did he?"

I frowned. Dr. Thomlinson swore Bailey

wasn't violent. Why was she worried? "Does Peter—has he—hurt people before?"

She shook her head. "No," she sniffled. "He's very sweet. But with his condition—well—you never know what might be coming next. Once, one of the other inmates at the halfway house, with the same disease, went after a counselor with a kitchen knife." She paused. Shuddered. "Up until then, he'd been a lamb—just like Peter."

I wanted to crouch beside her chair, take her hand, reassure her somehow, but it was one of those brittle moments when it seems best not to say too much. I reached into my bag and brought out the envelope containing the doll photos. "He brought me these."

Peter's mother hesitated, then accepted the packet, pulled out the first picture, and sagged back in her chair. With her free hand, she crossed herself, the motion hasty and practiced. "My word," she said, and closed her eyes.

Sonterra and I sat down, almost simultaneously, he on the couch, me in the chair nearest Mrs. Bailey's. We waited.

"I don't understand," Mrs. Bailey murmured, after a long time. "Peter was never interested in dolls."

Sonterra's tone was still gruff, but it had softened a little. "Mrs. Bailey," he said quietly, "we need to talk to your son. He's left the halfway house. If you hear from him—"

Mrs. Bailey nodded. "I will," she said, and I believed her, though I wasn't so sure about Sonterra.

I brought out a business card, added my cell and home numbers. "If you hear from him, will you please ask him to call me?"

Sonterra tossed me a look, and I ignored it.

Mrs. Bailey began to cry. Handed back the pictures. "Yes," she said. "Is—is Peter going to be arrested?"

"Right now," Sonterra said, "we just want to ask him a few questions." He produced his own card. "The sooner he gets in touch, the better."

She nodded, dabbed at her eyes with a corner of her apron.

Sonterra and I stood, said our good-byes, and left.

"You think she was telling the truth?" he asked, after several blocks of thoughtful silence.

"Yes," I said. "What about you?"

"Hard to tell," he answered. "I see Oscar-winning performances every day of my life."

When we got back to my office, Sonterra didn't come in. "If there's another incident, Clare," he said, "I want to know about it. Immediately."

I nodded, unhooked my seat belt. "How's the Judge Henry case going?" I ventured.

"We're spinning our wheels," he answered grimly. "That woman had more enemies than Harvey Krudd."

I was surprised that I'd gotten even that much out of him. It made sense to try for more. I was always curious about Sonterra's work—and he was always taciturn. "No leads at all?"

"None I would share with you, Counselor."

"His name was Kredd," I said, opening the door. "Harvey *Kredd.*"

"Whatever," Sonterra replied. He might have been sitting next to me, but his mind was already miles away. "I'll call you tonight. Stop by if I can."

"Whatever," I answered coolly. Then I got out and semi-slammed the car door.

David Valardi, computer whiz and client, was there when I went into the office. In fact, he was seated at my desk, working my computer keyboard at top speed. Shanda stood behind him, looking over his shoulder.

"What's going on?" I asked a bit snappishly, I'm ashamed to admit. I hadn't quite shifted gears.

"Mr. Valardi is tracing that email," Shanda said, with admiration.

David, the classic nerd, fifty pounds overweight, bespectacled, and wearing a short-sleeved plaid shirt in need of ironing, did not look up from the screen.

"Wireless," he said.

I was clueless. "Huh?"

"Whoever sent this used a laptop," David told me, fingers still flying, gaze still fixed intently on the screen. "He—or she—is a pretty good hacker. They've been into your home computer, and this one, too."

"They've been in my *house*—?"

David spared me a look of pitying indulgence. "Probably not," he said. "It's easy enough to tap in, if somebody knows what they're doing." He paused, evidently scanning his brain cells for a way to describe the process to a low-tech type like me. "Especially if their intended victims are careless with their passwords," he added, in blithe accusation. "Hope you're not storing credit card information, or your Social Security number, on your hard drive. Somebody could steal your identity."

I didn't use credit cards, and who in their right mind would want my identity? "Can you tell me who sent the email?"

"I'm working on that," David said.

Fifteen minutes later, he hit pay dirt. "The name's Kravinsky," he said, with an air of triumph. "The address is in Cave Creek."

Mrs. K. My former neighbor. My good friend.

Impossible.

TEN

"Mrs. Kravinsky?" Sonterra echoed, when I swallowed my pride and called him with the update. "You've got to be kidding."

"My reaction exactly," I replied.

"What are you going to do?" Sonterra sounded distracted. Maybe he was consuming a fast-food lunch, and maybe he was drawing a chalk line around a fresh body. With his job, it was anybody's guess.

"I'm going to ask her about it, of course," I said, feeling a bit peevish. It had been a difficult day, and it wasn't anywhere near over. I'd called in the report, as instructed, and that was a major concession for me, given that I'm not inclined to account to anyone for much of anything.

"Hey, Counselor?" His voice was low, and

a little gruff. A verbal caress that made parts of my anatomy tingle. "I'm on your side."

I sighed. "Yeah," I admitted. "I know."

"Don't let your guard down."

I laughed. "This is me you're talking to."

"Sometimes I forget. We really need to get away this weekend."

I fidgeted. Damn. I had to agree again. "Yeah."

"Don't sound so reluctant. I promise it won't be a heavy deal." He paused, and I heard paper crackling. Lunch, then. "Gotta go, Babe."

Babe? Before I could decide whether I was amenable to that term or not, Sonterra rang off.

At three o'clock, Dr. Thomlinson dropped in, looking beleaguered.

"Any word about Peter Bailey?" I asked, knowing what his answer would be.

Thomlinson shook his head. "I trust the police are looking for him?"

I nodded. "Detective Sonterra and I paid his mother a visit this morning, but she hasn't seen him."

Thomlinson digested the news, such as it was. "When Peter is questioned, I would like to be present. As I believe I've mentioned, a trauma like this could trigger a major psychotic episode."

At the moment, I was more concerned about having a psychotic episode myself, major or otherwise, but I felt a little sorry for the doctor. There was an air of quiet frenzy about him that made me wonder if he took all his cases as seriously as this one.

"I'll do what I can," I promised.

Thomlinson left again.

Shanda watched him go. "That guy is weird," she said.

"Given his line of work," I commented, going back to the file I'd been reading, "it's no wonder."

At five o'clock sharp, I locked the place up and Shanda and I went our separate ways.

I'd put off calling Mrs. Kravinsky all afternoon, but now I couldn't avoid it any longer. I got out my cell phone and speed-dialed her as I wove through the late afternoon traffic, inching toward the freeway.

After three rings, a man answered. That got my attention.

I dispensed with the usual preamble. "Who is this?"

"It's Rodney," came the grudging response. "Who are you?"

Rodney Gerring, Mrs. Kravinsky's bad-ass nephew. Last I'd heard, he'd been in Yuma, doing time for assault and burglary—not that Mrs. K kept me up to date on that particular aspect of her life. I'd met Rodney once or twice, marveled at the hazards of otherwise innocuous gene pools, and put him out of my mind. That day, I was in a suspicious state of mind, I knew classes of all kinds were offered in prisons, and I immediately wondered about his expertise with computers.

"This is Clare," I answered, in the most pleasant tone I was able to summon, given that I considered him a waste of vital organs other people could be putting to good use. "Is Mrs. K around?" *Tied up in a closet, maybe? Or on the floor, bleeding from her nose and mouth?*

"Ah, *Clare,*" Rodney said, with a smirk in his voice. "You're the most popular pin-up girl in prison these days."

No more Ms. Nice Guy. "You ought to know," I answered acidly. "I'd like to speak with your aunt, please."

"She's working." The second word had a mocking note to it.

Since when did Mrs. K have a job? She was in her sixties, living on Social Security, her late husband's pension, and the occasional fee for giving a tarot card reading. She wasn't rich, but she wasn't destitute either. Or was she? If she had financial problems, she probably wouldn't have mentioned them to me, lest I think she was asking for help. Help I would gladly have given. "When will she be back?"

"Who knows? It's not my day to watch her."

"What kind of job did she get?"

Rodney snorted. "Mystery shopper. Whatever that is."

"So, Rodney," I chimed, wondering the same thing, "how was prison? Did you learn any new skills? Say, how to send really disgusting pictures over the internet?"

He was silent.

"Yo, Rodney," I prompted. "I'm talking to you."

"I don't know nothing about computers."

"Somebody sent me a nasty email," I went on. "From your aunt's email address. I'm guessing it wasn't her."

"I told you, I don't know about computers."

"That's easy to check," I answered briskly. "Ask Mrs. K to please call me as soon as she gets back. She has the numbers."

More silence.

"Rodney?"

"All *right*." He slammed down the phone.

Next call: Sonterra.

"I'm beginning to think you like me," he said.

"Think what you like," I retorted. "I just called Mrs. K's place, and I got her nephew, Rodney. Last known address, the penitentiary in Yuma."

"Well, well, well," Sonterra replied.

"He claims he doesn't know how to use a computer."

"These guys would rather climb a tall tree and lie than stand flatfooted on the ground and tell the truth. What's his last name?"

I told him.

"Got it," Sonterra said. "I'll run a check and get back to you."

"Thanks."

"Go home, Clare. Do something mundane. Let me take this from here."

"I want to talk to Mrs. K. Make sure she's all right." *Find out what the hell she was thinking, letting Rodney step over her threshold.*

A brief silence. Then, "I think I can make that determination."

"But—"

"Trust me. For once in your life, Clare, will you trust me?"

This time, the silence was on my end. It, too, was brief. "If I don't hear from you within the next hour, I'm going over there."

"Fair enough," Sonterra said. "I'll meet you at your place in forty-five minutes. Pick up a bucket of chicken or something, will you?"

I couldn't think of a gracious way to refuse. I wasn't even sure I wanted to. "Okay," I said, and hung up.

I pulled onto the freeway and started swerving and braking my way toward my part of town. I bought the chicken, and Bernice tried to crawl into the bag.

When we stepped into the house, the phone was ringing.

"Right on time," I told Bernice.

Losing interest in the chicken, she rushed

the patio doors, yapping her head off. I let her out and reached for the phone.

"Sonterra?"

A whistling sound came over the line, and Bernice was still barking. I put my free hand over my ear.

"Don't tell me there's another man in your life?" a strange, distorted voice asked.

I stiffened, every sense on red alert. "Who is this?"

"The doll man."

Bernice upped the volume, and I went to the patio doors, the phone still pressed to my ear, to investigate. She was running back and forth along the edge of the pool. I squinted.

There was a floater in the water, and it wasn't a blow-up toy.

I dropped the receiver and ran.

Bernice raced to meet me at the threshold, then shot back to the edge of the pool.

A man. Arms spread wide. Unmoving.

Blood curling from his head.

I jumped in anyway, flailed my way to the middle, and grabbed the body by one arm. Heart pounding, adrenaline surging, I paddled my way to the steps, hauled my burden out of the water, and turned him over.

Peter Bailey.

Most definitely dead.

I turned my head and threw up under the bougainvillea growing at the edge of the patio.

ELEVEN

Maybe five minutes passed before I got to my feet, clutching Bernice against my sodden chest. I stumbled back to the kitchen and retrieved the phone from the floor. "H-hello?" I croaked. "Are you still there?"

"Of course," answered the doll man. "I'm closing in. You know that, don't you?" He paused. "Getting closer and closer. Don't mind too much about Bailey—I did him a favor by killing him. Have a nice evening, Clare."

He was about to hang up.

"Wait!" I cried.

The line went dead.

Leaning against the counter, dripping pink-tinged water onto the tiles, I dialed

911. I gave them my name and address, and told them I'd found a body in the pool.

I was still in the same place and position when the phone rang in my hand. Shaking, I read the caller ID.

Sonterra.

I pressed the button, but I couldn't say anything.

"Clare?"

I tried to answer, but all I got out was a raspy squeak.

Sonterra said my name again, and this time, there was an urgent note in his voice.

"I'm—" I set Bernice on the floor. "I f-found Peter B-Bailey—"

"Clare, are you all right?"

"No," I said. "Not exactly. He's dead, Tony. He was in my pool."

Sonterra swore. "I'm on my way. Is anybody in the house?"

I shook my head, forgetting, for a moment, that he couldn't see me. "No," I said. "I spoke to him on the telephone—the killer—"

"Go to the neighbors' place." Over the phone, I heard Sonterra's car door slam, then the engine starting up with a roar. "You did call 911, right?"

My body began to vibrate with chills. "Yes," I said.

"Get out of the house, Clare." With that, he was gone.

I flashed on a book I'd read once. The heroine was home alone, and the bad guy called her from another part of the house, using a cell phone.

I grabbed up Bernice and bolted for the front door.

The Witherspoons, the only neighbors I even remotely knew, were not at home. I stood in the middle of the street, waiting.

Sonterra and Eddie Columbia, his partner, arrived at the same time as the squad car. Eddie stopped to put an arm around me, while Sonterra and the two uniformed cops ran into the house.

An ambulance arrived, siren blaring.

"Let's get you inside," Eddie said gently. He took Bernice in one arm, and supported me with the other.

The EMTs practically knocked us over, rushing to the scene.

"There's no need to hurry," I said, to no one in particular.

Eddie sat me down at the kitchen table, put Bernice on her dog bed. "Catch your breath, Clare," he said kindly. "Put your head between your knees if you feel faint."

I wanted out of those wet, bloody clothes, and I craved a hot shower. I spent a few minutes recovering, then went into the laundry room, grabbed pink sweatpants and a T-shirt from the dryer, and proceeded to the downstairs bathroom. Eddie had the electric teakettle going when I returned to the kitchen, having scoured myself from head to foot.

"What happened?" he asked, getting down two cups and dropping a tea bag into each one.

Shivering again, even though I was warm and dry, I told him everything I could remember.

More detectives arrived, along with a crime scene crew. Through the patio doors, I could see Sonterra and the uniforms crouched beside Peter Bailey's body. The EMTs stood nearby, helplessly, waiting for instructions.

"I don't think it happened here," I told Eddie. I probably sounded pretty drifty, and I admit I was going by instinct. The house didn't *feel* as if a murder had occurred within its walls.

"This 'doll man' character—did you recognize his voice?"

I sipped my tea, hoping it would stay down. "No," I answered. "My God. I can't believe this is happening—"

Eddie patted my hand. He's a clean-cut type, Wally Cleaver all grown up. I wondered why his wife didn't love him anymore. "Try to stay calm."

Sonterra came in, touched my shoulder. "You okay, Counselor?"

"Oh, I'm great," I replied.

Sonterra had already turned his attention to Eddie. "Call the department. Have Rodney Gerring picked up."

My heart slipped a few notches down my spine. "Mrs. K will be frantic," I protested, but nobody seemed to be listening. In fact, Eddie was already on the phone to headquarters.

Sonterra crouched in front of my chair, took both my hands in his. I wondered if they felt as cold to him as they did to me. "We'll have the body out of here as soon as we can, Clare," he said gently.

"Did you see Rodney? When you went to Mrs. K's, I mean?" I asked. There was a corpse in my backyard, but suddenly all I could think about was Mrs. Kravinsky.

"Yes," Sonterra said. "And I ran the background check. He was telling the truth, at least about his computer skills. According to his prison records, he's functionally illiterate. One interesting note, though. He was in the same halfway house as Peter Bailey."

I tried to process that, but it was as if someone had stuffed my head with cotton batting. "Was Mrs. K there? You didn't upset her, did you?"

Sonterra squeezed my hands. "No and no. She was at work. Gerring was there by himself. Apparently, he's moved in."

"You think Rodney killed Peter Bailey?" Like I said, I wasn't tracking all that well.

"The halfway house connection bears looking into, but I'd say, probably not. Eddie and I were with him until an hour ago, and if he did the deed earlier in the day, there would have been blood. He'd have had to clean up, and believe me, this guy hasn't showered or bathed in at least a week."

I was baffled. "If you don't think he did it, why—?"

Instead of answering me, Sonterra spoke

to Eddie. "Ask for a warrant to pick up Mrs. Kravinsky's computer."

Eddie, about to hang up, complied with the request.

Sonterra focused on me again. "I don't want you to stay here alone."

"Then let me go with you."

"Not a chance."

"I rode along this morning, to Mrs. Bailey's place—"

Sonterra released my hands, rose to his full height. The set of his shoulders and jaw-line let me know he was going to be im-placable. "Error in judgment on my part," he said. "I could lose my shield for taking a civilian on a call."

I glanced at Eddie, who averted his gaze. In most respects, Eddie was no pushover, but Sonterra was the senior officer in their little team and, as the junior partner, he usu-ally caved.

Now that the adrenaline rush was subsid-ing, my brain was back in the argumentative mode. "But you couldn't legally stop me from going to visit my friend," I mused. "Driving my own car, I mean."

Sonterra lowered his brows. "Short of tying you up and throwing you into a closet," he intoned, "no."

I blinked at him, making it sappy. "You wouldn't do that. For one thing, I would never forgive you. For another, there is an officer of the law present. You'd come to my aid, wouldn't you, Eddie?"

"Shit," Eddie said miserably. My hero.

"All right," Sonterra conceded pettishly. "We'll take your car." It must have been some kind of record—Sonterra had given in, twice in one day. Maybe to save face, he waggled a finger at me. "Mrs. K is your friend, so I'll lay my badge on the line, but if you interfere, Clare—in any way—you'll have me to deal with."

I shrank back and widened my eyes, as if expecting a blow. "I wouldn't *think* of inter-fering," I said.

"Oh, right," Sonterra responded, holding out one hand. I knew what he wanted: my car keys. I gave them up gladly and scooped Bernice up in one arm.

Leaving Eddie to supervise the crime scene and removal of the body, Sonterra, the dog, and I set out for Mrs. K's condo in Cave Creek, saying little along the way.

When we arrived, her Buick was parked in

the driveway, and she opened her front door as we came up the walk, looking pleased and worried. She was clad in one of her collection of homemade caftans, dark blue with stars and moons, a microcosm of the known universe.

"Clare," she said fondly.

I kissed her cheek, taking care not to put an eye out on the Dear Abby curl jutting from the right side of her head. I've always regarded Mrs. K's hair as a lethal weapon.

Rodney loomed, shirtless, in the doorway behind her. His belly hung over his ragged sweatpants, and a huge geisha tattoo peeked through the jungle of hair on his chest. "You again?" he said, speaking to Sonterra.

"Rodney," Mrs. K scolded affectionately. "Mind your manners."

Just then, a squad car skimmed up to the curb, and an officer got out, papers in hand. The warrant Eddie had requested from my kitchen, I assumed. Sonterra and Eddie's earlier visit had been routine, based on the facts that the doll email had come from Mrs. K's computer, and Rodney and Peter Bailey had been housemates. Bailey's murder gave them reason to probe deeper.

Mrs. K looked at me. "Clare, what's happening?"

I took her arm. "You'd better sit down," I said.

Sonterra met the policeman in the middle of the driveway and collected the paperwork. Rodney stepped back, though grudgingly, to let Mrs. K and me come inside.

I settled her on the couch, sat down beside her, holding her hand. "Mrs. K, does anyone else use your computer, besides you and Rodney?"

She blinked rapidly. "I don't use it at all," she said. She looked up at her nephew, confused. "Didn't your girlfriend hook it up?"

Girlfriend? I tried to imagine what kind of woman would date Rodney Gerring, chronically unemployed and with a prison record. It wasn't a pretty picture.

Rodney grimaced. "Yeah," he said, as if the word had been dragged out of him. He'd claimed that he didn't know how to use a computer, and the prison records affirmed that he hadn't taken classes, but—duh—it appeared he'd been lying about that.

Sonterra came in, presented the warrant to Mrs. K. "I'm sorry," he said gruffly.

"Why do you have to take the computer?" she asked.

"We have reason to believe it might contain evidence regarding a crime," Sonterra replied. "It will be returned as soon as possible."

I knew that wasn't necessarily true, and gave Sonterra a look.

Mrs. K went frighteningly pale. "All right, then," she responded, sounding resigned.

The computer sat on the writing desk, in front of the window. Sonterra began unhooking the various cords. Rodney hovered nearby, clearly resentful but, evidently, smart enough not to open his mouth.

"Disks?" Sonterra asked him.

Grumbling under his breath, Rodney yanked open a drawer and handed over a box of 3.5 floppies.

"I didn't send no pictures," he said.

Sonterra ignored that. "Do you know a man named Peter Bailey?"

"No," Rodney said.

"Sure you do," Mrs. K put in innocently, still clinging to my hand. "You remember,

Rodney. I met him at your going-away party, when you left the home—"

Rodney silenced his aunt with a poisonous look, but of course it was too late.

"What's her name, Mrs. K?" I asked gently. "The girlfriend, I mean."

"Angela, I think," Mrs. K murmured. Her gaze seemed to turn inward as she searched her memory. "Angela Kerrigan."

Sonterra spared me an appreciative if slightly grudging glance, then nodded as if to say, *Good work.*

"Do you have an address for Angela?" I asked carefully.

Mrs. K shook her head. "Rodney?"

If looks could kill, Mrs. K would have been a goner for sure. I held her hand a little more tightly.

"I don't know where she lives now. They kicked her out of the halfway house for drugging."

"And you haven't been in contact with her since?" Sonterra pressed.

"Maybe in a chat room."

"But you don't know anything about computers," Sonterra said. He handed the computer tower to the policeman waiting just inside the door. "Put on a shirt, Mr. Gerring. We're taking you in for questioning."

"What in the world is going on?" Mrs. K pleaded.

I put an arm around her. "It's all right," I said. "The police want to ask Rodney some questions, that's all."

"What kind of questions?"

I looked at Sonterra, who nodded again, and turned my gaze back to my friend's fretful face. "There's been a murder, Mrs. K," I said. "When I came home from work today, I found Peter Bailey floating in my swimming pool."

Tears welled in Mrs. K's eyes, and she put a hand to her heart. "That poor young man," she murmured. "But why are they arresting Rodney?"

"We aren't arresting him," Sonterra said, but there was a silent *Not yet* attached.

Rodney had left the room, ostensibly to put on his shirt.

A thought struck me. Mrs. K's condo was a mirror image of the one I'd occupied before moving to the new house.

"There's a window in the second bedroom," I told Sonterra. "It's pretty small, but—"

"Thanks," he said, and followed Rodney's trail.

"I know Rodney wouldn't kill anyone," Mrs. K said anxiously. "He's been in trouble, sure, but he's never been violent. Why, when he was a little boy, he was the dearest thing."

I patted her hand, trying to imagine the hulking Rodney as a little anything, let alone dear. "Don't worry," I said, listening for a scuffle.

I wasn't disappointed.

Rodney started yelling, and Sonterra appeared in the doorway to the hall.

"The bastard is stuck in the window," he said.

TWELVE

I would have gone to look, but Mrs. K swooned.

"You're on your own," I told Sonterra, and hurried to get a cold washcloth.

Within a few moments, Mrs. K came around.

Sonterra and the officer extricated Rodney from the window, put him in handcuffs lest he try to escape again, and loaded him into the back of the squad car, along with the confiscated computer equipment and floppy disks.

Mrs. K was in tears by then. "He didn't do it," she said. "I know he didn't do it."

I recalled Sonterra's theory, presented at my house. Rodney probably *hadn't* committed the murder, since there would surely have been blood and he clearly hadn't been near a bathtub or a shower for some time. "There's no evidence that Rodney was directly involved," I told her, glad to be able to offer some small reassurance. I drew a deep breath. "Mrs. K, Peter Bailey brought me a packet of very disturbing pictures last night—dolls in various poses. Then, today, I received another photo, like the others, by email. It was traced to your computer."

Mrs. K looked as though she might faint again, so I put the moist washcloth against the back of her neck again. "Oh, my," she said.

"Tell me what you know about Angela Kerrigan," I urged.

She shook her head. "Not much," she said. "She's a skinny little thing, blond with black roots. I only saw her once, at Rodney's party. She was wearing torn jeans and one of those skimpy little tops—the stretchy kind? Oh, and her right eyebrow was pierced." She stopped, and a tear slipped down her powdery cheek. "Clare, Rodney will need an attorney. Will you represent him?"

I should have seen that coming, but I didn't. I was blindsided.

"I'm not sure," I said hesitantly.

"Please," Mrs. K whispered, and I could see by the expression in her eyes that she was prepared to call in all her markers, if necessary. Being one of my two best friends, she had plenty of those. "I—I know Rodney isn't very appealing, but he can't go back to prison. It would be the end of him."

I nodded, to show that I understood, and that I remembered all Mrs. K had done for me since we met, shortly after I went to work for Harvey Kredd. When Emma and I moved into our rented condo next door, she'd welcomed us with the first of many casseroles. She'd been a mainstay from the beginning, looking after Emma when the need arose, babying me when I was sick, even lending me grocery money when I was between paychecks. And that was just the beginning.

I owed her big-time.

"Will you do it, Clare?" she pressed. "Please?"

"Of course," I answered, stifling a sigh. Sonterra wasn't going to like this one bit, but what else was new? He would have to understand.

"You'll go to the police station with him? Be there during questioning?"

I nodded, albeit glumly. First a dead body in my pool, and now this. Another stellar chapter in the legend of Clare Westbrook.

Bernice, who had been exploring the condo since we came in, jumped up beside Mrs. K and licked her arm.

Mrs. K sniffled, managed a smile. "I knew I could count on you, Clare," she said, and petted Bernice.

Sonterra reappeared, standing in the doorway, rimmed in the last light of the day. "Will you be all right, Mrs. Kravinsky?" he asked.

She nodded.

He didn't move. "I'm sorry about this," he said.

"I know, dear," Mrs. K answered.

I got to my feet, collected my dog. I was about to invite her to come and stay at my place when I recalled that it was a crime scene. It was entirely possible that I wouldn't be allowed to stay there myself.

"As soon as I know anything, I'll call you," I promised, and turned to approach Sonterra.

He stepped aside.

"What do you mean, you'll call her as soon as you know anything?" he asked, as we headed for the Escalade.

Might as well get it over with. "I'm Rodney's lawyer now," I said.

Sonterra stopped in his tracks. *"What?"*

I faced him, and we stood like two Old West gunslingers, prepared to slap leather. "Mrs. K asked me to represent him. After all she's done for me, I simply couldn't say no."

Sonterra, it turned out, was full of surprises. "Okay," he said.

I stared at him. "'Okay'?"

He gave a semblance of a shrug. "In your place, I'd probably do the same thing."

My mouth dropped open. Sonterra grinned, took my elbow, and squired Bernice and me to the passenger door of my Escalade. The squad car pulled away from the curb, with my newest client handcuffed behind the inside grille.

"I don't envy you this job," he told me, as he got behind the wheel and turned the key in the ignition.

"Do you still think he's innocent?"

Sonterra backed out of Mrs. K's driveway, shifted into drive, and we were rolling.

"Sorry," he said. "I can't comment. Conflict of interest, and all that."

I frowned. "Come on, Sonterra. I'm entitled to full disclosure."

"That's your opinion," he replied. "You can't take the dog to headquarters. We'll drop her off at my place on our way."

"I was the one who tipped you off about the bedroom window," I reminded him. "If it hadn't been for me, Rodney might have gotten away. You owe me, Sonterra."

"Put it on my tab," he said.

It took fifteen minutes to drive to Sonterra's, and another ten to get Bernice settled.

When we got to Scottsdale PD, Eddie and a couple of technicians met us in the parking lot. The techs took charge of Mrs. K's computer stuff, and Eddie informed us that Rodney was waiting in an interrogation room.

"Are you guys finished at my place?" I asked hopefully.

Eddie shook his head. "The ME's people are there, looking for forensic evidence. I'm afraid it's off-limits for a while."

"Great," I muttered. "Where am I going to sleep?"

Sonterra smiled to himself.

Inside the police station, I went through a series of security checks. Eddie and Sonterra, of course, breezed right by.

When I got to Rodney, he was seated at a wooden table, his shaved head down, his meaty shoulders hunched. I pictured him stuck in the bedroom window at Mrs. K's and tried to work up some professional sympathy.

"I want some time alone with my client," I informed Eddie and Sonterra, who were conferring in a corner of the room.

Rodney looked up. "You're going to be my lawyer?"

"Yes," I said.

"I'm screwed."

Sonterra and Eddie left the room. Sonterra might have been smirking a little.

"Tell me about Angela Kerrigan," I said, sitting down across from Mr. Wonderful and getting a sobering whiff of his BO. "No bullshit, Rodney. No fancy footwork. You're in deep doo-doo here, and I'm your main chance, so you'd better cooperate."

Rodney folded his arms on the tabletop and laid his head on them. "You're on their side. You don't care what happens to me."

"You're right on one count," I said, pulling a pad and pen from my bag. "I'll leave you to guess which. Your aunt is one of my closest friends, and I'd do just about anything for her. So spill it. You said you spoke with Angela in a chat room. When was that?"

Rodney didn't lift his head, so his voice was muffled. "A couple of days ago, maybe. I'm not sure."

"Did she visit you at Yuma?"

"I didn't know her then."

"Where can I find her?"

Rodney was doing his ostrich number again. The top of his head gleamed through the stubble that remained of his hair.

"Rodney," I persisted.

"She stays wherever somebody will let her crash."

I put a shrug in my voice. "The police will find her."

Rodney lifted his head. "I didn't kill anybody," he said.

"I know," I replied.

"You really believe me?"

"About that," I answered, "yes. Angela knew Peter Bailey, I take it?"

"They were in the halfway house together for a while, before I got there. He showed her how to use a computer. He was one crazy mother. Always talking about helicopters and aliens and shit like that."

I thought of Bailey's mother. By now, she'd probably gotten the news of her son's death. I knew she would grieve, but I suspected she might feel some relief, too. Whatever he'd gone through before he died, he wouldn't have to be afraid of "bad people" anymore.

"Did Peter like to take pictures?"

Rodney scrunched up his face. Thinking was obviously an effort. "Who the hell knows?"

"Angela, probably. Help me out, here, Rodney. She might be able to get you off the hook."

Rodney sighed. "She hangs out at a club called the Headbanger sometimes. It's on First Street. That's really all I know. Are you going to get me out of here?"

A rap sounded at the door, and Sonterra and Eddie stepped back into the room.

"Are you planning to hold my client?" I asked Sonterra.

"Depends," Sonterra replied. He drew back a chair at the table and sat down, a small notebook and ballpoint pen in one hand.

The questioning began in earnest then.

Rodney didn't give up anything new.

"Can I go now?" Rodney asked, after about the third trip over the same old ground. "How am I going to get home?"

Sonterra leaned back in his chair. "You hungry, Rodney?" he asked. "My partner will get you a sandwich from the vending machine."

I looked from Sonterra to Eddie and back again. What was this—some twist on the old good cop/bad cop routine?

"I could eat," Rodney said.

Eddie went out, fishing for change in one pants pocket, and Sonterra folded his arms.

"You're holding out on us, Rodney," he said mildly. "That's not a good thing. A man was murdered. You either sent messages for him or let him use your aunt's computer to do it. Right now, you're all we've got in the way of a suspect."

"He was Angie's friend, not mine. I never let him do anything."

"Come on, Rodney."

"They might have come to my aunt's place a couple of times."

"Now we're getting somewhere," Sonterra said.

Eddie returned, handed Rodney a sandwich, wrapped in cellophane, and a can of cola.

I figured the timing was no accident. Shades of Pavlov's dogs.

Rodney's hands shook as he opened the sandwich, lifted the squashed white bread, and assessed the contents. Ham and cheese, and too much mayo.

I wondered if Sonterra ate from the vending machine and, if so, whether or not his arteries were clogged.

"Talk to me, Rodney," Sonterra said.

"Maybe they sent some emails," Rodney admitted, after poking a quarter of the sandwich into his mouth. "They were just fooling around."

"What were you doing all this time?" Eddie inquired. Musical chairs time. Sonterra stood up, and Eddie took his place at the table.

Rodney chewed and swallowed. "Watching TV."

"Where was your aunt all this time?" Sonterra asked.

"Working," Rodney said.

I glanced at the clock on the wall behind my client. It was almost eight o'clock, and Rodney's sandwich was beginning to look good. I thought my glance at the clock was subtle, but Sonterra caught me, and a faint smile rested briefly on his mouth.

"Give us Miss Kerrigan's address," Eddie said, "and you can go home."

Rodney tossed me an impatient but beleaguered look. "I already told *my lawyer* here. Angie doesn't have an address. She hangs out at the Headbanger sometimes. Once in a while, she gets a bed at one of the shelters, or sleeps on somebody's couch."

"So what do you do when you want to get in touch with her?" Eddie asked. "Send an email? Maybe she picks up phone messages somewhere?"

"She calls me," Rodney said, with a slight verbal swagger. "I don't call her."

God, yes, I thought. *You're such a catch.*

"Sounds like you've got a good thing going," Sonterra said. "You have a job, Rodney?"

Rodney shifted his bulk and looked put-upon. "Not much out there for a guy just out of jail," he replied. "Slinging burgers, mopping floors, stuff like that."

"And you're holding out for an executive position?" Eddie inquired.

Rodney glared at him, but Eddie didn't react, except to look genuinely interested in the answer.

"What do you do for money?"

My client turned to me. "Can they ask me questions like that?"

"Yes," I answered. I was Rodney's attorney, and I was supposed to be on his side, but it galled me that he'd rather live off Mrs. K than lower himself to work as a janitor or a fry cook. Not that I'd want to eat anything he'd touched.

Rodney squirmed again, reddening around the jowls. "I've got a place to sleep and plenty to eat," he said. "I'm all right."

"You don't mind letting an old woman support you?" Eddie prodded.

"It's not like I've got a choice," Rodney complained. "I've applied for a couple of jobs online. Soon as they find out I did a stretch at Yuma, they won't give me the time of day."

Go figure, I thought.

"That would be the burger joints?" Sonterra asked lightly.

Rodney clenched and unclenched his

hands, clasped on the tabletop. "Banks," he said.

"Banks," Sonterra repeated.

"I was trying to better myself," Rodney snapped.

"Please," Eddie said.

I looked at the clock again, and this time, it wasn't casual. "If you're not going to charge my client," I said, "how about releasing him?"

Sonterra pushed back his chair with an inordinate amount of noise. "Sure, Counselor," he said, without taking his eyes off Rodney. "He's all yours."

Rodney grinned. "I wish," he muttered.

I felt nauseous.

Sonterra took out his wallet, extracted a twenty-dollar bill, and tossed it onto the table. I knew why he was parting with his hard-earned cash. He didn't want to drive Rodney home himself. "Take a cab."

"Like any cabdriver's going to pick me up here," Rodney retorted, but he took the money. "I can go now?"

"Sooner the better," Sonterra said. "Don't leave town."

Rodney got to his feet, weaved a little.

"Don't worry," he answered. "I wouldn't want to get too far from my pretty lawyer."

Sonterra took a step toward him, stopped himself. Eddie steered Rodney toward the door, then out into the hall.

For a while, neither Sonterra nor I spoke. Then he said, "Buy you dinner?"

"Sure," I answered.

We drove to our favorite restaurant, the Horny Toad in Cave Creek, and had steaks.

Back at Sonterra's, we watched TV.

I sort of missed the old days, when we would have been making love as soon as the front door was shut.

THIRTEEN

Sonterra had already left for work when I woke up the next morning.

I used his shower, raided my stash of emergency underwear, and pulled on yesterday's clothes. While I was sipping reheated coffee and Bernice was having breakfast, I switched on the TV news and caught the middle of that day's big story.

". . . body was found at the home of Clare Westbrook, prominent local attorney," the anchor was saying. Sweeping shots of my minuscule backyard filled the screen. "Ms. Westbrook has not been charged with any crime."

"Maybe because I didn't commit one," I snarled, and shut off the set.

Collecting Bernice, I headed for the

garage, where my Escalade waited, with the keys in the ignition. There was a sticky note affixed to the steering wheel and a garage door opener on the passenger seat.

"The forensics people are through at your place," Sonterra had scrawled. "Better have the locks changed."

I crumpled the paper and stuffed it into my purse. My handbag is like a portable landfill but, hey, I don't litter. With my thumb, I jammed the button on the opener, and the garage door slid up with a clattering sound. I backed out, and almost hit a TV 220 news van broadside.

A cameraman stood in the shrubbery, film rolling.

I smiled woodenly and wished I dared give him the finger.

"You look awful," Shanda said, in greeting, when I banged into the office, half an hour later.

"Given that somebody was murdered in my backyard last night," I replied, "that's not surprising."

Shanda's eyes widened. "I didn't know that."

"If you're going to work here, Shanda, you will have to keep up," I said, somewhat impatiently.

She grimaced and got busy doing other things.

I'd barely settled at my desk when Dr. Thomlinson put in an appearance.

"It's a shame about Peter," he said sadly.

"Yes," I agreed.

"What was he doing in your yard?"

"That's a good question, Doctor," I responded, reaching for a stack of files. If I didn't get some work done, people's lives were headed down the tube. Shanda's court date was about to be set, and I hoped to get in touch with Barbara Jenkins, the accused murderess Sonterra had scared off the day before. I didn't like losing a client, whether they paid or not.

"Did you see anyone?"

I was distracted, and momentarily baffled. I reminded myself that Dr. Thomlinson had lost a patient he'd tried hard to help, and attempted to focus on the conversation.

"See anyone?" I echoed, still a little fogged.

"The killer," Dr. Thomlinson prompted. "Did you actually see the murder?"

I hesitated. Shivered. "No," I said, at some length.

The shrink managed a tentative, self-effacing smile. "Good. That would have been dreadful for you."

"If Peter had any enemies that you know of," I said carefully, "now would be the time to contact the police."

Dr. Thomlinson spread his hands, let them fall to his sides. Shook his head. "As far as I knew, Peter didn't have enemies—or friends, for that matter."

"He was apparently close to a young woman named Angela Kerrigan," I said. "And he knew one of my clients, as well. Rodney Gerring. Both of them did some time at the halfway house while he was there."

The doctor thrust out a sigh, squeezed the bridge of his nose between a thumb and forefinger. "He *did* mention Miss Kerrigan," he recalled. "As you said, she was a resident in the facility, periodically at least. He seemed to believe they were an item. I didn't take it very seriously. Peter wasn't capable of sustaining any sort of relationship."

I pondered that. He'd sustained *one* relationship that I knew of—with the doll man. And it had gotten him killed.

"What about Rodney Gerring?" I asked. "Didn't Peter ever talk about him?"

Thomlinson gave it some thought. "No," he said.

The telephone on my desk rang, startling me. I didn't wait for Shanda to pick up, but answered it myself, with a rushed and awkward, "Hello," instead of the usual spiel.

"Clare?" It was Sonterra.

"Hey," I said, my voice ringing with false cheer. "Did you see my backyard on the morning news?"

"No," he said, but from his tone, I knew something was wrong. "I just left my lieutenant's office. I'm off the Bailey case—officially, anyway."

I wasn't surprised. Technically, it would be unethical for Sonterra to investigate Peter's murder, due to his involvement with me. "Am I a suspect?"

"You'll be questioned," he said. "That's routine."

A fissure opened in the pit of my stomach, and fear bubbled up, like lava breaking through the ocean floor. "I was *already* questioned," I pointed out.

"By me," he specified.

"I don't like this."

"You're a person of interest, Clare. That's all."

"Only a 'person of interest.' Oh, well, that changes everything!"

"Clare," Sonterra said. "Get a grip."

I'd forgotten that I wasn't alone in the office, and when I remembered, I looked up anxiously. Dr. Thomlinson had gone, but Shanda was there, not even pretending not to listen.

"Now what?" I asked, shoving a hand into my hair.

"If I thought you'd do what I suggested, I'd say call Loretta, go have lunch, or shop, or something. Since I know you—see clients. Do your best not to stub your toe on another body."

"You're a *huge* help, Sonterra," I said, but I did feel better.

"Protect and serve," he replied. "That's my motto."

I could remember a number of times when he'd offered protection, but serving was another matter. In his mixed and motley culture, women did the honors in that department. "How's Eddie?" I asked.

"Not good," Sonterra said. "She wants to take the kids and move to Iowa, with lover boy."

"There are things he could do to prevent that," I pointed out. I wasn't much help, but I wanted to be. I liked Eddie, I knew he was a good father, if overworked, like most cops.

"Do me a favor," Sonterra said, "and don't get mixed up in this. I know you mean well, but you couldn't be objective."

"And I suppose you are?" It stung a little, the way Sonterra shut me out of things like that. I barely knew his family, and even though some of his cases were beyond traumatic, he didn't seem to trust me enough to let me carry some of the burden.

"I'm not his lawyer," he replied, with asperity.

I could see the conversation was not only going nowhere, it was degenerating. "I only wanted to help."

He sighed. "I know, Clare. I'll pass the word to Eddie. He might call you, and he might not. Fair enough?"

"Fair enough," I agreed.

"I'd like to have a look at your computer, by the way. Don't delete anything, okay?"

"Okay."

I guess you could say we ended on a positive note—if you were a Pollyanna type.

The rest of the day was crammed with work, and I didn't have much time to think about the various emotional roadblocks that kept Sonterra and me from really connecting. On a subliminal level, though, the machinery was churning away.

That night, when I got home, I immediately checked the premises for bodies and, finding none, filled the electric teakettle with water and plugged it in to come to a boil while I listened to my voice mail. Loretta had left a low-intensity howler, wanting to know why I hadn't bothered to mention finding a floater in my pool. Mrs. K had called, too; she knew about the corpse, of course, but she was concerned about Rodney's standing with the police. Emma, who kept up with the news by means of her laptop, tersely suggested that I read my email once in a while, if it wasn't too much trouble, and hung up with a brisk click.

Smiling a little, I brewed my tea, then carried the cup into the downstairs office. Bernice trotted at my heels.

I sat down at my desk and went online. My niece's cybermissive was long, with a lot of capital letters and exclamation points. She'd seen the latest on a news website and she was scared. She wanted to come home, immediately, so I wouldn't be alone in the house. Also, if I didn't mind, I could raise the daily limit on her ATM card.

I responded that I was fine, and so was the current spending cap. In hopes of reassuring her a little, I told her Sonterra and I were planning to spend the weekend at his cabin.

I clicked Send, and perused the long list of subject lines under New Messages. There were the usual pornographic offerings and sales pitches, all of which I consigned to Junk—despite Sonterra's earlier injunction not to delete anything—and I was just about to erase one bearing only an email address when my spine started to tingle.

I leaned forward a little and clicked.

The body of the message consisted of six words: *She was going to warn you.* And there was an attachment.

My hand trembled as I worked the mouse.

Another picture, but this was no doll. The subject of the piece was a woman, sprawled across a rumpled bed, with her throat slit from ear to ear.

I must have cried out, because Bernice gave a little yelp, jumped into my lap, and tried to lick my face.

There was a great deal of blood in the photograph, but that didn't keep me from recognizing the dead woman.

It was Melanie Witherspoon. My across-the-street neighbor.

I groped for the telephone on my desk, punched in Sonterra's number.

"Yo," he said, without waiting for me to speak. "I just picked up some Chinese take-out. I'll be there in fifteen minutes."

A tear slipped down my cheek. Frustration, horror, sorrow—I felt all those things and more.

Not again. Please, God, not again.

"My neighbor," I croaked. "I think she's dead."

"Jesus," Sonterra rasped. "What are you talking about?" I'm sure that last part was rhetorical; it was perfectly obvious what I was talking about.

Haltingly, I explained about the email. "I'm going over there," I finished.

"Don't you *dare,*" Sonterra snapped. "Did you call 911?"

The room was spinning. I held on to the edge of the desk with my free hand. "I called you."

"I'll take care of it. *Do not move* until I get there. Have you got that?"

"Sonterra, what the hell is happening?"

"We're going to find out, Babe. Stay on the line. I'll be back with you in a minute or so."

I nodded, forced myself to look at the email again while I waited. I saved the file, but that was about all I could do. I was oddly restless, wanting to bolt but, para- doxically, unable even to rise from my chair.

"Clare?"

Sonterra's voice was a lifeline; I wanted to reach out for it, wrap it around me.

"I'm just pulling onto the 101, and the cops are on their way. You're sure you're alone, right?"

That question made the small hairs rise on my forearms. For the length of a heart- beat, I was certain someone was standing directly behind me, but then common sense kicked in.

"I'm sure," I said shakily, though I didn't quite dare to look over my shoulder. "Bernice would have made a fuss if anyone else was here."

"Are the doors locked?"

That much I was sure of. "Yes."

"The squad car might get there before I do. Don't open up without making sure it's them, okay?"

"Okay," I agreed weakly.

As it happened, Sonterra and the squad car arrived at the same time. I had managed to get as far as the front door, and I had one eyeball to the peephole when they all braked at the curb.

I yanked open the door and dashed down the sidewalk. Flung myself into Sonterra's arms, and clung. He held me tightly for a few moments. I welcomed the warmth of his breath against my temple, and the way he steadied me until the trembling eased up a little.

"Which house?" Sonterra asked.

I pointed across the street. The Witherspoons' front door gaped open and, as we watched, their golden retriever, Waldo, crossed the threshold. His coat was drenched in blood.

I would have dropped to my knees, right there on the walk, if Sonterra hadn't grabbed me again.

The other police officers bounded in that direction. Sonterra followed, his strides long, and I was right behind him. I'd forgotten Bernice; she streaked past me to greet Waldo with a concerned sniff.

Sonterra stopped on the porch, turned to face me. "Stay here," he said.

I shifted my attention to Waldo, crouching to run my hands over him. They came away crimson, but there was no sign of a wound.

The retriever whimpered, his one brown eye full of pleading trust.

"Take it easy, boy," I said, stroking him. "Everything's going to be okay." Talk about whistling in the dark. He wasn't convinced, and neither was I. I'd seen the picture, he'd seen the body, and probably the murder as well.

And it must have been recent.

Sonterra came out of the house. I was covered in blood; the coppery smell of it stung my nostrils.

"It's bad, Clare," he said.

I'd been hoping against all reason that it was all a mistake, a sick joke of some kind.

"No," I whispered, remembering Melanie's shy but friendly manner.

A crime scene van and two more cruisers appeared, and Sonterra left me to go and speak with the officers.

Waldo made a whining sound, and I patted his head.

I'm not sure what made me do it, but suddenly, on some out-of-left-field impulse, I stepped into the house. Followed the voices into the master bedroom.

If I could undo that decision, I would. I will probably never get the grisly images out of my mind. The real thing was infinitely worse than the picture on my computer screen; Melanie lay across the bed, and the wound in her throat was so fresh that the blood hadn't congealed.

I put a hand to my mouth, maybe to hold back a scream, maybe to keep from vomiting. Or both.

Sonterra gripped my shoulders from behind, turned me around, and marched me back down the hallway, through the living room, and out onto the porch. Waldo was still sitting there, forlorn and panting, with Bernice beside him, lending canine moral support.

I sat down on the top step, off to one side, so I'd be out of the way, and draped one arm around Waldo. He gave a little shudder and leaned against me. Bernice scrambled into my lap.

Sonterra squatted beside us.

"Don't you have to be in there?" I asked, watching as another car arrived, and two men in plainclothes got out.

"I called in some backup on this one."

The detectives approached. Sonterra stood to greet them and give a few terse words of explanation. They nodded and went inside.

I put my face in my hands.

Sonterra leaned down, gripped my arm, and raised me to my feet. "Come on, Counselor," he said quietly. "This is no place for you."

I blinked at him. "Could we bathe the dog?"

He looked confused. "What?"

"Waldo—all that blood."

Sonterra hoisted Bernice, held her schoolbook-style against his side. "No, Counselor," he said. "The forensics people will want to run some tests."

"He can't stay here."

"I'll take care of it," he answered, and went back inside for a few moments.

Waldo followed us across the street, up the walk, and into my house. The last thing I was thinking about, at that moment, was the mess he might make.

"I'd better shower," I said, looking down at my stained clothes. The blood had soaked through my T-shirt and shorts, and it felt clammy against my skin.

"I want to look through the house first," Sonterra replied grimly, putting Bernice down. "After that, I'll need to see the email."

I nodded, and stuck to Sonterra like a piece of packing tape while he went from room to room, checking every window and door, every closet, every possible hiding place. Waldo sat patiently in the living room the whole time, Bernice beside him.

When Sonterra was satisfied that the doll man wasn't hiding somewhere in the house, waiting to finish me off, I pulled up the email and attachment, and left my self-appointed bodyguard to study them while I went up-stairs, took a shower and put on clean clothes.

Downstairs again, I found Waldo in the kitchen, nonchalantly lapping up water from a bowl, while a crime scene technician took samples from his fur. Sonterra poured me a cup of freshly made coffee.

His expression was understandably grim.

"'She was going to warn you,'" he quoted. "Maybe this was somebody she knew."

"That probably narrows it to a couple of hundred people," I lamented.

"What do you know about Dr. Witherspoon?" he asked.

For a fraction of a second, I didn't know what he meant, and it must have shown in my face, because he hit me with a prompt.

"Melanie's husband?"

"His name is Jack," I said, sipping my coffee and wishing Sonterra had laced it with a splash of Canadian Club. A shiver danced down my spine. The possibility that there had been two victims, instead of just one, had not occurred to me. Now I realized that Jack's body could have been lying in another room.

"Is he dead, too?"

"I doubt it," Sonterra said. "Did they get along? The Witherspoons, I mean?"

I was finally picking up what Sonterra was laying down. He was operating on the most-likely-suspect theory, and that was always the husband or boyfriend, especially when the murder was particularly violent. "I didn't know them very well," I said, watching as the gloved crime scene tech dropped bits of clipped fur into a plastic bag, using tweezers. "If there were problems, Melanie didn't mention them to me."

"I already checked the yellow pages and called his office," Sonterra mused, leaning back against the counter and folding his arms. "I got a recording. Instructions to call the home number."

"He was practicing out of his home," I said, "and only part-time. He had a heart attack a few months ago." Suddenly, a mental movie began to unreel in my mind: Jack, coming home to find the street choked with official vehicles, hurrying inside, seeing the blood, Melanie's body . . .

I sank into a chair at the table.

"Do you think he could have done it?" Sonterra pressed.

I shook my head. "It doesn't make sense. The doll man sent the email."

"It makes sense if Witherspoon *is* the doll man."

Anything was possible, of course, but the theory didn't resonate. "Why would Dr.

Witherspoon want to kill Peter Bailey, or Melanie, for that matter?"

"Could be it's random," Sonterra pointed out. "As in, serial killer."

The crime scene tech was waiting to say something. Sonterra and I both looked at him.

"Can we bathe the dog now?" I asked.

The tech nodded, holding up the gruesome bag with a few bloody tufts of hair in the bottom. "I've got what I need," he said. "I'll be going now."

Sonterra walked him to the front door.

I waited for Waldo to finish slurping up water, then led him out into the backyard, hooked up the hose, and cleaned him up as best I could, considering that it was dark by then. Bernice stayed close by, watching with the kind of fascination people exhibit after a car crash.

Sonterra appeared with towels, helped me dry Waldo.

Without warning, a lump formed in my throat and I began to cry. The dry, raspy sobs hurt, but I couldn't seem to stop them.

Sonterra took the towel out of my hands and set it aside with the one he'd been using. "We're leaving, Counselor. Let's go pack you a bag."

I looked at him in confusion. "Leaving?"

"For the cabin," he said.

The thought of such a refuge was a welcome one. I should have felt relief, I suppose, but I was too numb. Melanie Witherspoon had died horribly, and very possibly because she was my neighbor.

Sonterra dried my cheeks with his shirttail. "There's something else," he said huskily. "I was going to tell you over Chinese food. They caught the guys who shot up your office. It was some kind of gang initiation."

"Why did they pick me?"

"Just lucky, I guess."

"You mean, they simply drove by, decided I would do as well as anybody, and opened fire?"

"Your lights were on. That was probably a factor."

I bristled a little. "And if I hadn't been there in the middle of the night, someone else would have been the target?"

"I didn't say that."

"You were *thinking* it."

"No, I wasn't. I was wondering who the doll man is."

My shoulders went slack, and I felt a rush of weariness.

"I'll get your stuff," Sonterra said, leading the way inside. Waldo, Bernice, and I followed, like rats after the Piper.

"What about Waldo?"

"What about him?"

"We can't abandon him. What if Jack doesn't come back?"

"I'll leave word with the crew across the street that he's with us."

I relaxed, but only slightly. "Don't forget my toothbrush," I said, as Sonterra started up the stairs to throw some of my things into a suitcase.

I had to hold Melanie's murder at a distance, at least for a little while, so I shifted my thoughts onto another track. Sonterra and I were going to be alone, for a whole weekend, in his cabin. I was feeling needy and vulnerable, and when it came to sex, he was damn near irresistible.

Would I be able to hold out?

Should I even try?

FOURTEEN

Sonterra loaded us all into his SUV, then went across the street to bring the detectives up to speed. I called Father Mike from the car, since I knew I wouldn't be able to reach Shanda—I didn't want her going into the office the next morning. It was Thursday night; she could have a three-day weekend. I would check phone messages from the cabin. I wasn't sure there were any appointments scheduled, but if there were, explanations would be in order. As for walk-ins, well, they were just out of luck.

Father Mike's voice mail kicked in; not surprising, given that it was nearly eight o'clock. I left a concise message, asking him to convey the information to Shanda in person if necessary, and included my cell number. Knowing I was asking a lot, I settled back against the seat, closed my eyes, and let out a long breath. "I'm looking forward to some peace and quiet." I'd never been to Sonterra's hideout, though he'd owned it when I met him. I knew he'd taken his ex-wife and young stepson there for weekends and vacations, before his divorce; maybe that was why he'd never invited me before. Sacred ground.

We ate congealed sweet and sour pork and cold fried rice from Sonterra's take-out boxes, purchased hours before and forgotten, and said little.

Presently, I dozed off, and when I opened my eyes, we'd covered a lot of miles. Sonterra was on his cell phone, talking in low tones obviously calculated not to wake me up.

"Okay, Leanne," he said. "*Okay.* No, it's not a cold case. We're working on it. And, no, I do not think we should get together and talk it over." Pause. "You *know* why not."

I let him think I was still sleeping, watched him through my lashes. My heart was in the back of my throat, pounding with an emotion I wouldn't have claimed.

"Yeah," he finished tersely. "Good-bye." He glanced at me as he put the phone away. "Stop playing possum," he said. "I know you're awake."

I sat up, yawned, stretched. "The friend you met through work, I presume," I said lightly.

"Leanne is the relative of a victim. Her twin brother was shot to death four years ago."

I subsided a little. After all, I knew what it was to lose a sibling to violence. "And the killer was never caught."

Sonterra sighed, shook his head. "Things got dicey, and I finally had to hand it over to McCullough and Robbins—they're with Phoenix PD. Given their workload, they might get to it by, oh, 2050."

"So why is she calling your house and your cell phone, if it happened four years ago and you're not even working on the investigation?"

"People have trouble letting go in a situation like this. Their emotions get out of hand." He gave me a sidelong look. "I seem to remember another person who had a similar problem."

"I don't like it," I said, tilting my head back and closing my eyes.

"Come on, Clare. I've already told you. Leanne and I are not involved."

It had been a long day, and I guess my defenses were down. "It would seem that she doesn't see it exactly that way."

"I can't help what goes on in other people's heads, Clare."

"I hate that other women find you attractive."

He relaxed slightly. "If they didn't, you probably wouldn't either. Ever think about that?"

"Actually, no."

"Liar."

"I don't want to talk about this anymore." I pressed my lips together, hard.

"You're the one who brought it up."

"Whatever, Sonterra."

We left the freeway, passed through a town made up of a post office, a seedy café, eight run-down houses with junk cars and other detritus out front, and two convenience stores. One stop sign for the whole place, and I swear one of the mailboxes was a converted toilet.

The faint strains of dueling banjos strummed in my head.

"This could be a long weekend," Sonterra grumbled. He turned off onto a rutted road, and we bounced along between pine trees and stumps. I looked back to see if the dogs had been jostled to the floorboards. Waldo was sitting tight and panting, his one eye traveling between Sonterra and me. Bernice snoozed.

"Where do you buy groceries around here?" I asked. You know what they say about Chinese food. A couple of hours had gone by since we'd eaten, and I was getting hungry.

"Flagstaff is ten miles up the highway," Sonterra answered.

I bit my lower lip. I could have been more gracious, but my neighbor had been murdered and my emotions were raw. "Why don't you just get it over with, right now? Go ahead and say that you're tired of trying to work out the kinks in this relationship, especially with the moratorium on sex, and you want to date other people, get on with your life, all that."

Sonterra looked stunned. "Is that what you think this is about?"

"Yes," I said, a little surprised myself. I hadn't consciously realized how scared I was.

"So now you're inside my head? You've got me all figured out?"

The cabin came into view, rimmed in bright moonlight. It was made of logs, and there was a wraparound deck. The windows reflected the headlights, and Waldo began to bark. Bernice bestirred herself and contributed a halfhearted yip.

I glanced at Sonterra, but this time I couldn't read his expression. The shadows were closing in. "This is a great cabin," I said, in a flimsy attempt to change the subject and take some of the heat off. "Is it paid for, or do you have a mortgage?"

"None of your damned business," Sonterra retorted. "Will you stop with the diversionary tactics?"

I let out my breath. "Do you or do you not want to break up?"

"That's about the last thing I want," Sonterra answered somberly. He stopped the SUV with a lurch, shoved open the door, and got out. Waldo jumped to the ground, the moment he was set free, and ran in gleeful circles, woofing his head off. I hoisted Bernice off the seat and tucked her under one arm.

I didn't know what to say, so I just stood there with my teeth in my mouth, as Gram used to say.

Sonterra put an arm around my shoulder. "Truce," he said, with a husky note to his voice. "I'll show you around."

I nodded.

We clomped up the wooden steps and across the deck. Sonterra whistled for Waldo and unlocked the front door. A flip of the light switch, and the darkness receded a little.

The living room had hardwood floors and a gray stone fireplace. A framed photograph of a woman and a little boy stood on the mantelpiece—Sonterra's ex-wife and stepson, Ryan.

The kitchen was equipped with a wood cookstove and, conversely, a microwave. There was an oak table with four chairs, and a coffeemaker stood on the counter, next to the sink. Sonterra plugged in the ancient refrigerator, and it began to chortle and hum.

Waldo, clicking along at my heels, barked again. It sounded conversational, as though he were commenting. I put Bernice down, and she toddled after Waldo, nose in over-drive.

The bathroom was next on the tour—claw-foot tub, pedestal sink, standard toilet. Sonterra opened a door to reveal a hot-water tank, switched it on. More chortling and humming.

The master bedroom, which took up one whole end of the house, was simply fur-nished, with a view of the woods on three sides. Another stone fireplace nearly cov-ered the remaining wall.

Waldo sniffed all four corners, then jumped up onto the bed and settled himself in the middle of the mattress. Bernice hesi-tated, then joined him.

"Make yourselves at home," Sonterra said, with a crooked grin.

"Are there any other bedrooms?" I asked. I wanted to shut down, sleep for twenty years. Maybe when I woke up, my life would be normal.

"Yes," Sonterra answered, in a tight voice. "Two."

"Good," I said, but I didn't mean it, and I wondered if he knew.

"I'll get the stuff out of the car," he said, after a long, brittle silence. "How about putting on a pot of coffee? Unless it'll keep you awake."

I just rolled my eyes. My whole body screamed for collapse.

Sonterra schlepped in my suitcase and his gym bag, putting both in the living room, as if the separate-bedroom question had yet to be decided. "I'll backtrack to one of the convenience stores and pick up some grub," he said. "You need anything?"

I almost said tampons, just to hedge my bets, but then I decided to cut him some slack.

He left for downtown Deliverance, and I fired up the coffee-maker and searched the cupboards until I found a collection of mismatched mugs.

While the java was brewing, I took a quick shower and changed into my favorite sweats, which had seen better days. I was sipping coffee when Sonterra came back with a couple of grocery bags, a gallon of milk, and a ten-pound bag of kibble.

He checked out the sweat suit, shook his head, then started putting stuff into the noisy fridge: beer, eggs, cheese, a pound of bacon, steaks, butter. I poured coffee into a mug; black and strong, the way he liked it.

"So," Sonterra said, as I put the cup on the table, "what do you think?"

I was stumped. What did I think of *what,* exactly? The state of the economy? Nipple piercing? Randy Johnson's batting average?

"Of the cabin," he prompted.

"Nice place," I said, relieved. "Do you spend a lot of time here?"

"Dumb question," he replied. "If I'm not at work, I'm with you."

I drew back a chair. "It's so peaceful. Are there any neighbors?" I winced a little at the last word, remembering Melanie.

"Darryl and his brother, Darryl," Sonterra quipped, watching me with a sort of sad humor in his eyes. He was quiet for a few beats. "What is it about me that scares you so much, Counselor?"

I slumped into my chair, cupped my hands around my coffee. Suddenly, I felt chilled. The mountain air, I supposed. "We want different things. You want a live-in girl-friend and plenty of sex."

He cocked an eyebrow. "Oh, yeah? And what do *you* want, Counselor?"

I surprised myself again. "Maybe marriage. A genuine commitment."

Sonterra gave a low whistle. "I'll be damned," he marveled. "I thought you were as scared as I was."

Honesty time. Besides, I was too frazzled and too tired for fancy footwork. "I am," I said. "But I'm not getting any younger, Sonterra. I want babies someday."

He considered that, turning a matchbook end over end on the tabletop. "Don't look now," he said, at last, "but babies and a bad habit of getting shot at don't mix all that well."

That remark would have been ever so much easier to deal with if it hadn't been true. "Maybe I could break the habit," I heard myself say, and I instantly wished I could take the words back. Being this open, with just about anybody, and infinitely more with Sonterra, was like unzipping my skin and walking around with my vital organs exposed.

"Maybe," he said.

"Your turn," I recovered enough to say. "What scares you? About us, I mean? About me?"

He scrubbed his face with both hands. He was probably twice as worn out as I was. Why didn't we just go to our appointed beds and give it up for the night?

"When Eddie got married," he answered, after drawing a deep breath and sitting up a little straighter in his chair, "I was just getting divorced. I told him he was a fool. But he seemed to be happy—both of them did—and then the babies started coming. It was like something out of one of those braggy letters some people send with Christmas cards. It got better and better." He paused, looked away, then gazed straight into my eyes. "Then I met you. I started hoping we could make it work, even with all the things working against us—"

"Like what?" I prompted, when he fell silent. I knew, but I wanted to hear his version.

"My job. Your job. The way there's no in-between with us. We're either fighting, or having monkey-sex." He stopped again. "And then there's your bank account."

"We're not fighting right now, and we're not having monkey-sex," I pointed out. *More's the pity,* added the personal devil's advocate I carry around in my head.

"Only because we're both too wiped to get our hackles up." He grinned, breaking the tension a little. "Speaking of getting things up—"

Inwardly, I groaned. "No fair, Sonterra."

He sighed, but he was still grinning. "It was worth a try," he said.

I laughed, but the mood was fleeting. "Maybe we should just give up," I said. "Stop trying to make this work."

His eyes darkened. "Maybe," he agreed, at comforting length.

"On the other hand—"

Sonterra sighed again.

"Cut me a break, Sonterra," I said. I wanted to reach out, touch his hand, but I didn't quite dare. I wasn't sure what it would unleash. "Sure, I'm confused. I know I'm sending mixed messages. But I've never done this before. I don't think I know how."

"You've never done what? Driven a man crazy?"

"I've never been serious about anybody before. I had Emma, and school, and a job. Then I was building my career. I didn't have time to learn the dance."

He smiled, but his eyes were still troubled. I got the sudden and very distinct impression he wanted to tell me something heavy-duty. Instead, he picked up his mug, took a sip of coffee, set it down again.

"How about an omelet?" I asked brightly, because we weren't getting anywhere, and neither of us was up to making sensible decisions about the rest of our lives. "I make a pretty good one."

Typically, Sonterra wasn't ready to let it drop. "I hate your job," he reiterated. He got up, opened the refrigerator, and extracted the eggs and milk, along with a block of cheese.

I stiffened. "I'm not exactly wild about yours, either."

He set a frying pan on the stove with a clang. Maybe he'd forgotten it wasn't electric. "And I hate that you have a shitload of money in the bank."

"Yes, you mentioned that. And, gee, I'm all reassured now," I said.

Waldo trundled in from the bedroom, yawning. His sidekick trotted dutifully behind.

"What is it you want from me, Sonterra?" I asked, suddenly unable to bear the suspense any longer, even though I'd been keeping him at arm's length. By then, he was jamming newspaper and kindling into the belly of the stove.

He struck a match. "Besides screaming, clawing, sweaty sex?"

Damn, but he could be obstinate. I blushed furiously, looked away. "Yes. Besides that."

"I want you to quit your job and give away your money."

FIFTEEN

I stared at Sonterra, speechless.

"I'm kidding," he said.

I wasn't so sure he was. I decided to go with my instincts. "I can see why the job might be an issue," I said carefully, "but I don't understand about the money. Do you think it's changed me in any significant way?"

He pondered. "No," he said, finally, in the tone of an admission.

I braced an elbow on the tabletop and rested my chin in my palm, watching as he added wood to the fire. "You're always telling me I'm a coward where our relationship is concerned, and maybe that's true. But until tonight, you conveniently overlooked the fact that you're afraid, too—you don't want people saying you were after my money. And you think because your first marriage didn't work, and now Eddie's is on the rocks, there's no hope of getting it right."

He thrust out a sigh, and avoided my gaze. He also avoided the reference to his take on the perils of matrimony. "I have money of my own, Clare. From an inheritance. I invested most of it, and I've done well. I don't need you to support me."

"I know that, and you know that," I persisted, but quietly, with none of my all-too-usual confrontational tactics. "But do your buddies at the station know it? Or the guys at the gym?"

Sonterra caved, but not entirely. The stove wasn't hot enough to cook on, but he busied himself cracking eggs into a skillet. "Okay, so I admit it. I'm a private type. I don't want everybody speculating about the financial situation, tallying up the cost every time we buy something, or go on a trip."

"That's just pride."

"Maybe it is, but it's the way I feel."

I waited. Then, "So where do we go from here?"

Sonterra didn't look at me. "We could live together. See how it plays out."

"No way," I said. "You get to keep one foot in and one foot out, ready to jump if things go sour. No wedding ring, no deal, buddy."

He turned slightly. "You'd marry me, if I asked you?"

"I honestly don't know."

"Great. I love a definite answer."

I left the table, found plates and silverware, rinsed them at the sink—who knew how long they'd been sitting in the cupboard—and set a place for each of us.

The silence seemed to create a vacuum, our own private black hole, right there in Sonterra's kitchen.

I relented first. "It's been a hard day." I crossed the room, laid a hand on his shoulder. He concentrated on the omelet. "Can't we talk tomorrow?"

He turned, spatula in hand, and landed a kiss on the top of my head. "Okay," he said. "Okay."

We made short work of the omelet, and Sonterra took the dogs outside while I washed the dishes.

I brushed my teeth, and when I stepped

into the bedroom to say good night, he was standing in front of the fireplace, staring into a crackling blaze. Obviously, he hoped I'd change my mind about the sleeping arrangements, and I wished I could.

Sonterra's shoulders were slightly stooped. I wanted to comfort him, and searched my lawyer mind for something poetic, maybe even poignant.

"I'm through in the bathroom," I said.

He nodded and left the room.

"I have a way with words," I told the dogs. Then I backtracked, made my way upstairs, and tumbled into bed, very much alone.

Hell, even the dogs didn't join me.

Next thing I knew, sunlight was pouring into the room, Bernice was standing on my chest, and Waldo was nuzzling my arm with his ice-cold nose.

I felt a flutter of panic, not knowing where I was, before downstairs kitchen-type sounds registered in my brain.

He was cooking. Definitely a point in his favor.

I moved Bernice, got up, and padded to the upstairs bathroom. After washing up and brushing my teeth, I wandered down to the kitchen.

The floor felt cold under my feet, but the wood stove was going and Sonterra was frying bacon.

"About time you rolled your lazy but very attractive ass out of the sack," he teased.

I made a face and poured myself a cup of coffee.

"Sit down," Sonterra said. "Breakfast's almost ready."

I sat. "I like a man who cooks."

"Given your limited culinary repertoire," he replied, "I'm not surprised."

Still wearing the clothes I'd slept in, I shoved a hand through my sleep-rumpled hair. "So what's the plan?" I asked, and yawned.

"Nothing heavy," Sonterra said. "Breakfast. A walk. I'd like to show you what the place looks like in the daylight."

"Sounds nice," I said. A little fresh air and exercise would do me good. I didn't get a lot of either one in my regular life, and I was on the high side of the ten pounds I've been gaining and taking off ever since I got out of high school. Maybe I would go whole hog, deal with the problem once and for all, sign up at Loretta's gym. I had never been a joiner; I belonged to the bar association, and that was it.

We consumed bacon, eggs, toast, and the rest of the coffee. Sonterra did the dishes while I went up to my bedroom to pull on jeans, a sweater, socks, and tennis shoes.

The dogs were ecstatic at the prospect of an outing.

When Sonterra took my hand, I felt pretty good myself. *Live in the moment, Clare,* I thought. *It might be all you have.*

Although most of the trees around Sonterra's cabin were evergreens, there were a few oaks and maples, too, and their leaves were on fire with autumn shades of gold, crimson, rust, and pale yellow. They crunched beneath our feet as we strolled, a little apart, with just the backs of our hands touching.

There was a clearing at the top of the hill, and we climbed a rickety rail fence to get into it, Waldo running ahead, Bernice sticking close. The grass was waist-high, but here and there a crooked grave marker peeked through.

"Pioneer cemetery," Sonterra said. "Some

of the first people to settle in northern Arizona are buried here."

I paused and crouched to read the mostly worn-away letters on an ancient headstone. "Eudora Baker Mackaby," I read aloud. "Born 1840, died 1882." Still on my haunches, I looked up at Sonterra. "Forty-two years," I reflected. "Not a very long run."

"Back then, forty-two was old," Sonterra said, with a shrug that communicated resignation, rather than a lack of caring. Once again, I was reminded that he was used to death; it was part of his day-to-day life.

I straightened. "How do you stand it? All the bodies and the blood?"

"Part of the job," he said simply. "Sometimes, I just check out of my brain for a while."

I looked up at the sky, blue and crisp, unmarred by urban smog. "Do you think anything comes afterward? After death, I mean?"

He pondered the question. "Yeah," he said, with a ghost of a grin. "I was raised Catholic, remember?"

I had never known Sonterra to attend Mass, but he did wear a small gold medal most of the time. I wasn't sure, though, whether he really believed St. Christopher would protect him. There were a lot of things we never talked about. "So you believe in God?"

"I believe in something," he said, and took my hand. Waldo explored the cemetery, and his tags jingled happily as he moved through the dry grass. Bernice pawed at Sonterra's shin, and he bent to lift her with his free arm. "What about you, Clare? What do you believe in?"

I considered. "I believe in personal responsibility," I said. "God or no God, it all comes down to the choices we make."

Sonterra merely nodded. We came to the edge of the cemetery, and found ourselves facing a deep ravine, a red gouge in the landscape, cut by some passing glacier, millennia ago. For some reason, the small hairs stood up on the back of my neck.

Sonterra must have sensed my sudden inner freeze, because he let go of my hand and slipped his arm around my waist, holding me close against his side. Bernice clung to his other shoulder. "Picking up vibes?" he asked.

I bit my lower lip and nodded. I've never

been particularly afraid of heights, but I wanted to get away from that place. Only my pride stopped me from backpedaling—my pride and Sonterra's hold on me.

"Sometime in the early 1900s, a family made camp down there," he said. "They had a covered wagon and a few cattle—the story goes that they were on their way to stake a claim on some land up in Utah. Coming from the Midwest, they probably didn't know to avoid low ground. A flash flood wiped them all out."

I shuddered.

Sonterra's arm tightened around me, and I liked the feeling.

"Ready to head back?" Sonterra asked.

"Yes," I managed. In my mind's eye, I could see that wagon, a woman in long skirts and a bonnet, cooking over a camp-fire, the cattle grazing on scrub grass while the man of the family unhitched the team, and a couple of kids, ostensibly picking up dry wood for the fire, played chase. I almost heard the roar of rushing water, a dirty, glimmering wall, coming out of nowhere. I saw the ill-fated travelers pause at the sound and the sight, knowing it was too late to escape.

Sonterra gave me a squeeze. "Come on," he said.

"Why did you show me that place—tell me that story?" I asked, as we walked back through the cemetery, Waldo following reluctantly at our heels.

"I guess I wanted you to know it was here," Sonterra answered, after some thought. "So you wouldn't go out wandering and fall in. Several hikers have made that mistake."

I felt the chill again, and I must have shivered. When we got back to the cabin, Sonterra immediately started a fire blazing in the living-room hearth. Waldo circled the rug in front of the fireplace a couple of times, then plopped himself down for a nap. Bernice joined him.

I waited for Sonterra to make a move. He didn't. And I was pretty sure I didn't want him to, but I began to feel restless again, just the same.

"Did you own this place—when the hikers were killed, I mean?" I asked.

Sonterra, sitting on the raised hearth with his back to the fire, bent to stroke Waldo's head, then Bernice's. "No," he said. "I bought it while I was married. When Ryan visits, we come here to fish and just hang out."

I nodded toward the photograph on the mantel. "Do you miss them?" I asked.

Sonterra's gaze locked with mine. "I miss Ryan," he said.

I gravitated to one of the bookshelves against the far wall, opposite Sonterra. There were plenty of old books, and stacks of board games in tattered boxes.

"Feel like getting beat at checkers?" I asked.

Sonterra's chuckle was low and raspy. "You are entirely too confident," he said. "About all the wrong things."

I pulled the game from the stack, drew a deep breath, and turned, holding it in both hands. "Are you trying to start an argument?"

"Just making an observation."

I let it go. For just one weekend, I wanted life to be ordinary.

He got up from the hearth and pulled the rustic coffee table a little farther from the couch. I took a seat on the overstuffed sofa, he sat cross-legged on the floor, on the other side. Bernice jumped up beside me, while Waldo opened his one eye, surveyed the proceedings, and went back to sleep.

I chose the red pieces, leaving Sonterra with the black. We lined our men up on the appropriate squares, ready for battle.

"How do you know so much about the history of this place?" I asked, thinking of that long-ago family again, wiped out in the bottom of the hidden ravine. It was better than thinking about our personal impasse, the doll man, and Melanie's brutal murder.

Sonterra slid one of his men out of line with the tip of a forefinger. "Research," he said.

The fire crackled cheerfully in the grate, filling the room with its pleasant, singular fragrance. I sent a red man out to meet his black one. "Somehow, I can't picture you in some dusty library." That seemed like a safe statement. I was on a roll, in the safe statement department.

"There are a few old-timers around, and I got the rest off the internet."

"Why?"

He jumped two of my game pieces and swept them off the board with a slightly cocky flourish. "Ryan was curious about the graveyard—kids his age are usually fascinated by things like that. To them, death is something that happens on TV, or in the movies, or in video games. They see the same actors pop up alive and well a week later, so it isn't real to them. As for taking him to the ravine, that was a cautionary measure."

I pictured Sonterra and Ryan standing at the edge of that crevasse, Sonterra's hand resting lightly on the boy's shoulder, ready to grab if the edge gave way. "Does Ryan ever ask you about your work?"

Sonterra's cell phone chirped before he could answer. He grimaced, but pulled it from his belt, flipped it open, and identified himself.

He looked at me ruefully as he listened, and I found myself praying that he wasn't being called back to duty because of some emergency. I was enjoying the relative peace and quiet.

"That's great," he said, into the phone. "Thanks for letting me know." His gaze locked with mine. "Yeah. Thanks, Eddie. I'll see you next week."

I waited with raised eyebrows as he closed the cell again and put it back in its customary place.

He cleared his throat.

"What?" I prompted.

"Eddie picked up my mail this morning," he said, running a hand through his hair and looking away for a moment, then back again, by an obvious act of will.

I flashed on a moment the night before, when I'd sensed he was about to drop something on me. "And?"

"A few months ago, I put in an application with the FBI," he said. "I've been accepted. I leave for Quantico in a month."

I stared at him. In all the time we'd been involved, roughly three years by then, including a few gaps, he'd never mentioned changing jobs, not seriously, anyway. His career as a homicide detective was bad enough—but the Bureau?

"I should have told you I was thinking about it," he said.

Waldo, snoring on the hearth rug, lifted his head, suddenly as alert as a bomb dog catching a whiff of something explosive. Bernice laid her muzzle on my thigh and looked up at me. If she'd had eyebrows, she would have raised them.

"Yeah," I answered. "You should have." I

leaned back, forgetting the checkers game, and folded my arms. "Especially since you've apparently already made the decision."

"Clare—"

I measured my words out carefully. "What kind of work will you be doing?"

"Antiterrorist stuff, mostly."

I should have known it wouldn't be a desk job.

Sometimes, as a homicide detective, Sonterra got shot at. Mostly, though, the people he dealt with were already dead. Terrorists were a whole other thing, alive and dangerous. Open season on anybody—especially if they were carrying a shield. "Undercover work?"

Again, that wicked grin, though it was a bit flimsy. "Some," he said. "Agents don't accomplish much, as a general rule, if they announce themselves."

I thought of the World Trade Center, and the Pentagon. Rubble. Bodies falling out of the sky. I wanted to throw up. "Why?" I asked, and it came out as a croak.

"Why do I want to join the Bureau, or why didn't I tell you?"

"Both, I guess," I said, stroking Bernice

for comfort. Waldo laid his muzzle down on his forelegs, but he was watchful, and his floppy ears were perked.

"The Bureau: because maybe I can keep a few people alive, instead of drawing chalk lines around cold corpses all the time. Not telling you: because I knew you wouldn't like the idea."

"I *hate* the idea."

Sonterra's jawline tightened. "You think I ought to become an insurance agent, maybe a car salesman?"

"Works for me."

"Well, it doesn't work for me. And may I point out that *your* job seems to be as dangerous as anything I'd encounter with the Bureau?"

I had no answer for that. Most lawyers go through their whole lives without a single death threat, never mind finding bodies in their pools and getting their office walls strafed with bullets. And that was just the last week and a half.

"Tell you what, Counselor," Sonterra said earnestly. "You give up your law practice, and I'll get a nice, safe job."

"I don't think I can do that," I said. I'd

worked so hard to get my degree, sacrificed so much. Without my practice, my career, I wouldn't know who the hell I was.

"Then we've got a standoff."

I closed my eyes. What else was new?

Sixteen

Leaving Waldo and Bernice behind at the cabin, Sonterra and I drove down to Deliverance Junction to have lunch at the diner, and when I saw the inside of the place, it crossed my mind that he might be out to poison me.

Sitting across from me at a booth in front of the grimy window, hands folded, he grinned. "The food is good here, Clare," he said. "Trust me."

I held my fork up to the light and inspected it for water spots—or worse. "I think my feet are stuck to the floor."

Sonterra laughed, shook his head. "They don't cook on the floor," he pointed out.

I set the fork down. Enough chitchat.

"What if the cops don't find the doll man before you leave for Quantico?" I asked.

The waitress chose that moment to amble over and hand us each a menu. Mine had egg yolk stuck to the front. Sonterra ordered ice tea for himself, and diet cola for me, while I opened my purse and brought out a small bottle of hand sanitizer.

Sonterra rolled his eyes.

"Then I won't go," he answered, when the waitress departed, as if there had been no interruption in the conversation.

I studied him over the top of my menu. "Really?"

"I could take the next training cycle," he said, fiddling with the lemon slice perched on the edge of his glass. It looked a little droopy to me, like it might have been recycled. "Anyhow, I plan to nail this bastard before I have to leave."

I closed the menu as the waitress approached. "I can't decide," I said. "Order for me."

Sonterra asked for cheeseburgers, no onions, while I used the hand sanitizer. "What if you don't find him?" I asked. "The doll man, I mean?"

Sonterra clenched his jaw. "I'll find him," he said.

I picked up the sugar bottle and peered at the little grains of rice in the bottom. I get the reasoning—rice absorbs moisture and keeps the sugar from getting lumpy—but it still grosses me out. Especially when the rice turns brown. "So do you think the Bureau will assign you to some other city?"

Sonterra took the bottle out of my hand and set it down with an irritated clunk. "I don't know," he said. "Homeland Security is a unique animal, and either way, I'll be traveling a lot. Will you stop with the obsessive-compulsive stuff, please?"

I sighed, sat back, and folded my arms. "You would just pull up stakes, then?" Sonterra had a life in Arizona, a large extended family, and lots of friends. Ryan lived in California with his mother, but I knew he visited occasionally.

"I'd prefer to stay where I am, but I may not have a choice."

"Emma's going to be devastated if you leave," I said. I couldn't quite bring myself to meet his gaze. Or to admit that I was going to be devastated, too.

"Don't borrow trouble, Counselor. For all

we know, I'll wash out of the training program and none of this will be an issue."

Sonterra was exquisitely fit, and his mind was one of the best I'd ever run across. He wasn't going to wash out of anything.

The waitress brought the cheeseburgers, and they looked pretty good. I checked under the sandwich, just in case.

Sonterra shook his head, popped open a catsup bottle, and covered his French fries in red goop. "Suppose my base of operations *is* in some other city," he said carefully. "You and Emma could go with me."

I felt a little leap in the base of my throat. "I'd have to close my office," I said.

"Bingo," Sonterra replied. "Just think about it, Clare. You could start a new practice, or take up corporate law." He was picking up speed. "Leave behind all the people who want to kill you."

"Now there's a plus," I answered.

Sonterra took a bite of his cheeseburger, and when he didn't keel over, I reached for mine. It was delicious.

He chewed, swallowed, sucked up some ice tea. "Maybe we could start a kid, or something."

I put my cheeseburger down. Stared at

him. "A baby? You're talking about making a baby?"

He pulled a wry grimace. "Yeah."

"Holy shit."

"Not exactly the reaction I was hoping for."

I laid a hand to my heart, which felt as if it was spinning like a hamster wheel. "What about the money?"

"What money?"

I leaned forward, lowered my voice. The other customers in the diner—two truckers and a guy in a cowboy hat—were ignoring us so studiously that I figured they were probably listening to every word we said. "Damn it," I said. "You *know* 'what money'!"

"Oh, that." Sonterra bit off another chunk of his cheeseburger.

I waited.

He shrugged, wiped his mouth with a paper napkin. "If you can compromise, so can I."

"And exactly what compromise would that be?"

"Eat your lunch," Sonterra urged. He munched a few more French fries before addressing my question. "If you gave up your practice and moved to—wherever—that would constitute a compromise."

I pushed my plate away. "It sure would. And I never said I'd do it."

"I'm aware of that, Clare. I'm throwing out ideas here."

"You expect me to leave Loretta, and Mrs. K?"

"Loretta's jet-setting half the time anyway. Mrs. Kravinsky would be *delighted*, and you know it. Are you going to eat that cheeseburger?"

"Take it," I said. "I'd have to let Shanda go if I closed the practice."

"You could help her find another job."

"You should have been a lawyer, Sonterra."

"Oh, yeah. I'd rather milk cobras."

"Gee, thanks."

"Anytime." He started on my French fries.

"Do you have a tapeworm or something?"

He laughed. "I might have to fight crime at any moment," he said. "I need my strength." He signaled the waitress, and she brought the check, which he paid.

Once we were out of the diner, and in his SUV, I used the hand sanitizer again.

"Why don't you just bathe in that stuff?" Sonterra inquired, starting the ignition.

I ignored the jibe, pretended an interest in the gravel parking lot.

"We'd better drive up to Flag and pick up some more groceries, now that you're a picky eater."

I felt defensive, uneasy, and distinctly fluttery. Sonterra wanted a baby. With me. I'd entertained the idea myself, but that was different. Safe, in the privacy of my own head. "We could just go back to Scottsdale."

"Not a chance. We're staying until Sunday afternoon, just like we planned."

Sonterra drove out of the parking lot and whizzed past the road leading to his cabin.

"What about the dogs?" I asked.

"They'll be all right for another hour, Clare."

We found a supermarket on the outskirts of Flagstaff and laid in some supplies. Sonterra filled his gas tank, and then we went back to the cabin.

The front door was open.

Bernice and Waldo.

I was out of my seat belt and ready to hit the ground running before Sonterra got the rig to a full stop. Just the same, he shot past me like the proverbial rocket.

"Bernice!" I yelled. "Waldo!"

Nothing. Sonterra came to a sudden stop, and I almost collided with him from behind.

"Son of a bitch," he whispered.

I scrambled around him, one hand to my mouth.

There was a doll in the previously empty plant pot next to the porch step, buried up to her neck.

"Oh, my God," I gasped, and bounded for the door.

"Clare!" Sonterra grabbed for me and missed, and I was over the threshold before he caught up.

"Bernice!" I sobbed. Lord, if anything had happened to that dog, or to Waldo . . .

"Stay here," Sonterra said, and this time, he had a grip on my wrist. "I mean it, Clare."

I bit my lip, and nodded, and he let me go.

He crossed the room, opened a little cabinet next to the fireplace, and took out his service revolver. After giving me a warning look, he started down the hall.

I waited five seconds, then followed.

He was standing just inside the doorway when I got there.

The bed had been slashed, blankets,

sheets, mattress. It looked as though someone had gone after it with a buzz saw.

"Waldo," I whispered. "Bernice."

I heard a whimper.

Sonterra heard it, too, and he pinpointed
the direction before I did. He stuck the revolver in his belt and approached the bed.
Dropping to one knee, he lifted the shred-
ded bedspread.

Waldo crawled out, and then Bernice.

I gripped the door frame so hard that my
knuckles throbbed.

"They're all right, Clare," Sonterra said.
"They're all right."

I hurried across the room and knelt to
gather Bernice into my arms. I buried my
face in her fur and wept with relief.

Sonterra, meanwhile, stroked Waldo's
head.

"He was here," I said, quite unnecessarily.
I guess it was hysteria.

Sonterra put his arm around me, pressed
my face into his shoulder.

I don't mind admitting that I clung to him
a little.

SEVENTEEN

Sonterra went through the rest of the house, but he didn't find the doll man, or any other vandalism.

He was outside with the dogs when my cell phone rang, and I nearly jumped out of my skin. Part of me wanted to let the voice mail pick up, but I rifled through my purse for the thing and answered anyway.

"Clare Westbrook," I said.

"Where are you?" Emma demanded. "I've left three hundred and fifty messages on your machine at home."

I sagged into a chair. Through the open doorway, I watched Sonterra throwing sticks for Bernice and Waldo. Something tightened inside me.

"Emma," I whispered, boneless with relief.

"You sound weird, like you never expected to hear from me again or something."

"Of course I expected to hear from you. And I'm fine."

"Except for finding a guy floating face-down in the pool, and the neighbor getting slashed, you mean," Emma parried.

Damn the internet, anyway. Was there a website, for Pete's sake? Clare'sBody Count.com? "I was going to tell you," I said, somewhat lamely.

"Sure," Emma said. "If it weren't for my laptop, I'd never find out anything." She took an audible breath. "Once again— where are you?"

"Sonterra's cabin."

Instant thaw. "Awesome," Emma enthused. "I guess I forgot about that."

I sighed. Tears filled my eyes. I missed Emma with every breath I took, but I was glad she was thousands of miles away, on another continent. I'd been so scared when I'd thought something might have happened to Bernice and Waldo. How much worse to be afraid for Emma.

"Clare?"

I sniffled. "How's school? Are you enjoying Europe?"

"School is school, and I *might* enjoy the trip if I didn't have to worry about you all the time."

Sonterra appeared in the doorway, and the dogs followed him inside.

"You don't need to worry about me," I told Emma, making eye contact with Sonterra. "I've got a bodyguard."

Sonterra wiggled his eyebrows.

"Cool," Emma said, apparently cheered. "So what's with the dead guy in the pool? And the lady across the street—yeesh. That must have been gross."

I frowned. Remembering Peter Bailey, and especially Melanie, I felt sick. Good thing I hadn't eaten the cheeseburger. "How do you find all this stuff?"

"Easy. I just type your name in and ask Jeeves."

"Well, stop doing that, will you?"

"In your dreams," Emma replied. She's not my niece for nothing. "Is Tony there? I want to talk to him."

I extended the phone to Sonterra. He'd been building a pot of coffee while Emma was grilling me. Now, he flipped the little switch to On and took the receiver.

"Hey, kid," he said. "How's it going?"

I watched him. Silently dared him to tell Emma he was joining the FBI.

He didn't.

I went outside, to take another look at the doll in the flowerpot.

A shudder ran down my spine. What kind of pervert would even *think* of something like that?

Sonterra was on my trail, the receiver still pressed to his ear.

"Don't touch that," he said.

I pulled back my hand.

"Never mind," he told Emma, in response to the inevitable question, and sat down on the top step. "Yeah. I'll tell her. Behave yourself, okay? Right. Good-bye, Gomer." He pressed the disconnect button and handed me the phone.

"Tell me what?" I asked, dropping the cell into my shirt pocket. Actually, it was Sonterra's shirt pocket, but it was on my body.

"To stay out of trouble. Poor kid. She actually thinks that's possible."

I glanced at the doll, with only its head and part of its neck showing above the dirt. "She's my greatest vulnerability—I love her so much. If she'd been here, she might have been caught in the crossfire somehow—"

Sonterra squeezed my shoulder. "She *wasn't* here, Clare. Emma's perfectly safe where she is."

"But eventually she'll have to come home. Live with me."

"One day at a time, Babe."

I stared out at the dusk. "Love is a terrible risk," I almost whispered.

"Yeah, but I'm beginning to think *not* loving is even more dangerous."

I wasn't ready to wander into that particular part of my psyche, so I shifted direction. "Since when do you call her 'Gomer'?"

"Since she decided to call me 'Goober,'" Sonterra answered, after a few moments of profound silence, during which he was probably deciding whether or not to let me off the emotional hook.

He was looking at the doll, and I could almost see the cogs turning in his head.

"Are you planning to call the cops?"

"I *am* the cops," he said.

"Maybe there are tracks," I speculated. "From his car, or where he walked in from the woods."

"I've already checked, Sherlock. We're

not dealing with a first-time criminal. This is a psycho, of the virtuoso variety."

"What does your gut say?"

Sonterra hesitated for a long time. He met my gaze, but I could tell it was an act of will. "This doll bit really creeps me out," he said quietly. "In my opinion, he's a serial killer. He's good with computers, and he likes to play games. I'd bet anything Peter Bailey wasn't his first victim."

I shivered, scanned the edge of the woods. There was already a purple tinge to the light; soon, it would be dusk. Was he out there somewhere, watching? Gloating? If he was a game-player, he'd want to keep an eye on the scoreboard.

"Why me?" I whispered.

"There isn't necessarily a reason. Not one a sane person would comprehend, anyway. Lots of times, these assholes spend weeks, months, even years, picking a victim. It could be as simple as the color of your hair, or maybe you just caught his eye at the supermarket."

"You don't think it's someone I know?"

"I'm not ruling that out. He could have been somebody Melanie knew, if she was going to warn you, like he said."

"What am I supposed to do now?"

Sonterra sighed. "What do I think you should do, or what do I know you'll do instead?"

I tried for a smile, but it wobbled and fell off my mouth. "Both, I guess."

"All right. I think you *should* lock up your house and office and join Emma in Europe, or at least hole up at one of Loretta's palaces until things cool off. I think you *will* carry on as usual. It's stubborn and it's stupid, but I kind of admire your go-to-hell approach."

"Kind of?"

He smiled, kissed my forehead, pulled me to my feet as he stood. "My admiration is tempered by the stubbornness and the stupidity," he said.

My gaze fell to the doll again. "Why do you suppose the dogs hid when he came in, instead of barking their heads off? In town, Bernice yaps at anybody who crosses my property line."

Sonterra was still. Cop brain in overdrive. "Maybe she took her cue from Waldo. And he knew who was there because it was the same person who murdered Melanie Witherspoon." He opened the door and stood back to let me step inside first. "On the other hand, the doll man might have known they were here all the time. He could have killed Waldo when he murdered Mrs. Witherspoon, but he didn't."

I was skeptical. "He's an animal lover?"

Sonterra shrugged. "So is bin Laden. He'll do anything for his horses." He sighed, surveyed the woods. Perhaps he was thinking the same thing I was: that the doll man might be within watching distance, lurking in the gathering darkness.

We went back inside, leaving the doll, and Sonterra proceeded to the kitchen, washed his hands, and started making dinner. A man who cooked. Had to love it.

I felt braver after a plate of Sonterra's spaghetti. We washed the dishes together afterward, then we took the dogs outside for a potty break. When we came back inside, Sonterra dug up a Scrabble game, and set up the board in the middle of the kitchen table.

We ate vanilla ice cream, argued over the more inventive words, but we didn't get into anything heavier than that. I guess we needed a rest from the doll man, Sonterra's career plans, and the gnarlier aspects of our relationship—like whether or not we had one in the first place.

Nothing we did was particularly sensual and yet, somewhere along the way, my nerves worked their way to the outside of my skin, and my insides started humming at high decibel. It was a visceral thing with me, urgent and picking up speed. Maybe it was my biological clock, maybe it was a sense of time going by, coupled with irrefutable proof that my next moment could be my last.

After the ice cream, Sonterra meandered into the kitchen and poured wine. It was no quantum leap to figure out that his thoughts were following a similar path to mine.

When he came back with the glasses, he sat down beside me on the couch, his thigh touching mine. We toasted Scrabble, vanilla ice cream, and faithful dogs, and each of us took a sip, watching the other over the rim as we did.

"I really want to make love to you," he said. "Right now."

I took another gulp of wine. "It wouldn't have to mean either one of us was promising anything, exactly," I ventured.

Sonterra nodded, but I thought he

looked mildly disappointed. "Before, it was always a spur-of-the-moment thing," he said slowly. "Impulsive."

I couldn't disagree with that. Not once in our tempestuous relationship had Sonterra and I formally *decided* to make love. "Do you think it would be different, if we—well—did it on purpose?"

He smiled. "Only one way to find out. Are you game, Counselor?"

I set down my wineglass. "Yes."

He put down his wine, caught my face between his hands, and kissed me, not hard, not fast, but slowly and deeply. I felt a hook catch the middle of my heart, and tears burned my eyes.

He drew back, frowned. "You're crying. If you don't want to do this—"

"I do," I said.

He kissed me again. I could have gone for faster, and harder, but Sonterra was going in slo-mo, for sure. And with every light pass of his lips, every move of his tongue, I was more eager.

At last, he slipped a hand inside my shirt, under my bra. Cupped my breast, chafing the nipple with one side of his thumb. He knew that drove me crazy, and he was taking full advantage.

My knees were weak by the time he pulled me to my feet and led me toward the stairs. I hadn't forgotten the slashed mattress in the master bedroom, and I knew Sonterra hadn't, either. There had to be an inherent message in that, but this was for us, a time out of time, and the doll man was outside the perimeter, where he belonged.

We are alive, I thought, with fuzzy defiance. *We are not afraid.*

I hadn't made my bed. The sheets were rumpled.

Sonterra shut the door on the dogs, who would have followed, and I sagged to the edge of the bed.

Sonterra grinned, planted his knees on either side of my hips, and eased me backward onto the mattress. He began nibbling at the hollow beneath my right ear, then the length of my neck.

I groaned and wrapped my legs around his middle, and even though we were both still fully clothed, the contact was electrifying.

"I guess I don't need to ask if you're sure about this," Sonterra muttered, working his way down the front of my shirt now, nipping at my breast through the fabric.

I arched my back. "This is what I look like when I'm sure," I answered.

He chuckled, started unfastening my buttons, all the time maneuvering me to the middle of the bed. He got my shirt open, and worked the front catch on my bra, ready to capture a nipple when my breasts sprung free.

The pleasure went through me like a shard of near-molten steel; I cried out, clasped the back of his head in both hands.

"Do something," I pleaded.

"I—am—doing—something," he replied.

"I mean, oh, God, Sonterra—"

He popped the front of my jeans, lowered the zipper, and put his hand to me. I squirmed, half-frantic. Damn it, my panties were in the way—didn't he know my panties were in the way?

"Take it easy," he breathed, on his way to my other breast.

"I'll take it easy *later*," I gasped. "Right now, I need—"

He kissed a whispery trail down my sternum, over my navel, to the edge where I was hanging by my figurative fingernails, quivering and wet. He slipped to his knees beside the bed, tugged my jeans down and off.

I tore at my panties as if they were on fire, but he caught my wrists and held them aside, and nibbled at me through the nylon.

I called him a name.

He laughed, and touched me with the tip of his tongue.

Just like that, I exploded, my hips airborne, choking on one long sob of frantic, ecstatic release.

He teased me with little flicks until I sagged to the mattress, utterly spent. I thought it was over then, that he'd take me, carry me to another peak. I was half right. He pulled off my panties and had me in earnest, his hands caught behind my knees now, holding my legs apart.

He made me wild with need, stopped just short of satisfying me, and then tasted me again. He made me beg, and I loved it.

Three orgasms and counting, and I wanted him more than ever, the bastard. He let me rest awhile, catch my breath, and then he took off his clothes, stretched out beside me, and worked me with his fingers until I came apart in his arms.

Only then, when my eyes had rolled back

into my head and I thought sure I would die of the relentless pleasure, that I surely couldn't take another climb, did he finally enter me. The thrust was deep, and it blazed with a whole new fire.

I cried out, and gripped the bottom of the headboard with both hands, certain I would drift off into outer space if I didn't hold on for dear life.

Sonterra rasped something, beginning to lose control, and delved deeper still.

I rose to meet him. This was no graceful twining, it was a collision, followed by another collision, and then another.

He moaned, and I felt his restraint snap. He moved faster still, and so did I, matching him stroke for stroke.

The final moments were apocalyptic. We split the atom.

The descent was long and slow, and fraught with powerful aftershocks.

At last, Sonterra fell to me, and we lay trembling, sweaty, flesh to flesh.

The light shifted, and shadows crept in, and still neither of us moved.

I played with his hair. He slipped down to take a few languid licks at my nipples, then rested his head on my belly. We fell asleep, awakened, and made love again, this time, not so urgently. It was easy, it was exquisite, and it was heartrendingly sweet.

We slept again.

The dogs woke us, whining in the hall.

"Real life," Sonterra sighed, and got out of bed. "I'd better let them out and feed them." He leaned to kiss me. "I'll take the first shower."

I didn't stir, for fear I'd end up sharing his shower. Both of us under the spray, naked and soapy? No possible way. One more nuclear climax and I'd melt and slither down the drain.

I dozed, wakened, and dozed again.

Sonterra knelt on the side of the bed, fully dressed, hair still damp from the shower. "Hey, sleepyhead," he drawled. "Unless you're angling for breakfast in bed, you'd better get up."

"I'm not sure my legs still work," I said.

He chuckled. "Oh, they work just fine. I think you bruised my shoulder blades with your heels."

"Very funny."

"Who's kidding?" he replied, and pulled me upright. "Get up. You're too much of a temptation, lying there like that."

I dragged myself to my unsteady feet, wrapped the top sheet around me. Sonterra smiled at my belated modesty, pointed me toward the bathroom and gave me a swat to get me moving.

When I came downstairs, twenty minutes later, he had scrambled eggs on the table and orange juice poured.

"I don't know what's better," I said. "The sex, or the fact that you cook."

I was wearing his bathrobe, the kind of plaid flannel number you might expect to find in a mountain cabin. Behind me, he slid a light hand down the side of my neck and under the fabric to caress one of my breasts.

"Don't you?" he asked.

"Definitely the sex," I whispered—after I caught my breath.

After the food, we went back to bed.

I wouldn't have thought we could manage another round, but we did.

Sonterra fell asleep before I did.

I lay in the early morning silence, thinking of all that I cherished, all that I wasn't about to let the doll man, or anybody else, take away from me.

On the nightstand, Sonterra's service revolver glinted nickel-blue.

EIGHTEEN

At mid-morning, Sonterra's cell phone woke us both with a start. He grabbed it from its place beside the service revolver, flipped it open, and barked his name, while I sat up, pushed back my hair, and reoriented myself. Brassy sunlight filled the room, and the dogs whimpered to be let out again.

"Christ," Sonterra snapped. "When did this happen?"

I had been about to throw back the covers and usher Waldo and Bernice as far as the back door, with a short detour at the bathroom down the hall, but Sonterra's words stopped me cold.

"I'm out of town," he told the person on the other end of the line. His bare shoulders were rigid, his face hard. "No, no—I can be there in a couple of hours." Long pause. "On my way," he finished, and hung up.

"Bad news?" I asked. Sometimes, it just helps to state the obvious.

He didn't look at me. "Eddie's in the hospital," he said. "Carbon monoxide poisoning."

I couldn't take it in. "What?"

Sonterra stared into some imaginary scene, probably picturing his longtime partner dead, or dangerously close to it. "The meter reader found him in the garage this morning, sitting in his car, with the motor running."

My stomach did one of those little acrobatic leaps. "Eddie tried to kill himself?"

"No way," Sonterra said grimly. "Not Eddie."

"But how else—?"

At last, Sonterra met my gaze. "It was attempted murder," he said. "The EMTs found a doll on the passenger seat—with duct tape wrapped around its head."

I ran for the bathroom, and it wasn't to pee.

Half an hour later, we were on the road, barreling south.

First stop, Paradise Valley Hospital. We

left the dogs in the car, with a couple of windows cracked, and rushed inside.

Eddie was in room 423. His skin was a strange shade of pale apricot, and he was hooked up to IVs and various monitors, but he was awake. His estranged wife, Jenna, rose from her vigil chair as we entered.

"Tony," she said, and sagged against Sonterra.

He put his arms around her, hesitated for a moment, then hugged her fiercely.

"Hey, buddy," Eddie said weakly, from the bed. He was trying to smile, taking us both in. "Hi, Clare. Sorry to interrupt your weekend."

Sonterra put Jenna gently aside and walked to his partner's bedside. "What the hell happened?"

Jenna mouthed a sheepish "hello" to me, and we joined the circle.

I noticed the dressing taped to the back of Eddie's head.

"Somebody called the house, around midnight, with a tip in the Judge Henry case," Eddie said. "It was time-sensitive, so I decided to get right on it. I started the car and I was reaching for the button to open the garage door when my head exploded. That's the last thing I remember."

"You didn't see anybody?"

"Nope. The suspect must have been hiding in the backseat."

"The side door had been jimmied," Jenna put in. She was small, slender, blond, and brave. That last part goes with being a cop's wife, soon-to-be-ex or not. "The one that opens onto the patio."

Eddie extended a hand to her, and she took it. She wanted to cry, I could see that, but she was holding herself in check, probably for her husband's sake. She and Eddie had had a nice life together, quiet and ordinary, with a house, two kids, and a stack of bills. In my lesser moments, I'd envied them.

Now I just felt sad.

"It's going to be okay, Snook," Eddie told her tenderly.

She withdrew slightly.

Sonterra turned to Jenna, raked a hand through his hair. "When you called, you said the EMTs found a doll."

Jenna shuddered visibly. "The officers were bagging it when I got there." She blushed. She'd been with her new love, then.

"But you must have gotten a fairly good look," Sonterra persisted. "You described it to me."

Jenna nodded, still keeping that little distance from Eddie. "It was pretty ratty—made of cheap plastic, and naked. Its whole head and face were wrapped—"

It didn't take a rocket scientist to draw the parallel. Eddie's head hadn't been wrapped in duct tape, thank God, but the objective had certainly been the same.

"Congratulations on getting into the Bureau," Eddie told Sonterra, maybe to break the conversational deadlock that followed Jenna's description of the doll. "I'm going to miss you, man. And I'm jealous as hell."

"Never mind the Bureau," Sonterra said, and then brought Eddie up to speed on the incident at the cabin. Clearly, the maniac of the hour was having a busy weekend.

Eddie let out a long breath when Sonterra got to the doll, buried to her neck in the planter on his front porch.

"Same dude," he concluded.

A nurse stepped into the room, beaming, carrying a floral bouquet in both hands.

"Somebody's thinking of you, Mr. Columbia," she said cheerfully.

I glanced at the flowers, like everybody else, and did a double take.

A doll rose out of the middle of a huge cluster of carnations, roses, and daisies, like Venus from the sea.

Jenna sank into a chair, one hand over her mouth.

Eddie stared at the offering, befuddled. No doubt his synapses were still sluggish, firing delayed rounds.

Sonterra jerked the whole shebang right out of the nurse's hands, plunked it onto Eddie's bedside table, and rooted through the blossoms. I figured he was looking for a bomb, or maybe a note.

"No card," he said grimly.

Tension makes me peevish. "Did you expect a name, address, and phone number?"

Sonterra froze me with a glance.

"Is everything all right?" the nurse asked, in a worried singsongy tone. Her large blue eyes widened, flitted from one of us to the other.

"Just great," Sonterra snapped, jerking the doll out of the bouquet to examine it. "I don't suppose you were around when this was delivered."

"It would have come in downstairs," the nurse answered slowly. "Probably at the reception desk." She waited a moment, wringing her hands. "I could call them—"

"Never mind," Sonterra told the nurse. "I'll talk to them in person."

The angel of healing fled.

Eddie's gaze found its way to Jenna, groping. Full of carbon monoxide, he could be forgiven for slow tracking. His tone, however, was urgent, and just the slightest bit confrontational. "Where are the kids?"

"At my mom and dad's," Jenna answered. "They're safe, Eddie."

"I'm taking this to the lab," Sonterra announced, referring, of course, to the bouquet. I could tell by his bearing that he didn't hold out much hope of learning anything useful by going that route. The doll man could have phoned in the order, and never actually touched the arrangement, let alone delivered it. On the other hand, his kind likes to be directly involved, savoring the rising alarm of his victims. He could have assembled the thing personally, and added a sprinkle of something nasty for good measure.

Thanks to the internet, recipes for poisons of all types are readily available.

Sonterra wasn't one to leave i's undotted or t's uncrossed. When he got his figurative teeth into something, his jaws locked like a pit bull's, and he didn't let go. "You'll be staying at your folks', with the kids, right?" he said to Jenna.

A charge crackled in the air.

She had moved to Eddie's bedside. "When I'm not here with Eddie," she said, with a lift of her chin.

"Good," Sonterra replied brusquely. He picked up the flower arrangement.

I resisted a sudden and primitive urge to grab Sonterra and yank him away from the flowers. The doll lent them a malevolence that altered the atmosphere.

"Take care," he told Eddie. "I'll stop by again later."

I turned to Jenna. "Is there anything I can do?"

She smiled tentatively, and shook her head. "Thanks, but I'm okay."

I wanted to do something for her, for Eddie, to make some kind of difference, however small. In a way, it was my fault that this terrible thing had happened in the first place.

"You're sure?"

She nodded.

Sonterra and I left the room, headed for the elevator. "I'm dropping you and the dogs off at my place," he said. Before I could protest, he blocked me. "No arguments, Clare. You wouldn't be safe at your house, and I've got things to do."

"I wouldn't be safe at your place, either," I pointed out.

"Loretta's, then."

"I could help," I ventured.

He stabbed at the elevator button with one forefinger. "If you want to help," he said crisply, "do as I ask."

The dogs were glad to see us when we got back to Sonterra's car.

He started the engine and screeched out of the lot, onto Bell Road, traveling east.

"What are you going to do?" I asked, as we waited at a red light, where Bell Road intersects with Tatum Boulevard. There was a Wal-Mart a block back; I began to tick off a shopping list in my mind, things Jenna might need at the hospital. I could borrow

Loretta's car, if she wasn't using it, and double back.

"After I get you and the dogs behind locked doors," Sonterra replied, his gaze fixed on the traffic, "I plan to get back to work." The light changed, and he hit the accelerator, but only after looking both ways. Phoenix and Scottsdale are notorious for red-light runners.

In some sense, I was still back at the intersection. "This is not about me," I said.

"Of course it's about you," Sonterra said, navigating the traffic with a skill born of long hours on the road, first in squad cars, then in his capacity as a detective. If cops got frequent-flier miles, he'd have enough to ring the equator a couple of times. "Call Loretta."

I did, reluctantly, and I was not-so-secretly pleased when I could honestly say she wasn't home.

Sonterra didn't take the news all that well. "Shit," he said, whipping into the right-hand lane and making a turn onto Hayden Road. "Then it's my place."

"And what am I supposed to do while you're out playing Holmes?"

"Play Watson," he said.

"How come you always get to be Holmes?"

"I've got a badge." We turned into his driveway, and he pushed a button on his visor to open the garage door. I couldn't help thinking of what had happened to Eddie.

Silly me. I was still hoping he'd let me tag along. "If the doll man went to the cabin, and to Eddie and Jenna's, then he surely knows your address, which means I'm not safe here, either."

"You have your .38 in your purse, don't you?"

I nodded. I'd been carrying it on a steady basis since the strafe attack on my office. "Yeah, and I'd have it at my place, too."

Sonterra ignored this reasoning. I knew it was a territorial thing, his wanting me under his roof, even if he wasn't there—he might as well have pissed in a circle and put me in the middle. Alas, I also knew I was wasting precious time arguing with him. "Keep it handy. Short of locking you in a holding cell, this is the best I can do right now. You've got the dogs for company."

"They'd just hide under the bed," I answered disconsolately.

Sonterra left the garage door up, a sure

sign that he wasn't planning to stick around very long. "You could always join them. Make for a long day, though."

"It would be simpler if I went with you."

"For you, maybe."

I sighed, unlocked the car door, and shoved it open. "I could get a cab to my place, or call Mrs. K for a ride. Catch up with you at the cop shop and tail you."

"You do," Sonterra said flatly, "and I *will* throw you into a holding cell."

I'm a lawyer. I *have* to argue, even when it isn't productive. "On what charge?"

Sonterra let the dogs out of the car.

"Don't worry, I can trump something up in no time. By the time you unwind the red tape, I'll have put in a full day's work."

"You're such a bastard."

He came around to my side, planted a cocky smacker on my forehead. "You'd better believe it."

We went inside, followed by the dogs.

Sonterra made the rounds, making sure the doll man hadn't gotten inside the yellow circle, I suppose.

I was washing my hands at the sink, getting ready to make coffee, when Sonterra checked his service revolver.

"Let's see the .38," he said.

I took the pistol out of my purse, somewhat gingerly, and handed it over.

Sonterra popped it open, spun the cylinder. Fully loaded, with hollow points. Satisfied, he set it on the table.

"Call me," I said. "I want regular updates, Sonterra."

He gave me a thin smile, kissed my forehead again. "Don't do anything creative," he said.

Since pacing and wringing my hands didn't qualify as creative, I could make that promise without guilt. "Hurry back, okay?"

He nodded, then went out.

I listened with a sinking heart as he started the SUV, backed out into the street, and the garage door went down with a grinding rumble.

"This must be what it's like to be a housewife," I told the dogs.

NINETEEN

Sonterra hadn't been gone five minutes when my cell phone rang. Thinking it might be the doll man, I didn't pick up right away, but by the third ring, curiosity got the better of me.

"Hello?"

"It's Shanda," my assistant said. "I hate to spoil your weekend, but—"

The muscles in my shoulders bunched painfully. "But?"

"I stopped by the office this morning. Some asshole spray-painted the front window."

I caught my breath. In comparison to some of the things that have happened to me, this was relatively small potatoes.

"Don't worry about it, Shanda. I'll have it cleaned tomorrow."

"Maybe I wouldn't worry, if I couldn't read," Shanda replied. "Clare, it says, 'Die Bitch.' And it's red paint. Like blood."

Since I hadn't bothered to charge my phone since before Sonterra and I left for the cabin Thursday night, the signal was weak. I wandered into his living room, hoping for better reception.

"Okay," I said. "That's probably not good. Anything else?"

Shanda hesitated, then the words tumbled out. "I got a letter. My court date has been set—it's a week from next Friday."

Sonterra has a leather recliner in his living room, facing the big-screen TV. Hey, no man is perfect.

I sank into the cushions. "It'll be okay, Shanda," I said, but I took too long.

Shanda started to cry. "I'm scared. I've got a bad feeling about this."

"I'm going to fight for you, Shanda," I said with certainty. "How you think is important. If you set up a lot of bad vibes, they might come back to bite you in the—well, to bite you. Most likely, you'll get community service."

Sniffles. "What kind of community service?"

"Could be anything from sorting donations in a thrift store to visiting old people in a nursing home."

"I could deal with that."

"Sure you could."

A pause, another sniffle. "Are you having fun up there at the cabin?"

"I'm not at the cabin," I said, and let it go at that. I didn't feel like giving Shanda or anybody else a blow-by-blow, and anyway, I was losing her, satellite-wise. "Look, my phone is dying." I gave her Sonterra's home number. "If you need to talk again, call me here."

"Thanks, Clare," she said. "Is—is everything all right on your end?"

The phone made a chirping sound, and the conversation was over.

I went back to the kitchen, found Sonterra's charger on the counter, and plugged it into my cell. I waited a couple of minutes for his landline to ring, and when it didn't, I was relieved. I was also famished, since Sonterra and I hadn't taken time for breakfast.

I opened the refrigerator and found a

plastic container with egg salad inside. I lifted the lid, sniffed, and dumped the stuff down the disposal.

Further investigation turned up half a loaf of bread, which I inspected closely for mold, and a can of potted meat. I made a sandwich for myself, and because both dogs were staring at me pitifully, I whipped one up for them, too.

"I refuse to watch soap operas or do laundry," I told my canine companions.

I thought they looked sympathetic, but it was hard to tell, since they were both busy snarfing up morsels of potted meat sandwiches.

"Okay, maybe I'll wash some clothes," I relented. "But that's it." Out of fidgety boredom, rather than any desire to wax domestic, I sorted the pile of T-shirts, jeans, socks, and underwear on the floor of Sonterra's laundry room by colors and filled the washer to the brim, pushed the appropriate buttons, and stepped back.

That process took all of two minutes.

Sonterra's computer was in his den, next to the front door. After steeling myself, I logged on to check my email.

No doll pictures. No threats.

So far, so good.

I decided to run a Google on my clients. Sonterra's serial killer theory aside, I hadn't completely ruled out the idea that the doll man was someone I had defended, refused to defend, or failed in some way. I win most of my cases, but there were a few clinkers. I checked the ones that had gone to jail first, starting at the beginning of my career with Kredd & Associates and working my way forward. There were a lot of names I couldn't remember, but more than a dozen stood out in my mind.

The lost causes were still in jail.

Loretta's screen-name popped up with an instant message.

WHAT ARE YOU DOING ONLINE? YOU SHOULD BE WALKING IN THE WOODS OR, BETTER YET, MAKING MAD, PAS-SIONATE LOVE WITH TONY.

I smiled. I'VE BEEN DITCHED, I typed. STUCK AT HIS PLACE, DOING LAUNDRY. I CALLED EARLIER, BUT YOU WEREN'T HOME.

Loretta replied with a smiley face icon and, I WAS SHOPPING, SANS CELL PHONE, AND KIP'S IN D.C. ON BUSINESS. I COULD SPRING YOU.

I considered Sonterra's threat to put me behind bars if I left the house. I MIGHT AS WELL STAY PUT. FINISH THE LAUNDRY.

More smiley faces. WHO ARE YOU, AND WHAT HAVE YOU DONE WITH CLARE?

At that moment, a thunderous clunking sound met my ears, seeming to rattle the very walls, and the dogs began to bark.

The washing machine was off balance.

I bolted from the desk chair and raced toward the laundry room. The clunking got louder, and I hit the kitchen at a dead run. The floor was awash in soapy water; I slipped, went down, and landed hard on my right forearm.

I actually *felt* the bones splinter, and the pain was swift and ferocious. My stomach rolled up into the back of my throat like the long end of one of those paper noisemakers employed at kids' birthday parties and, for a moment, I thought I was going to pass out.

Waldo whimpered, high-footed his way through the rising water, and licked my face. Bernice was more reticent.

I sat up, tried to move my arm.

The pain struck again, this time with the impact of a sledgehammer.

I lowered my head to my knees, waited

for the wave of agony to pass. It grew more intense, instead, then waned just as quickly, leaving me spinning in a dizzy wake. Water continued to surge in from the laundry room like a sudsy river. I was soaking wet, and in serious danger of spewing up my sandwich.

Using my left arm, I levered myself to my feet, clung to the counter edge until I was sure I could stand.

Go figure—the phone was right there, but I groped my way into the laundry room and turned off the dancing washer. My right arm immobile, I was soaking up the water with dirty towels when it occurred to me that I needed medical attention.

The pain was horrendous.

I slogged through the flooded kitchen, passing both Sonterra's phone and my plugged-in cell without a thought. All I could think about was getting to the computer— where I'd left Loretta. My brain was busy with suffering; there was no room for rational thought.

Her messages hung on the screen.
ARE YOU THERE?
CLARE. ANSWER ME.
CLARE????????
Ordinarily, she probably wouldn't have

freaked like that, but given my track record, and recent events, she was probably picturing me with an ax in the middle of my head.

I sat down in Sonterra's desk chair. Tried to type. The resultant ache flashing through my fractured arm put me back in touch with reality.

HELP, I pecked out, with my left index finger. ARM IS BROKEN.

Was she there? I waited, swamped by pain, battered by nausea, fighting not to black out.

The desk extension rang. And rang. And rang again.

Finally, I managed to get hold of the cordless receiver, press the answer button, and croak out, "Loretta?"

"I'm on my way," my best friend said. "Is there a homicidal maniac in the house, or is this just your regular, everyday broken arm?"

I laughed, in spite of the rising throb, now radiating from my fingertips to the center of my solar plexus. "The washing machine overflowed, and I slipped on the kitchen floor, running to shut it off."

"Wait till you see me pull up, then unlock

the front door. I'll call Tony on my cell, on the way over."

"Don't," I said quickly, and waited for another smothering wave of sickness to pass. "He's—he's busy." I laid my head down on the keyboard, too dizzy to sit upright. "Please, Loretta. I'll call him myself—later."

"Whatever," Loretta said. "Sit tight." With that, she was on her way.

Waldo appeared at my side, lapped at my rapidly swelling arm with his long, scratchy tongue.

"It's okay, boy," I said.

He whined.

When Loretta squealed up to the curb in her Lexus, I worked the locks and flung open the door.

"The dogs—" I began, as she took my uninjured arm.

"Never mind the damn dogs," Loretta snapped. "They'll be fine." She hustled me to the car, steered me into the front seat, and fastened my seat belt.

I tilted my head back and closed my eyes.

Loretta got behind the wheel. "How did you get from a romantic weekend at Sonterra's cabin to here, with a broken arm?" she demanded.

Slowly, in halting words, I caught her up—the break-in while Sonterra and I were eating at the E. coli Café. The doll, buried up to its neck in the flowerpot. The slashed bed. Eddie's brush with carbon monoxide poisoning, and the strange bouquet he'd received at the hospital. Sonterra leaving me at his place to go off and fight crime.

"Amazing," Loretta said, shifting into gear and peeling out. "In less than two weeks, you've been shot at, threatened, found two bodies, and broken your arm. That's more than I've been through in my whole life!"

I tried for a smile. Even that hurt. "Want to trade places?"

Loretta took a corner on two wheels. I guessed we were headed for the Scottsdale Healthcare Center at 90th and Shea. That was the nearest emergency room. "Not a chance," she said.

A squad car whipped in behind the Lexus, and the blue-and-red lights splashed into Loretta's car.

"Loretta, you're speeding," I said.

"No shit," Loretta replied, and hit the gas.

"That policeman wants you to stop."

"He'll have to wait."

We zipped up to the emergency room

exit. Loretta stopped the car, shut off the engine, and erupted from the driver's door.

The policeman approached. "I'd like to see your license and registration, ma'am," he said politely. He was about nine years old, by my pain-fogged calculations. Tall for his age.

"Get in line," Loretta replied. "I have an emergency here. Which would be why I was speeding to the *emergency room!*"

"Loretta," I protested. "This is a broken arm, not a heart attack."

She rounded the car, wrenched open my door, and leaned in to unsnap the catch on my seat belt. "With you, it could be anything from bubonic plague to a brain tumor."

A nurse and an orderly came out of the hospital doors, inquired what the problem might be, and gently shifted me into a wheelchair.

Loretta stayed to argue with the policeman.

Perhaps twenty minutes later, when I was lying in an examining room, mildly drugged and waiting to be x-rayed, she stomped in.

"The bastard gave me a ticket!" she fumed.

"Sorry," I said. I feel personally responsible for just about everything that happens in the universe, especially if it's negative in nature.

She smoothed my hair back from my forehead. "Your arm is the size of a yoga bolster," she said, and grimaced.

I felt as though all my vital organs had stuffed themselves into that arm, every one of them pulsing in time with my rapid heartbeat. "Always a cheery word," I teased.

Loretta paced. "When are these people going to *do* something?"

"They're busy, Loretta."

"Don't they know you're in pain?"

"I threw up on the nurse's shoes. I think they're up to speed on the pain question."

"Damn it, this is an emergency! You should be a priority."

"I'm not sure the average head-on collision victim would agree."

"Oh, hell," Loretta said, and sank onto a little round stool. "Did they give you a shot, at least?"

"'Least' is the operative word," I answered. "It must have been aspirin."

The curtains slid back on their noisy metal rod. "Ms. Westbrook?"

"It's about damn time," Loretta said, glowering at the young man who entered, clad in green scrubs and a stethoscope.

By my blurred assessment, he might have been a doctor, an X-ray technician, or a high school kid making the most of Career Day. Maybe he and the policeman outside were classmates.

Ignoring Loretta's sarcasm, he began prodding and poking at my arm.

"It's broken, all right," he concluded.

"Duh," Loretta said.

The next few hours were fuzzy. I was x-rayed, given more drugs, and, because I'd been right about the bone-splintering, stripped, washed, and finally wheeled into the operating room. When I opened my eyes, Sonterra was standing on one side of my bed in the recovery room, Loretta on the other.

"The dogs are home alone," I told Sonterra.

He smiled. "They're okay," he said. "What about you? How do you feel?"

"Like an elephant is standing on my arm," I answered. "When can I go home?"

Sonterra stroked my hair. It felt different than when Loretta did it earlier. "Tomorrow or the next day," he said. "You need to rest, Babe."

"Did you find the doll man?"

He shook his head. "Not yet."

"What about Eddie's flowers? Any anthrax or fingerprints?"

"Clean as a whistle."

"I think your washing machine is broken."

"Good call, Counselor. Forget the freaking washing machine."

"Probably didn't do your floors any good, either."

"No big deal. Go to sleep, Clare."

"Somebody wrote 'Die Bitch' on my office window with red spray paint," I said, holding on to consciousness.

"What?" Loretta asked sharply.

Sonterra frowned. "I'll check it out."

I was reluctant to drift back into the darkness, even though it pulled at me. There were monsters lurking there, in a forest of bad dreams. "Loretta got a ticket today. Can you fix it?"

"Oh, for pity's sake," Loretta said.

Sonterra closed my eyes, first one, then the other, with the tip of his index finger. "Sleep," he repeated, like some stage hypnotist.

I remember thinking that was what you did with dead people. You closed their eyes with your finger.

Cool air kissed my eyelids. I hoped like hell Sonterra hadn't laid pennies on them.

TWENTY

I remained hospitalized until the following Wednesday morning—a long time, by today's HMO, *Gong Show* standards. Considering that the medical establishment had been known to perform a mastectomy and send the patient home the same day, as if they'd had a wart removed instead of a breast, I found this remarkable.

It was also restorative—if it hadn't been for the pain, which sometimes reached breathtaking crescendos, the whole experience would have resembled a visit to one of Scottsdale's legendary spas. During this time-out-of-time, nobody shot at me. I didn't stumble across a single corpse, and not one serial killer called to inform me that they were getting closer.

What luxury.

Sonterra brought flowers. Loretta brought books, and grumbled about her speeding ticket. Even Mrs. K put in several appearances, each time in costume for some mystery-shopper gig. She didn't make a lot of money, but the work suited her adventurous nature, and lent a touch of drama that Rodney and bingo simply couldn't provide.

I was happy for her.

Alas, her infamous nephew was still unemployed, still under police surveillance, and still sleeping on her couch. There had been no sign of the missing Angela, which worried me. When a person is mixed up with bad people, and then disappears from the radar screen, it is not a good sign.

By the time I was released, I had my equilibrium back, and most of my perspective.

Sonterra picked me up at four-thirty in the afternoon.

"I want to go straight home," I announced, as soon as my cast and I were settled in the front seat of his SUV. I was braced for an argument, but Sonterra is full of surprises. He gave in.

Turned out, he'd had all the locks changed at my place. The dogs greeted us with happy yelps as soon as we stepped over the threshold.

On the drive over from the hospital, Sonterra had filled me in on Eddie—out of the hospital, back at work. He and Jenna were still on the outs, though the attack might have drawn them closer. No sign of the doll man, either—he'd apparently gone underground.

I stood at the front window for a few moments, gazing at the house across the street. The yellow crime scene tape had been removed, and the place seemed normal—if you didn't know a savage murder had been committed there.

Sonterra came up behind me, put a hand on my good shoulder, and gently turned me toward him.

"Any news about Dr. Witherspoon?" I asked.

Sonterra set his jaw. Shook his head. "Still missing. We've turned the whole county upside down. Not a trace of him."

"Do you think he's dead?"

Sonterra steered me to the couch, sat me down. "Maybe. If he's alive, he's probably in hiding, which would make him look good for the murder."

"The doll man killed Melanie," I said. I was certain of that much, anyway.

"Yeah," Sonterra agreed. "But Witherspoon might *be* the doll man."

I barely knew Witherspoon, but he'd struck me as rational.

"How come you're so willing to let me come back here?" I asked, unable to hold the question in any longer.

Sonterra grimaced, averted his eyes, looked back at me again. "Isn't it time for you to take a pill?"

"Stop hedging, Sonterra. Something happened."

He sighed, sat down beside me, and took my hand. Chafed the knuckles lightly with the pad of his thumb. "There was a break-in at my place," he admitted. "It was ransacked, among other things."

My mouth dropped open. I consciously closed it. "When?"

"Sometime after Loretta took you to the hospital on Sunday." If I'd dragged those words out of Sonterra with eight mules hitched to a logging chain, they would have come more easily.

"The dogs were there alone," I fretted.

"I found them under my bed, hiding out."

I bit my lip. "And there was a doll, wasn't there?"

Sonterra did the jaw-clamping thing again. It's a wonder he doesn't suffer from TMJ, or have to wear a night-guard to keep from grinding his teeth in his sleep. "Yes," he admitted.

"Tell me," I insisted.

He stared into space, remembering. "It was nailed to the wall, over the living-room fireplace, hands and feet, like some kind of weird crucifix."

Dizziness swamped me. "My God," I whispered. "My *God*." I studied his face, scrambling to regain my inner balance. "There's more, isn't there?"

Sonterra's eyes were as flat as darkened windows, and as opaque. "The doll looked—like you. Dark hair, even a little briefcase slung over one wrist." He grimaced. "If this wasn't so damn bizarre, it would be funny."

I felt a chill. "So far, I'm not seeing much humor in any of it."

"If you did, I'd take you back to the hospital. You need to take a pain pill."

I nodded. Sonterra handed me my purse, and while I was pawing through it for the prescription I'd been given on release, he went to the kitchen for a bottle of water.

Bernice climbed up beside me, huddled close. Waldo laid his muzzle on my thigh and looked up at me, a furry and adoring Cyclops.

Sonterra watched while I swallowed a dose of codeine. "This is making me crazy," he said. "Why can't we be normal people?"

I smiled ruefully. "Got me," I replied. I'd made the same wish, a thousand times, but reality is a stubborn beast. All the finger-crossing and denial in the world won't change it. "Did you find out anything about the graffiti on my office window?"

He looked grim, and intensely frustrated. Shook his head.

"We could try," he said. "To be normal, I mean."

"Waste of time," I said. "This is our destiny."

"God, I hope not," Sonterra replied.

The doorbell chimed. Bernice yapped halfheartedly, and Waldo perked up his ears. Sonterra did the honors, and Loretta blew over the threshold when he opened the door, carrying a bag from a Chinese

take-out place in one hand and a small suitcase in the other.

"I'm spending the night," she said, level-
ing a look at me, as if she expected a challenge, and planting her feet.

I glanced from her to Sonterra. Obviously,
this was something they had cooked up together. *Clare needs a keeper.*

"What's in the bag?" I asked, because I
knew any argument would be futile, and because I didn't mind the company. Besides,
I'd lost five pounds on institutional cuisine,
and I was starving.

"Dinner," Loretta said. She set down her
suitcase and headed for the kitchen. Plate
rattling and silverware jingling ensued.

Sonterra bent, kissed the top of my head.
"Gotta go," he said.

"Crime never sleeps," I agreed.

Sonterra sighed, plainly exhausted.

"Maybe you should get another job," I
ventured, looking around for my actual
briefcase, which I use when I want to get
myself into a really professional state of
mind. Shanda's court date was drawing
near, and I wanted to go over the prepara-
tions I'd already made, see if I could add
something. My game plan, where her case

was concerned, was simple but effective. Whatever she'd done in the past, she was living responsibly now. She was a good mother, and a taxpayer. I intended to show the judge her reference letter from Father Mike and her grades from his computer class, along with some positive statistics from similar cases.

"Maybe you should, too," Sonterra retorted, with a weary twinkle in his eyes. "You could join the Israeli Special Forces, for instance. You've got the personality for it."

"Thanks," I said, with irony. "Have you seen my briefcase?"

"Never mind your damn briefcase."

The phone rang, and Loretta picked it up in the kitchen. She brought the receiver to me. The savory scent of something sweet-and-sour, being reheated in the microwave, teased my nostrils. My stomach growled.

"I need my briefcase," I told her, before taking the call. "Please."

Sonterra rolled his eyes. Loretta nodded and went looking for the requested item. The bell on the microwave dinged, a wonderfully normal sound.

The caller was Shanda. "How's your arm?" she asked.

"Utterly useless, but still attached to my body," I answered. "Are you calling from the office?" I'd put her on paid leave, from the hospital, but she had a key, and I suspected she'd been putting in eight-hour days the whole time I was confined. I didn't want her there alone, especially since the front window had been desecrated again—this time with spray paint.

There was a defensive quaver in her voice. "Yes," she confessed. "Somebody had to answer the phone, read the mail, and reschedule all the appointments. There's some important stuff you need to handle. Paperwork, I mean."

"Messenger it over here," I said, "and go home."

"My court appearance is coming up." She sounded as though she was on the verge of tears.

I felt a rush of sympathy. "I know, Shanda," I said gently. "I'll be there, and I'll be ready."

Bravely, "Father Mike says everything will be all right."

I wished I could hug her. "Father Mike is right, Shanda. Anyway, we still have more than a week."

"And I'm still scared."

I couldn't blame her; she had a lot to lose, starting with her personal freedom, ending with her baby. "Of course you are," I said. "That's understandable."

Sonterra waved good-bye and left the house.

Loretta plunked my briefcase down on the coffee table in front of me, and motioned that she would bring my dinner.

I nodded gratefully. "Anything else going on?" I asked Shanda.

"Well," Shanda said hesitantly, "there *was* a small fire."

"What?"

Loretta, in the process of setting a plate of sweet-and-sour chicken, fried rice, and wontons down in front of me, froze.

"It was only the filing cabinet," Shanda said.

"When did this happen?" I think I can be excused for being a little terse.

"About twenty minutes ago," Shanda replied. "It's okay, Clare. Dr. Thomlinson and I put it out before the fire department got here."

"How did it happen?"

"Must have been spontaneous combustion, or something. I went into the restroom to fix my lipstick, and when I came out, the thing was in flames and Dr. Thomlinson was running for the fire extinguisher. He said he saw the flames from the street." She paused. "Most of the files are toast."

I speared a piece of sweet-and-sour chicken. As I have said before, nothing much wrecks my appetite. "But no one was hurt?"

"No," Shanda assured me. "But of course there was smoke damage." Her voice brightened. "One of the firemen asked me out. His name is Mike."

"There's always a bright side," I said, but I don't think Shanda caught the sarcastic note. I looked up at Loretta, who was watching me with her hands on her hips.

"The sprinkler system came on, though," Shanda went on. "Drenched everything. I can't get the computer to boot up."

I swore under my breath. Most of my files were gone, and, if the computer had been doused, so were the duplicate records on my hard drive. My practice, my identity, was at ground zero.

"Your insurance will cover it, right?" Shanda inquired tentatively.

Collecting on my office policy was the least of my concerns. Without those files, and the corresponding computer records, the whole thing was swirling in the bowl, sewer-bound.

Maybe it was ordinary vandalism. And maybe someone had something to hide, something that was contained in those files.

"Shanda," I said, "I want you to get out of that office, now. It's long past quitting time anyway. Lock it up and go home."

"What about the stuff you wanted messengered to your place? I could bring it over, if you'll pay my cab fare."

"Bad idea," I said. "It can wait until morning. But I'm glad you managed to save something."

"Some of the files and your appointment book were in your desk drawer," Shanda said, with a note of pride. "Stuff I thought you'd want to see right away."

"Tomorrow," I said, with a sigh.

We said our good-byes and hung up.

"What now?" Loretta wanted to know.

I told her the latest.

"It's a message from the gods," Loretta decided. "You're supposed to close that place and marry Tony Sonterra."

"Funny," I said, eating again. "I didn't get that from it at all." That wasn't entirely true, of course, but I don't tell Loretta *everything*. Just almost.

"You wouldn't," Loretta said.

I concentrated on my dinner.

"Aren't you going to call Tony?" my best friend prodded.

"No," I said, "I am *not* going to call Tony. He's up to his fine ass in alligators as it is. I'll tell him about it later." I flipped the catches on my briefcase.

Loretta glared. "Please tell me you're not going to work. You just got out of the hospital, for God's sake. Your whole life is a train wreck! How can you possibly think about depositions and briefs and all that other lawyer crap?"

"I'll go crazy if I don't," I answered simply, and opened the case.

In the next instant, the poles changed places, and the earth froze.

There was a doll inside the briefcase, one of those eleven-inch numbers, anatomically correct and naked. There were thumbtacks where her eyes should have been, and her right arm was bound in a tiny sling.

"Oh, *shit*," Loretta said.

It wasn't the doll that stopped my heart, and made my breath seize in my throat. I was developing an immunity to that kind of shock.

"He's been here," I murmured. *"In my house."*

"I'm calling Tony," Loretta said. "And then we're blowing this joint."

"This is my *home*, damn it. I won't let him scare me away. I'm *not* leaving!"

"Give me that phone," Loretta said. I handed her the receiver. "At least we can report it."

While she punched in a series of numbers, I slowly closed the briefcase.

"Who the hell are you?" I whispered. "And what the *fuck* were you doing in my house?"

TWENTY-ONE

When Loretta got Sonterra's voice mail, she turned testy. "Where's a cop when you need one?"

The doorbell rang. Sonterra, having just left, wasn't likely to have doubled back so quickly. Loretta and I looked at each other in worried silence.

Finally, she went to the door and peeped through the hole.

She looked back at me. "Mrs. Kravinsky," she said. "At least, I *think* it's her."

"Let her in," I prompted, carefully closing the briefcase.

Loretta opened the door, and Mrs. K swept in, wearing a floral print cotton dress, a long blond wig, and granny glasses with pink lenses. Apparently, she'd been on assignment.

"I called the hospital for an update," Mrs. K said, "and they told me you'd been released. I came to see for myself."

"What's with that getup?" Loretta asked, shutting and locking the door. Apparently, she hadn't heard about Mrs. K's new career as a secret shopper.

Mrs. K was lugging a large tote bag, with a sequined picture of Lucille Ball gracing one side. "I was checking out a new Wal-Mart," she said. "I wanted to blend in with the clientele."

"I see," Loretta said, though I could tell she didn't. But, then, Wal-Mart is only a vague memory for Loretta. She shops at Neiman-Marcus and Saks now.

Mrs. K gave her a brief rundown on her job description. "I'm not getting rich," she finished, "but it's a living."

"You must spend most of your paycheck on costumes." Loretta's tone was dry.

I gave her a look, and she gave it right back.

"Maybe you ought to look into this mystery shopping thing, Clare," she said sweetly. "It would certainly be an improvement over what you do now."

"Bite me," I replied.

If Mrs. K registered that little exchange, she gave no sign of it. "I get them all at thrift shops." She frowned. "My costumes, I mean. Too bad nobody would believe a pirate wanted to pay a light bill or get some dry cleaning done. I would love to dress up like Johnny Depp in that Disney movie."

In spite of my broken arm, the burned files, and ruined computer at my office, not to mention the doll with thumbtacks in its eyes and a sling on its arm, the image of Mrs. K as Captain Jack Sparrow made me want to laugh. "It would take too long to do your hair," I said reasonably. "All those beads."

The woman of a thousand faces took a seat beside me on the couch, leaving Loretta to plant her bony butt on the stone hearth. Mrs. K laid a motherly hand on my knee. "You look terrible, dear," she said. "Absolutely dreadful."

"Thanks," I said, cheered by her presence. "I *feel* pretty terrible."

Mrs. K brought a purple candle out of her bag, set it on the coffee table, and lit it with a flick of her Bic, assuming a dreamy expression. "Why don't you make us all some tea, Loretta?" she asked, sounding distracted.

Loretta came back with what I thought was a great suggestion. "How about martinis instead?"

"I never drink and drive," Mrs. K replied. I was relieved. She and that Buick of hers were a lethal combination anyway, without adding alcohol to the mix.

Booze and painkillers wouldn't make a good blend, either, I decided, with no little regret.

"Mrs. K and I will have tea," I said. "I wouldn't mind a couple of olives, though."

Loretta gave me a narrow inspection. "Tea and olives? Have you been taking your birth control pills?"

I ignored her.

Loretta made for the kitchen, where I kept my limited stock of firewater and about a hundred kinds of herbal tea, and Mrs. K reached into her Lucy bag again for more candles. Soon, six of them sat in a circle on my coffee table. Mrs. K made another dive and brought out a swatch of what looked like sage. I knew she'd light it on fire and wave the smoke around, to clear out any negative energies. The last time she used that stuff, Sonterra almost busted me for possession of a controlled substance.

Loretta brewed and served the tea first, then went back for her martini and a small bowl of green olives for me.

Mrs. K's eyes were closed now, lids quivering. She swayed back and forth, waving her hands around, and I gave Loretta silent points for not laughing.

Mrs. K looked like an aging hippie with a snout full of hashish. When she opened her eyes again, she seemed a little dazed.

"The dog saw everything," she said, in the voice of an oracle, and looked sadly at Waldo. It took me a few moments to realize she was talking about the murder across the street. Old news, in my fast-moving life, but Mrs. K had been busy coddling Rodney and making sure Wal-Mart toed the line. She was playing magical catch-up now.

Loretta took a swig of vodka and vermouth, and her eyes danced above the rim of her glass. I gave her another quelling glance, just in case her good intentions were slipping.

"This is very bad," Mrs. K continued.

I bit my lip, since I had an impulse to state the obvious.

"How's Rodney?" I asked, after a pause. I felt guilty about neglecting his case, not so much for his sake as for Mrs. K's.

She sighed. "The poor boy is distraught. The police are watching him, and he hasn't heard a word from Angela."

"That's his girlfriend," I told Loretta. "Sort of."

Mrs. K poured me a cup of tea, then one for herself. The steam fogged up her pink lenses. "He can't seem to find his place in life. A job would do him so much good—raise his self-esteem."

Not to mention leaving him with no excuse for mooching off his aunt.

"Maybe he could become a mystery shopper," Loretta offered, from behind her martini.

"Oh, no," Mrs. K said, with innocent good cheer. "No one would ever take a check or a credit card from Rodney."

Recalling his shaved head, offensive tattoos, dirty jeans, body odor, and surly attitude, I had to agree. He wouldn't look good in a blond wig, either, and forget the pink specs. "Maybe the moving company would rehire him," I said, though I didn't think there was a chance in hell that he'd get his old, pre-prison job back. I was just trying to console Mrs. K, recalling how proud she'd been when her nephew was bringing in a steady paycheck.

She looked thoughtful. The candle flames danced, and the smoke shifted in the air like wraiths at an orgy. Loretta coughed.

"I don't think they would," Mrs. K mused. "I never told you, but some things disappeared from one of the loads. Rodney was blamed—that's how he ended up in jail. He doesn't fit in very well, you know. Doesn't relate to people."

God bless Mrs. K. It had probably never crossed her mind that Rodney might lift the odd stereo system or wide-screen TV before it was officially time to unload the truck.

"How long is he staying?" Loretta asked.

"Just until he gets work," Mrs. K answered. I hoped she was lighting a lot of job candles, because Rodney was likely to be a hard sell, even to the Universe. She fixed Loretta with an unblinking gaze, suddenly all business. "You are staying the night, aren't you? Clare mustn't be alone, with that broken arm, and I really can't sleep over.

Rodney has an appointment in the morning, and I'm scheduled to investigate a supermarket."

"What are you going as?" Loretta asked, clearly intrigued. God knew what Mrs. K's conception of the average supermarket customer entailed.

"I'm afraid that's confidential," Mrs. K said importantly. She got to her feet and gazed down at me fondly. "Well, now that I've gotten the candles working, I'd better be on my way." I started to rise, intending to walk her to the door, but she stopped me by placing a hand on my shoulder and bending to kiss the top of my head. The tenderness of the gesture invoked memories of my grandmother, and sudden tears came to my eyes. "Don't get up," she added, pretending not to notice my emotional state. "Loretta will see me to the door."

They left me in the living room, and I heard them conferring, in whispers, in the entryway. No doubt they were lamenting my unprecedented talent for attracting calamity in every shape and form. Fires, bullets, broken bones—I was a one-woman Armageddon.

Loretta walked Mrs. K out to her Buick,

came back, and locked the front door, throwing all the bolts. Sonterra had added a few in my absence.

"You do have an extra bed in this mausoleum, don't you?" my friend asked, when she returned, after pausing to finish off her martini. "No way I'm going to sleep on that couch. Didn't you have that way back when you worked at Nipples?"

"You can spend the night in Emma's room," I said, ignoring the couch comment. By that time, I'd blinked away the tears of nostalgia brought on by Mrs. K's display of affection, but I don't think Loretta was fooled. Maybe my eyes were puffy or something.

"Did they give you anything for sleep before you left the hospital?" she asked.

"No," I answered. Eight hours of oblivion sounded good, right about then.

"I brought some tranquilizers," Loretta answered, nodding toward her suitcase. "I'd be happy to share."

"Thanks," I answered, getting to my feet. "If I decide on an overdose, I'll let you know."

At ten-fifteen that night, I woke to find Sonterra standing next to the bed. He set his service revolver on the nightstand, stripped to his briefs, and crawled in beside me.

"Did you get Loretta's voice mail message?" I asked tentatively. I hated to bring up the latest doll visitation, but if he hadn't gotten the word for some reason, he'd be understandably pissed that I hadn't told him.

"Yeah," he said grimly, stretching, slipping an arm around me. My cast was like a plaster log between us. "Loretta showed me the thing when I came in. I wish the chickenshit mother would come out of hiding. I'd like to put him out of his misery. In the meantime, I bagged the doll for evidence. It can keep the others company down at the station."

I let my head rest on his shoulder. "I'm sorry, Sonterra," I whispered, and maybe there was a slight catch in my voice.

He rose onto one elbow to look into my face. "For what?"

"For being so damned much trouble."

He grinned, albeit wearily. "You *are* a lot of trouble," he said. "But you're kinda cute, and you've got a really good ass."

I laughed, and then I cried.

Sonterra held me until I went to sleep.

TWENTY-TWO

It took some doing to get to the office the next morning.

I had to wait until after Sonterra left the house, and then work fast to get away before Loretta finished her beauty sleep. With one arm in a cast, it wasn't the easiest task I'd ever undertaken, but I managed to perform the usual ablutions and get myself into slacks and a blouse. My hair, arguably my best feature, cooperated.

When I got to Presidentsville, I found that Shanda had arrived ahead of me, put the coffee on to brew, and generally started the place humming.

After shaking my head over the charred contents of the file cabinet, I checked the voice mail messages, putting the phone on speaker mode, and I was chagrined, if not surprised, by the common thread of concern running through all of them, in varying degrees. There was an angry diatribe from David Valardi, who wondered at high decibel how I could be giving his case proper attention when I'd missed an appointment and he couldn't get me on the telephone. Other clients were equally disquieted. Only Barbara Jenkins, she of the husband found facedown in the family fishpond, was remotely positive. She apparently regretted fleeing my office after the encounter with Sonterra, and hoped I would not resign as her defense attorney.

The doll man got in the last word.

"You are a whore," he said, in that strange, flat voice of his. "Your time is running out."

I looked up. Shanda was in suspended animation, gaping at me, coffee carafe in one hand, cup in the other. Both of them shook as she set them both aside.

"Holy crap," she said, hugging herself. "My skin is crawling!"

I bit my lower lip, thinking. Shanda was young, and she had a daughter to raise, a life to live. What if something happened to her, because of her association with me? "This is a dangerous place for you to be," I mused.

"Not as dangerous as the bus stop in front of our apartment complex," she answered quickly. "Have you noticed how weird that guy sounds? Like he's a robot, or something. Maybe 'he' isn't even a dude—maybe he bought one of those voice-distorter things on the internet or at a spy shop or something, and he's really a woman. Have you thought about that? That he could be a she?"

The telephone rang before I could answer her. The possibility had occurred to me, but I'd rejected it almost immediately. Peter Bailey might have been slight, but he'd been wiry, too, and he'd had mental illness on his side. Such people are often formidably strong. Melanie Witherspoon hadn't exactly been Ms. Universe, but I remembered her as fit and loose-limbed. She'd been willing to risk her own safety by approaching the night Bailey presented himself at my door with that first batch of doll pictures, which indicated a certain confidence in her own strength. Most women would have had a hard time overcoming either one of them—unless, of course, she'd taken them by surprise.

Shanda grimaced and reached for the receiver. "Clare Westbrook's office," she chimed, after switching off the speaker. Her eyes narrowed as she listened. "Yes," she said tersely, "we *are* open for business, Mr. Valardi. And since you're getting Clare's services for free, you might want to do something about your tone of voice."

I paused in the act of pouring coffee, my eyebrows raised.

"I'll see if she's in," Shanda said, with scathing dignity, after what seemed to be another verbal barrage from Valardi's end. Cupping one hand over the mouthpiece, she asked stiffly, "Are you here?"

I smiled, nodded, and held out my hand for the phone.

"David," I said pleasantly. "How are you?"

Valardi let out a ragged breath, propelled by irritation. "I go on trial in three weeks," he replied. "I hear from my lawyer every other blue moon. How do you *think* I am?"

While I could certainly acknowledge that David Valardi had a point, and ample reason to work himself into a dither, it wasn't as if I'd been scattering rose petals along a wooded path since our last conversation. Except for a few interludes with Sonterra, I hadn't been out there having *fun*.

"You need to calm down, David," I said. "Judges pick up on attitude, and you can't afford to have one."

He huffed out another blast of wind. "I don't want to go to prison," he said.

"Of course you don't," I answered reasonably. "Can you come in? I've had some ideas about your defense, and I'd like to go over them with you."

I sensed his relief, though he was still a bit bristly. "I'll get there as soon as I can. Did you know they can make it a crime for me to even *touch* a computer, if this thing doesn't go our way?"

"Yes," I said. To David, this was surely a dire prospect. Giving up his computer would be like severing a limb, and worse, probably, than going to prison. "If you *did* create the Barabbas virus, you need to tell me right now. I don't want the prosecution blindsiding me with something they downloaded from your hard drive."

"That isn't going to happen."

I frowned, troubled by the fact that he hadn't denied any wrongdoing. That was the first impulse for most people, whether they were telling the truth or not.

Before he could speak again, I planted both feet on well-trodden ground, which is largely what the practice of law is all about. Hashing and rehashing, wringing the last quivering drop of meaning out of every tedious detail. "But they have hackers of their own—or, at least, access to them, especially if they've brought in the FCC. All they need is a starting point—something that steered them to some other element—and they can build a case. For instance, if you posted anything incriminating on a website—"

"I do a lot of research," David said, sounding defensive and, at the same time, deflated. I had a bad feeling in the pit of my stomach. "I've been to lots of websites."

"Any that I should know about?"

My client was quiet. Too quiet.

"David?" I prompted.

"There were some porn sites," he said.

"Normal, for a guy your age," I replied, wondering why I wasn't even mildly relieved. "No kiddie porn, though, right, David? No how-to-build-a-bomb stuff, no down-with-society-as-we-know-it?"

He swore. "Of course there was no kiddie porn," he replied angrily. "What do you think I am?"

I knew from earlier interviews that David lived with his mother, that he couldn't hold a job, that he was seriously overweight and had no discernible social life. None of which necessarily made him guilty, but such circumstances can foster resentment, among other things—look at the root of most crimes, and you'll find bitterness, a desire to right wrongs, be they real or imagined. "I'm merely trying to make sure we're on solid footing, from a legal standpoint," I told him. "If the DA's office rolls out a big gun, I don't want to be standing in the open. Bring me a list of every website you remember visiting."

He sounded petulant. "Why do you need to know all this stuff?"

"Because the prosecuting attorney will know it," I retorted. "I have to know what he or she knows, down to the last bid on eBay."

He was silent.

"David," I urged. I felt as though I were standing in an elevator, in free fall.

"All right," he spat out. "But just because I looked at a few kinky sites doesn't mean I broke the law. What about freedom of speech, freedom of the press?"

"Sticky questions, where the internet is concerned," I answered crisply. "There aren't a lot of rules, and that applies to the other side, as well as to us. Don't forget the list—and don't try to sugarcoat it."

Shanda let out a sigh as soon as I said good-bye and hung up. "You play hardball," she said.

"Believe it," I said. "So does the DA."

She made an undulating motion, like some magnificent, brightly colored bird shrugging its feathers smooth, and averted her gaze just long enough to make me worry.

I gave her a narrow look. "Is there something you want to tell me?" Her rescheduled court date was almost upon us and, while there would be no jury, I didn't want some eager clerk from the prosecutor's office trotting onto the scene at the last minute with a file full of secret Shanda-sins under one arm.

"Diego came back," she said.

"Who, pray tell, is Diego?"

Shanda pushed her shoulders back and stuck out her chin. "He's Maya's daddy," she answered.

If it weren't for bad vibes, I reflected, I'd have no vibes at all. "Ah," I said noncommittally.

"He's changed," Shanda threw out.

"From what?" I countered.

"He used to deal a little."

"Oh, shit," I said. "Shanda, you can't expect the judge to be lenient if you're hanging out with a pusher." It went without saying that I wouldn't be too pleased, either.

"People change," she insisted.

"Sometimes," I admitted, with reservation.

"Maya needs a father."

"Like a hole in the head, if he's using or dealing. Do you really want a man like that around your child?"

Tears welled in her eyes. "I told you, he's changed. He found God."

"Right," I said.

"You sound like Mama."

"Then you have a smart mother."

"Oh, yeah? Then how come she makes minimum wage and we can't even have a telephone?"

I leaned back in my desk chair and folded my arms. "Listen up, Shanda. You and I, we had a deal. You have to keep your nose clean. One brush with the law, and you're going to be out of here so fast, your heels will leave skid marks."

"You're firing me?"

"No," I said. "But if you get into trouble, I will. In a heartbeat."

"It isn't so easy, being alone. And Diego's clean. He's not dealing. He even has a job."

"Doing what?" In my head, I'd pretty much tried and convicted the guy, sight unseen. I have a thing about drug dealers; in my experience, they're like child molesters. They don't reform, they just lie dormant, like mushroom spores in a bed of dung.

Shanda's chin went up another notch. "He runs a nightclub."

"What nightclub?"

She hesitated. "The Headbanger. But you can't go by the name of the place—"

"Can't I?" I asked, experiencing a déjà vu moment. The Headbanger was the club Rodney Gerring had mentioned. His girlfriend, Angela, hung out there. I wondered if the police had followed up on the lead, and made a mental note to find out. "What's Diego's last name?"

"Are you going to run a background check on him?"

"Maybe," I said. *Definitely*, I thought. I didn't want Shanda to lose custody of Maya, let alone go to jail, but if Diego was the kind of yardbird I suspected he was, the child would be better off in foster care.

"Sanchez," Shanda said reluctantly, but I thought I saw something else in her eyes. Relief, perhaps. "Diego Sanchez."

TWENTY-THREE

Life is full of surprises. If only more of them were good ones.

Call me jaded, but I would have bet sheepskin and shingle that Diego Sanchez was bad news.

I spent the next two hours returning phone calls and reassuring disgruntled clients. My arm throbbed, inside its hard cast, and I guess I could have used it as an excuse, but I didn't. I don't whine.

Shanda kept busy, trying to salvage something from the scorched file cabinet, but she was subdued. Good. Maybe she was thinking.

I called in an order for two computers, hoping one of them wouldn't become superfluous. I'd taken a hard line with Shanda, but I still had confidence in her. She was intelligent, as well as street smart. She loved her daughter, and she had goals: night school, a car, an apartment of her own.

She would make the right decisions.

All this time, I was concentrating on the business at hand, at least on one level. In the boiler room of my brain, though, I was still gnawing at the Diego problem—if indeed it *was* a problem. Maybe all my instincts were wrong. Maybe he really *was* a changed man.

Maybe the Pope shopped at Victoria's Secret.

At ten-fifteen, David Valardi arrived for our appointment, armed with a handful of lists and an attitude.

I was not in a mood to mollycoddle. "Why don't you have a job?" I asked, the moment he took the hot seat on the other side of my desk.

"What happened to your filing cabinet?" he countered, taking in the damage.

"Spontaneous combustion," I said. "Answer my question, David."

"Whose side are you on, anyway?"

"That wasn't an answer, it was a question."

He sighed. His hair hadn't been combed, there was a film on his teeth, and his sweat-suit looked as though it doubled for pajamas. "I'm disabled."

"By what?"

He frowned. "Bipolar disorder."

"You didn't mention that before."

"It didn't seem important."

It was my turn to sigh. "I'm your lawyer. I'll decide what's important."

"I don't get along with people."

"Neither do I," I said. "Do you take medication?"

He shifted uncomfortably. "Most of the time."

"Did you or did you not create the Barabbas virus, David? And keep in mind, whatever you tell me is confidential."

He glanced nervously at Shanda, who was at the other desk, sifting diligently through blackened files, seeing what she could salvage. Her original assessment, unfortunately, was pretty much right on—there wasn't much.

I opened my desk drawer, pulled out my purse, extracted a bill from my wallet, and sent my reflective assistant off in search of lunch for three. There were plenty of fast-food places in the neighborhood.

"I wrote the virus," David said. "But I didn't put it out on the net. I swear I didn't."

I squeezed the bridge of my nose, focusing on the confession, not the disclaimer. "Why?"

Valardi didn't pretend to misunderstand. "I wanted to see if I could do it," he said. "That's all."

Strangely, I believed him. Go figure. He'd been lying to me from the first. Still, I could picture him in some dark corner of his mom's basement, his bulk rimmed in the bluish gray glow of a monitor screen, pudgy fingers flying over the keyboard. Maybe a little smile touching down on his mouth, every once in a while, as he tried one code, and then another, boldly going where no hacker had gone before.

I reminded myself that the virus was predatory, lurking in emails, sliming its way over phone lines, satellite dishes, and cable, gobbling up hard drives, multiplying itself to the nine-millionth power. The specialty seemed to be wiping out accounts receivable in the credit card departments of banks and certain retailers, but there had been incidents with utility companies as well, and even local and state agencies.

"This thing did a lot of serious damage, David. How did it get out there, if you didn't turn it loose?"

More shifting. "I might have shown it to a couple of people."

"Great." I reached out for the website list, which he was clutching in one meaty fist, and found it damp with sweat when he handed it over. "Do these people have names?"

Valardi looked miserable. I wondered if he could pull off an insanity plea. If he was a manic-depressive, and unmedicated . . .

"I only know them by their screen names," he lamented. "BoogerBrain243. Flasher. HumpDoggy."

"I am not looking forward to telling that to the judge, David." I set the list down. I wasn't going to like what was on it, and I couldn't check it out until the new computers arrived anyway. Or until I went home and logged on. A double bummer, with one useless hand.

If possible, I would give the job to Shanda.

He sniffled, then his big face crumpled, and he began to cry. "They promised they wouldn't try it out. BoogerBrain and Flasher and HumpDoggy, I mean. They *promised*."

"People lie," I said, in a testy tone. I was not unsympathetic—like I said, I basically believed him—but we were in deep shit. Stupid as their screen names were, Valardi's cyberbuddies were probably smart enough to cover their tracks. I doubted, too, that they'd set out to destroy half the hard drives in Arizona. Most likely, the original objective had been to wipe out the balance on their mothers' Visa cards, and after the first few experimental forays, the thing had gotten out of hand.

"What am I going to do?"

"Tell the truth when the assistant DA puts you on the stand," I suggested. I have my fanciful side. "And find out exactly who these guys are. Names. Addresses. Anything and everything."

David wiped his face with the hem of his sweatshirt. It was an oddly vulnerable gesture. "I could stand going to jail," he said tearfully. "I wouldn't like it, but I could cope. But if they take away my computer—"

"You're in big trouble, David," I said, but I got up and got him a box of tissues and a bottle of water from the minifridge.

He blew his nose copiously. I thought of BoogerBrain.

"I've got a question," I ventured.

David blinked. "What?"

"You're obviously smart. Why write a program like Barabbas in the first place, instead of something constructive? Or at least legal, like a video game? You could have stayed on the right side of the law and maybe even gotten rich."

He shrugged. "I guess I didn't think of it," he said.

I closed my eyes for a moment. When I opened them, Shanda was peering through the front window, which had been cleared of spray paint while I was in the hospital, holding a pizza box in both hands.

I gestured for her to come in.

"I don't think I can eat," Valardi said.

Shanda breezed over and plunked the box down on top of her desk. "Well," she said, "you'd better work up an appetite, because this thing is the size of a manhole cover."

Between the three of us, we ate every crumb.

"So how did it go?" Shanda asked, when David left. Either Diego had dropped off the face of the earth, or the food had raised her spirits. Since the first instance was too good to be true, I was betting on the second.

"I assume you're asking about Mr. Valardi." I crumpled my paper napkin and tossed it into the trash. "I'll be lucky to keep him out of the state pen."

Shanda winced. "Bummer," she said.

I was reminded of Emma, who was the subject of much industry on yet another floor of my brain. I hadn't heard from her since before I wiped out on Sonterra's kitchen floor, and that bothered me. I hadn't checked my email since before the accident, but Emma usually communicated by telephone.

I glanced at my watch, calculated the time—it would be around nine P.M. in Italy—and dialed her hotel in Florence.

"Emma Westbrook, please," I said, when a receptionist answered in cheerful Italian. "She's with the American school group."

The desk clerk switched to English without a hitch. "I am sorry, Signora. They have checked out one week ago."

I was taken aback, even though moving on was the nature of this particular beast—the curriculum was planned around twelve different European cities. I had an itinerary at home, where it was no help at all.

"Do you know where they went?"

The answer surprised me. So many things had been going wrong lately that I was already clenching my back teeth.

"Si, Signora. They are in Roma. But who is calling, please?"

I identified myself as Emma's legal guardian, and asked for the name and telephone number of the hotel in Rome. Italians are more trusting, it would seem. She gave me the information without hesitation.

I placed the second call immediately.

"Hello?" inquired a young girl's voice, when the Roman desk clerk rang Emma's room.

"This is Clare Westbrook," I said. "I'd like to speak with Emma."

Hesitation. "This is Emma."

Instant tension. "No," I countered. "This is *not* Emma. Where is my niece?"

Transatlantic tears. "I told her this wouldn't work."

"Excuse me?"

"Emma ran away. She said she was going home. I've been covering for her."

The pizza churned in my stomach. "Good

God," I breathed, dizzy. "When did she leave? Why didn't she call me first—?"

"She isn't home?"

"No," I said, terrified and furious, both at once, "she isn't. *When did she leave?*"

"Night before last. She took a cab to the airport. I let her use my dad's credit card."

I tugged at the collar of my blouse. "And the chaperones didn't notice she was gone?"

"Like I said, we've been covering for her. So she wouldn't get in trouble."

"Oh, she's in trouble, all right," I said. *Please, please, let her be all right. Just let her be all right!*

I hung up without a good-bye and promptly redialed. While I waited for the connection to be made, I flipped awkwardly through my day-timer, one-handed. When another happy Italian voice answered, I had the name of the woman heading up the school tour, and asked for her.

She answered sleepily. "This is Stella Tittle."

"Clare Westbrook," I said, to get it out of the way. "Emma Westbrook is my niece. Are you aware, Ms. Tittle, that she took off for home night before last, according to her roommate?"

Stella sucked in a horrified breath, which was answer enough. "That's impossible! We keep very close track of our girls—"

"Apparently," I broke in, "you do not. I just called her room, and I was told that Emma intended to buy a plane ticket and come home."

"We don't permit our girls to travel unaccompanied."

"You've been hoodwinked, Ms. Tittle. But the point is, my niece has evidently been in transit for forty-eight hours!"

"They said she was sick—"

"And you didn't bother to look in on her?"

"Ms. Kahn tried, but she was in the shower."

The top of my head must have been rattling like a lid on a boiling kettle. "If anything has happened to that child, Ms. Tittle, you are going to wish you had never been born!"

She got huffy. "Emma may not be suited for our school," she said.

"You're right about that much," I responded, and slammed down the receiver.

Shanda's eyes were as big as the pizza we'd just devoured. "What's wrong?"

"My niece is missing," I said, as I punched in a familiar number.

"Hey, Counselor," Sonterra said. "What's up?"

"Emma ran away from school. I don't have a clue where she is and—"

"Relax. She's at Loretta's place."

Relief swamped me. My palm was so sweaty that I thought the phone would slip out of my hand. *"What?"*

"She got bumped a couple of times, traveling standby. She called me when she landed, and I picked her up. I didn't want to leave her alone at your house, so I dropped her off at Loretta's."

"And you didn't bother to *tell* me?"

"She wanted to surprise you."

"Oh, she did that all right. Thanks a *lot*, Sonterra!"

"Take a breath, Clare. All's well that ends well. Emma is home, and she's safe."

Two people had been murdered, and the only thing they'd had in common was an association with me. The doll man had been inside my personal boundaries, and he wanted me to know it. I was under siege, and my love for Emma was my greatest vulnerability.

Yes, my niece was home. But was she safe?

TWENTY-FOUR

"Emma's asleep," Loretta said, when I called her, the moment I'd hung up on Sonterra. I was annoyed, yes, but I also didn't want to give him time to jump all over me for coming to work. "The poor kid is exhausted. I'm not going to wake her up, and I'm not about to let you do it, either. And by the way, that was sneaky, leaving your house before I woke up this morning. You knew I'd talk you out of going."

"Exactly," I said, distracted. My strongest impulse was to drive to Loretta's, storm inside, and shake Emma awake. The rationality of my best friend's statement—and, okay, Sonterra's—was all that stopped me. "Did she tell you—did she say anything?"

"Yes. She said flying standby sucks. She

spent three times as long cooling her heels in airports as she did in the air. They served 'four and a half pretzels' on the flight, and she was starving when she landed. She called Tony as soon as she got off the plane, and while she was waiting for him, she consumed three cheeseburgers in one of the restaurants at Sky Harbor."

"Why him?" I lamented, half to myself. "Why did she call Sonterra, instead of me?"

"That's easy, Clare. She knew you were going to be pissed. She wanted to give you a while to regain your perspective."

Guilt washed over me. "Did she *say* that?"

"Not verbally. But the old cliché is true: actions speak louder than words."

I shoved the fingers of my good hand into my hair, and rested my forehead on the palm. My right arm ached savagely, in rhythm with my speeding heart rate and rapid, shallow breathing. "I'm a total failure. An unfit aunt."

Loretta laughed. "Wrong again. The kid loves you. That's why she left school—she wants to protect you."

"Protect me? She's thirteen!"

"Going on forty," Loretta said. "Finish out

your workday, Clare. Maybe it will calm you down. Rosa will have dinner ready when you get here, and you and Emma can talk then."

"Dear God, Loretta, when I think of all the things that could have happened—"

"But they didn't," Loretta interrupted firmly. "Emma is *fine*. Let that be good enough."

"Thank you, Dr. Phil."

Loretta laughed. "Get back to work."

We hung up, and I made one more call—to Ms. Tittle, in Rome. While I would have snatched her bald-headed if we'd been face-to-face, I wasn't angry enough to leave her wondering about Emma's safety. Our conversation was short, terse on my end, defensively relieved on hers.

Hours later, when I got to Loretta's, Sonterra was there, too, swilling iced tea on the patio, beside the pool. Rosa brought me a glass, as well, and I used the first couple of sips to wash down an overdue pain pill. Emma was nowhere in sight.

"You shouldn't have gone to work," Sonterra said, looking grim. "Driving with one hand is not the most prudent thing in the world."

I wasn't about to be deflected. "Where is Emma? For that matter, where is Loretta?"

Sonterra's jawline bunched, and his fingers tightened around his glass. "Emma is taking a shower. Loretta is giving us space."

"I still can't believe you didn't call me. Let me know Emma was back."

"She asked me not to."

"What if he hurts her?" I whispered.

"I plan to see that he doesn't," Sonterra replied. "But I need your help, Counselor. For once in your life, you're going to have to cooperate."

I met his gaze. "Do you have a plan?"

"Yes. You and Emma are moving in with me."

"Your place isn't a fortress," I said quietly. "He was there, too—the doll man, I mean— while I was in the hospital."

"Yeah, but not when there was a chance of running into me."

"You can't stand guard over the place 24/7, Sonterra—or over me."

"Hide and watch," he said. "When this perverted mother comes in for the kill—and he will, Clare, make no mistake about that— he's going to meet up with 185 pounds of pissed-off cop."

I moistened my lips. I didn't want Sonterra putting himself between me and the doll man—for all his macho confidence, he was not immortal. He could be killed—like Peter Bailey and Melanie Witherspoon and God knew who else. Thinking of Melanie made me think of Jack, her missing husband. "Any sign of Dr. Witherspoon?"

Sonterra let out his breath, rotated the sweating iced tea glass with one hand. "Oh, yeah. He turned up in a landfill this morning, with a bullet through his head."

I had been in the process of raising my glass to sip. At this news, I set it down again. "My God."

"It gets worse. His hands and feet were bound with duct tape. According to the ME, the killer probably hauled him there in the trunk of a car, dumped him out, and shot him."

I put a hand to my stomach, in a fruitless effort to settle it. "Why? Why not kill him in the house, along with Melanie?"

"Who knows? Why kill either one of them in the first place?"

"I think I'm going to throw up."

Sonterra nodded in the direction of the

patio doors. "I'd wait," he said. "Emma is about to step onstage."

I forgot my churning stomach and whirled in my chair.

Indeed, there was Emma, short blond hair still wet from the shower, face set with determination.

"Don't start on me, Clare," she said, before I could get a word out. "I had to come home. And I had to run away from school, because you would have made me stay, and so would the teachers."

I stood up slowly, put an arm around her, and awkwardly drew her close.

"You are in so much trouble," I said softly, and through tears.

She smiled, hugged me back, clinging a little. "Give it your best shot," she said. "Whatever happens, we're in this together."

"You're a brat," I sniffled. "What am I going to do with you?"

"Probably ground me for a year."

I laughed. "Probably." I stood back to assess her. "You look good."

She took in my cast, and then her gaze rose to my face. "And you look like hell. I should have come back sooner!"

I wiped my eyes with the back of my left

hand. "I appreciate your concern, Emma, but you've just complicated matters by ditching school. I really wish you'd stayed in Europe."

Emma spread her hands—the gesture was Tracy's, and her words were Gram's. "Wish in one hand—"

Sonterra lowered me back into my chair. "Enough tender sentiment. Rosa comes, bearing tacos."

I turned my head and, sure enough, there was Rosa, carrying a platter and beaming. Loretta was right behind her, with plates and paper napkins.

As always, I ate with good appetite, and even though I was terrified for Emma, I was also happy that she was home.

Paradox, thy name is Clare.

"Where do we go from here?" Emma asked cheerfully, when we'd all eaten our fill of Rosa's world-class food.

"To my place," Sonterra said, looking at me, daring me to argue.

"Awesome," Emma said. "Are we going to live there?"

"For all practical intents and purposes," Sonterra answered, "yes."

Emma's face glowed. "It's about time."

"It's temporary," I felt compelled to add.

"Whatever," Emma said.

An hour later, we pulled into Sonterra's garage, leaving my Escalade behind in Loretta's driveway. This, of course, was a part of Super Cop's big plan—he figured I'd stay put if I didn't have a car.

He should have known better.

TWENTY-FIVE

After a brief stop at my house, where Emma and Sonterra did some hasty packing, we made the move. While I certainly resented being commandeered, there was also a sense of taking shelter in a storm.

It was an illusion, I knew, because the doll man had already proven that he could penetrate even this stronghold, but that night, with Emma back and the pain pills not quite working, I needed to feel safe, even if it *was* only a pretense.

"Tell me about the trip," I said, sitting on the end of Emma's bed, while she made herself at home in Sonterra's guest room. He was outside, with Bernice and Waldo.

Emma was pinning a poster on the wall. Some guy who made Alice Cooper look like

Donny Osmond. "A geezer tried to pick me up on the plane," she said, with an offhand shrug. "I told him to buzz off or I'd tell the flight attendants he was trying to light his shoe on fire."

I refrained from comment. "Were you scared?"

She considered the question, head tilted to one side. How beautiful she was, I thought. How young, and how vulnerable. Like most kids, she probably expected to live forever. How could she know that the doll man might have other ideas?

"A few times. Mostly, I was wondering what was going on with you. The stuff on the internet kept getting worse and worse, and then I emailed some people and found out about your broken arm. That's when I decided I had to get home, but it took a while to come up with a plan. My friend let me use her credit card to buy the ticket— you owe her dad some money."

I would send the man a check in the next day's mail. Having decided that, I shifted my attention to the poster. "Just how long do you think we'll be staying here?" I asked moderately.

"Forever, I hope," Emma said brightly,

and for a moment, she resembled my sister so strongly that I wanted to hug her again, hard and for a long time. Missing Emma had been a temporary thing; missing Tracy was permanent.

I cleared my throat, looked away, looked back. "Don't read too much into this, Emma," I warned. "Our bunking in at Sonterra's, I mean. It's more a matter of expediency than anything else."

Emma screwed up her face. "Yeah. Heaven forbid you should move in with the hottest man in the world unless there's a mad killer after you."

"Emma."

Her hands came to rest on slender hips, and her expression was full of challenge. "Why can't you ever just let yourself be happy, Clare? Why can't you let *me* be happy?"

I sighed, rubbed my left temple with the corresponding fingertips. "I'm happy on my own," I said, as gently as I could, "and much as I love you, Snookums, I can't make a decision like this based on your preferences."

I might as well have been whistling Jiminy Cricket's happy tune.

"And why do you call Tony 'Sonterra'?" Emma demanded, on a roll. "No, wait—you don't have to tell me, because I already know. It keeps him at a distance."

I stood. "We'll talk about this another time," I said evenly, on my way to the door.

Emma was on my heels, not to mention my case. She followed me to the threshold. "Yeah," she blurted. "Like never!" Before I could formulate a reply, she slammed the door in my face.

I went downstairs. No sign of the dogs. No sign of Sonterra.

I tracked them to Sonterra's den; they were lying on either side of his desk chair, while he stared at the computer screen. He turned slightly, a beat or two after I entered the room.

"Emma settling in?" he asked, distracted.

"A little too well," I answered, rubbing the upper part of my right arm, where the cast didn't get in the way. I craned my neck a little, trying to see if there was another ugly doll image on the monitor; instead, I saw the logo of a well-known financial institution. He'd been tracking his investments.

He gave the chair a spin and faced me. "Meaning?"

I did a half-shrug. "She's got her hopes up. About us."

"Maybe she's not the only one," he said.

I didn't know how to handle that remark, so I let it pass. "How can I protect her?" I fretted. "She's so independent, and she's got to go to school—"

Sonterra stood with a graceful motion of his body, crossed the small room, and laid a hand on either side of my waist. "She's going to be all right. We'll make sure of it, Clare. You and I, together."

I let my forehead rest against his shoulder, smelled his laundry detergent and the deodorant soap he uses in the shower. "I keep thinking about something she said," I murmured. "That I call you 'Sonterra' because it keeps you at a distance."

He chuckled, kissed my temple. "Out of the mouths of babes," he said.

"I'm sorry," I whispered. "I don't seem to be able to—"

"It's okay," he told me. "If you called me 'Tony' I probably wouldn't realize you were talking to me."

I laughed and sniffled at the same time. Lifted my head to look up into his dark eyes.

"I have to go to work tomorrow. My schedule is packed."

I expected an argument but, as I've said before, Sonterra is a man of surprises. "Take a cab. Or get Loretta to drive you. Until that arm is healed, you shouldn't be driving."

I opened my mouth, closed it again.

Sonterra laughed. "See? You don't always know what I'm going to say, do you?"

I slid my arm around him, cuddled close. After all, nobody was looking. "You keep me guessing, all right."

"You love it."

I did love it, but I wasn't ready to admit as much. "That solves one problem. What about Emma? I can't take her to work with me—what if somebody shoots up the office again?"

Sonterra touched the tip of my nose. "Send her to school. She'll be safe there, and it's important to keep things as normal as possible."

I sighed. Even school wasn't completely safe these days, but Emma was a young woman, not a hothouse plant. Much as I would have liked to keep her with me twenty-four hours a day, I couldn't. I laid my head against Sonterra's shoulder again, and trembled. His arms tightened around me.

"I talked to someone at the Bureau today."

I stiffened. "And?"

"And they're holding a spot for me in the next training class. It starts in early December."

"You're still joining up?"

I felt him nod. "The good news is, I'll probably be assigned to the field office in Phoenix. They're keeping a closer eye on the flight schools these days."

"What's the bad news?"

"There isn't any," he replied. "Unless you're not going to let me make love to you tonight. That would definitely be bad news."

His erection pressed into my belly. Heat weakened my knees.

"Not to worry," I answered.

Sonterra was gentle that night, because of my arm and recent stint in the hospital, and because we were both a little self-conscious, with Emma just down the hall. Still, he was inventive, and Emma's music was loud.

Who needed sleeping pills? After four

seemingly endless orgasms, I lapsed into a near coma.

"I brought you guys something," Emma announced, the next morning at breakfast. With that, she bounded to her feet and dashed out of the room, returning a few moments later with her backpack. She delved in, first with one hand, then the other, producing two souvenir snow globes.

Mine had a little replica of Westminster Abbey inside, Sonterra's the Leaning Tower of Pisa.

"Cool," Sonterra said.

I turned the thing upside down and watched the little plastic flakes drift down. Suddenly, my throat was tight.

"Don't you like it?" Emma asked. In that way of teenagers, she'd apparently gotten over our disagreement the night before.

"I love it," I said, and started to cry.

"Stress," Sonterra explained to Emma, and got up to fetch me a bottle of water from the fridge.

Emma approached slowly, as though she expected me to disintegrate, and laid a hand on my shoulder. "It's okay," she said gently. "I'm here now. I'll take care of you."

I cried harder, and Emma glanced worriedly at Sonterra as he set the water bottle in front of me.

"Give us a minute," Sonterra told her quietly.

After a moment's hesitation and a reluctant nod, Emma scooped up Bernice and left the room. Waldo, who had taken to her immediately, trotted after them.

Sonterra crouched beside my chair, holding one of my hands. "Hey," he said gruffly, with a hint of a grin. "The day's off to a good start. Last night finished on a high note. You just got a present. And nobody's tried to kill you."

I snuffled. Dried my face with a paper napkin. "It's still early," I answered.

TWENTY-SIX

For a full week, my life was pretty normal. In my day-timer, I marked each of those seven days with a smiley face, hoping my run of good luck would last.

Emma went back to school in Cave Creek, and settled in nicely, if a bit grudgingly.

The prosecutor's office dropped the charges against Barbara Jenkins when two of her late husband's drinking buddies came forward to say Jenkins had told them he wanted to die, and if he could find a way to make Barbara take the blame, he'd do it.

Maybe it was a desire to lighten their case load, and maybe they didn't think they could win. Whatever the reason, the DA decided not to pursue the matter.

Sonterra and Eddie collared Judge Henry's murderer—a guy she'd sentenced to hard time early in her career.

We didn't hear from the doll man.

I was beginning to think we were living charmed lives.

Cue the cartoon birds and the whistling elves.

On the day of her hearing, Shanda was waiting on the courthouse steps, as agreed, when I arrived at twenty minutes till ten. Sonterra, still in protective mode, had dropped Emma and me off at Loretta's on his way to work, and as soon as he was gone, I'd gotten into the Escalade and headed south—driving carefully, as any one-armed woman would. I'd spent a few minutes at the office checking phone messages, and then headed for the halls of justice.

A woman I correctly took to be Shanda's mother was there, looking staunchly respectable in her homemade dress, and holding little Maya by the hand. Following Shanda's nervous gaze as I mounted the steps, briefcase tucked under my cast and clasped against my side, I spotted a bad-boy type sitting on a nearby cement planter, smoking a cigarette. He wore torn jeans, a muscle shirt, and tattoos on both forearms.

Diego Sanchez, of course.

My mouth tightened.

"This is my mother," Shanda said quickly. "I don't think you've met."

I put out my left hand, shuffling to keep from losing my hold on the briefcase and smiling. "Hello, Mrs. Rawlings," I said. "I'm Clare."

Mrs. Rawlings's eyes shone with hope as she looked at me. She wore her black hair in a tidy chignon, and if she'd noticed Sanchez, she gave no indication of it. "My Shanda is a good girl," she said urgently.

I glanced at Shanda, silently conveying the message that I wasn't pleased that Diego was in attendance. "Yes," I said. I turned what I hoped was a reassuring smile on little Maya, who was clinging to her grandmother's hand. "Hello, Pretty Baby."

Maya gave a gurgling laugh and buried her face in Mrs. Rawlings's skirt.

Mrs. Rawlings led the way into the court-house, with Maya toddling at her side. I hung back to walk beside Shanda.

"What is he doing here?" I whispered.

Shanda looked back over one shoulder. "I

asked him not to come," she said distract-edly. "He said I shouldn't have to go through this alone."

Inwardly, I rolled my eyes. Oh, yeah, he'd be lots of help.

We went through the security check, came out the other side.

"If he wants to lend moral support," I told Shanda, "why doesn't he come inside?" I paused for effect, watching as Mrs. Rawlings lifted Maya up so she could press the call button on the elevator. I'd had a great week, but seeing Diego Sanchez reminded me that all good things come to an end. "Oh, wait, I know. He couldn't get past the metal detector—those pesky guns and knives. Or maybe he's afraid he'd be arrested."

Shanda's chin quivered. "It's not like that."

"Please."

The elevator arrived, and we stepped inside, after Mrs. Rawlings and Maya. Because of their close proximity, I dropped the subject of Diego, but it wasn't the end of the discussion, and Shanda knew it as well as I did.

The doors were closing when someone

stuck an arm between them, and they popped open again.

Ted Adams, boy nerd. I'd known him professionally for a long time. He was pesky as a horsefly, and basically inept.

Shanda stared at her former public defender.

He smiled winningly and gave a little salute. "Hello, Shanda. Mrs. Rawlings. *Clare*."

"I hope this isn't an omen," I said.

Ted grinned. "Did I tell you that I'm with the DA's office now?"

Shanda looked as though she might slide down the elevator wall. Mrs. Rawlings frowned and clasped Maya's hand a little more tightly.

"No," I said, with acid good cheer. "You didn't mention it."

Adams focused on my cast. "What happened to your arm?"

"I was bitten by a shark."

Mrs. Rawlings crossed herself. Maya sucked her thumb.

The elevator started to rise.

"Wasn't that Diego Sanchez I saw out there?" Adams asked, perky as hell.

Apparently, with her daughter and granddaughter's fates hanging in the balance, Mrs. Rawlings hadn't noticed Sanchez lurking outside. At the mention of his name, she put a hand to her throat, and her gaze shot to Shanda, who made a point of staring into space.

"I wouldn't know," I said. "You're not attending Shanda's hearing, are you, Ted? Because that would definitely be improper."

He sighed dramatically. "Alas," he said. "No. I've got other fish to fry."

I didn't like the emphasis he put on the word "fry." But then, I didn't like anything else about him, either. He'd tried to pick me up too many times, at too many social functions.

He got off at the seventh floor, humming to himself, and nobody bothered to say good-bye.

"Diego is here?" Mrs. Rawlings hissed, taking a clawlike hold on Shanda's arm.

Shanda swallowed, but she didn't try to pull free. "He's Maya's father, Mama."

Mrs. Rawlings pretended to spit. At least, I hoped she pretended. "Father! Are you stupid? You know what that man is! What has he ever done for you but cause you grief and misery? What has he ever done for Maya? And you promised me, Shanda—"

I cleared my throat, nodded toward Maya, who was watching the exchange with enormous, frightened eyes.

Mrs. Rawlings subsided, but her eyes glittered with fury.

The doors opened onto our floor. "Is Father Mike here?" I asked, to change the subject. I'd notified him of the new court date, and he'd promised to be on hand.

Shanda lowered her head.

"He knows about Diego," Mrs. Rawlings said, with a note of angry triumph.

We stepped off the elevator in a pack.

I glanced up and down the hallway, searching for any sign of a clerical collar. Maybe Father Mike was in plainclothes.

"Where is he, Shanda?" I asked, as we walked toward the appointed courtroom.

A tear slipped down Shanda's cheek. "He was angry when I told him Diego was back," she confided softly. "But I thought he'd be here."

I looked at my watch. We had five minutes, and Father Mike was an important character witness. In fact, he was the only one we had, since mothers and defense attorneys are notoriously biased, but if he'd been delayed by some problem at the church, which seemed more likely to me than Shanda's theory, we'd have to cope.

We stepped into the throne room of justice, and I looked up to see one of my least favorite judges on the bench.

Maybe Ted Adams *had* been an omen.

TWENTY-SEVEN

Judge Albert Ryan was a legend in his own right. Owlish and small, he had one agenda: clean up the streets. Get the riffraff behind bars, and keep them there. Fine objectives, but Ryan rarely tempered his decisions with mercy. Extenuating circumstances? Not in the judge's world of absolutes.

We took our seats, as near the front as possible, to wait our turn.

"He looks mean," Shanda whispered.

I didn't answer.

The bailiff called for the next case, in the usual legalese, and a biker type approached the bar, accompanied by his attorney.

The charges were driving under the influence, reckless endangerment, and resisting arrest. It was the third offense. Within fifteen minutes, the biker was on his way to Sheriff Joe's famous Tent City, beside Highway 17 North, and this would be no camping trip.

My stomach quivered. Mrs. Rawlings, holding Maya on her lap, leaned out to give me a questioning look.

I shook my head, leaving her to divine her own meaning.

The next few cases were equally depressing. A woman who had embezzled twenty-five hundred dollars from the convenience store where she worked was sentenced to a year in jail. A teenage boy, having broken probation, went to Juvenile Hall for eighteen months. His mother was easy to spot—she was a row ahead of us, and sobbing into both hands.

"The State of Arizona versus Shanda Rawlings," the bailiff boomed.

I hoisted Shanda to her feet, and we made our way to the front of the room. The judge loomed over us.

"Ah," he said inscrutably. "Ms. Westbrook."

I stood straight. "Good morning, Judge Ryan."

He shuffled through the files before him. "If you say so," he said.

I could feel Shanda trembling beside me. I squeezed her hand.

Ryan's gaze shifted to her, rather, I thought, like that of a lizard tracking an unwary fly. "And you must be Miss Rawlings."

"Yes, sir," Shanda said, with an audible gulp.

He perused the court documents again. "You've been charged with writing bad checks. What do you have to say for yourself?"

"I did it," Shanda replied staunchly. "And I'm sorry."

"Yes," the judge intoned, "I would imagine you are."

"If I could go back, I wouldn't do it," Shanda argued.

I nudged her. The message: *Let me do the talking.*

"Give me one good reason why I shouldn't toss you into the hoosegow."

Shanda looked at me.

"Ms. Rawlings is gainfully employed in my office, Judge Ryan," I said. "She is a good worker, and she's intelligent. She has goals. And she sincerely regrets breaking the law."

"I wasn't talking to you, Ms. Westbrook," Judge Ryan replied.

"I don't want to leave my baby," Shanda told him. "She didn't do anything wrong."

More judicial perusing of papers. More frowning. "No, she didn't, Ms. Rawlings, but you did. What's your excuse?"

"I don't have one."

"Refreshing," the judge said, but he sounded skeptical. He turned his gaze on me. "Now, Ms. Westbrook, you may speak if you wish."

I would have curtsied, if Shanda's future hadn't been on the line. "Shanda has a job," I reiterated. "She's paying taxes. If she goes to jail, she'll be a burden to society, rather than a contributor. Her child, instead of being raised and supported by a loving parent, will be put into foster care, also at state expense. Ms. Rawlings's own mother helps out, but she works full-time, and would be unable to care for her granddaughter or afford day care."

"If this child has a thief for a parent, Ms. Westbrook, she would be better off in a foster home. State expense be damned."

"I agree," I said, and I did. "But Shanda deserves a second chance. She's trying to get her life together, and she's making steady progress." Except, of course, for

Diego Sanchez, the unknown element. I hoped I wasn't stone wrong in believing Shanda had the good sense to take care of herself and her daughter. Maya would pay the price if I was.

"According to my notes, this isn't a second chance," Judge Ryan maintained. "It's a third."

I said nothing. It would be good if I could show the same restraint in the rest of my life but, alas, I mostly reserve it for the courtroom.

"Which child is yours?" the judge asked, looking at Shanda. Unfortunately, the room was full of them, some accompanied by social workers, others by the nonoffending parent, grandmother, or family friend. They, the innocent ones, would serve time as surely as their mothers or fathers.

Mrs. Rawlings stood up, holding Maya. She looked regal in her home-sewn dress, and suitably solemn.

Judge Ryan waggled his fingers at Maya, and she waggled back, shyly, before burying her smiling face in Mrs. Rawlings's neck.

"Ms. Rawlings," the judge said, "I do not give a tinker's damn for fools who run afoul of the law for any reason. That would be you. On the other hand, I care very much for the little children who are too often caught in a web not of their own making. Therefore, I am going to give you that third chance— along with probation and three hundred hours of community service— but write this down in your day-timer. If you come before me again, on any charge greater than a parking violation, I *will* put you away. Have I made myself, as they say, 'abundantly clear'?"

Tears shimmered on Shanda's cheeks, but her smile blazed like a floodlight. "Yes, sir."

Judge Ryan slammed down his gavel. "Get out of here," he said. "I'm tired of looking at you."

I turned to Shanda and we engaged in a three-armed hug.

"As for you, Ms. Westbrook," the judge went on.

Everything stopped. I met his eyes.

"You're giving a young person an important opportunity. I appreciate that."

"Thank you, Your Honor," I said equably. Secretly, I liked him, but ours was a naturally adversarial association. I closed my file folder and Shanda and I left the bar to hook up with a weeping Mrs. Rawlings and a confused child.

We made our way through a crowded hallway, into an elevator, down to the lobby. I was braced for a confrontation with Diego, but when we got outside, he was gone.

I gave Mrs. Rawlings cab fare, and she and Maya went home, leaving Shanda and me to ride back to the office in my Escalade.

"Maybe I should drive," Shanda said, eyeing my cast.

"Do you have a license?"

"No," she replied.

"That decides it." I rounded the driver's side, juggling my briefcase and my keys— and saw the words scratched into the door.

Lawyer Bitch.

I groaned and rested my forehead against the cool glass of the window, recalling Sanchez's unfriendly stare in front of the courthouse.

"What?" Shanda demanded, hurrying around the front end of the car. Her eyes widened when she saw the artwork. "Diego didn't do it," she said.

I merely looked at her. It could have been the same person who defaced the office window but, somehow, I doubted it. Diego, after all, had been in close proximity to the courthouse.

"He *didn't*," Shanda insisted.

"At least he can spell," I answered, and unlocked the vehicle. I got behind the wheel and waited until Shanda was in the passenger seat, belt buckled.

We dropped the subject after that. There was plenty to do at the office.

Shanda made coffee, then we both got busy at the new computers, one on her desk, one on mine. Slowly, we were rebuilding the database lost after the fire.

I sent Shanda home at 2:30, since there were no appointments on the books, and she had something to celebrate. Sonterra called at three, to inquire, in a suspicious tone of voice, how I'd gotten to work.

"You're slipping," I told him. "I expected that question long before now."

"I've had a busy day," he answered. "What happened with Shanda?"

I took a moment to exalt in the victory. "Probation and three hundred hours of community service. No jail time."

"Good work, Counselor."

I flashed on Diego Sanchez, and the graffiti on my car door. Maybe I was prejudging him, but my instincts told me the ditty wasn't the work of the doll man, or a passing vandal. Experience has taught me to trust my gut.

"There was a little incident with my car," I said carefully. Sonterra would see the scratch job anyway.

"Such as?"

"Somebody wrote on the door with a rock or a key or something. 'Lawyer Bitch.'"

"Shit," Sonterra said.

A motion at the office door caught my eye, and I looked up to see Mrs. K and Rodney about to make an entrance.

"Clients," I said. "Gotta go."

"Clare—"

We'd been making plans, through the week, to head up to Sonterra's cabin that night. He wanted to go, so I figured this was my chance to alter his mood.

"What time are we leaving for the enchanted cottage?"

Sonterra was silent. He didn't like evasive action, but in this case, he couldn't do anything about it.

"Six o'clock," he said, at considerable length. "I'll pick Emma and the dogs up at Loretta's, then we'll swing by the office for you. Don't even think about navigating rush hour with one arm, Clare. I'm still a cop, and I'll hit you with enough traffic citations to paper a wall."

I believed him. "Okay," I said, with as much meekness as I could drum up. "You are my lord and master. I live to obey."

Mrs. K and Rodney were standing in front of my desk by then, Mrs. K smiling eagerly, Rodney looking as though he'd rather dance with the devil in the heart of hell.

"Good-bye," I told Sonterra, and hung up, effectively damming up a river of words I was better off not hearing.

Mrs. K assessed the office, frowning only once, when her gaze fell on the incinerated file cabinet, which I hadn't gotten around to replacing.

"Sit down," I said.

"Nice place," Mrs. K commented, arranging her caftanned self in the appropriate chair. She looked like a kitchen-table fortune-teller, which was normal for her, and I wondered if the Mystery Shopper thing had fallen through.

Rodney sat down too, though with reluctance and much shifting of bulk.

"What can I do for you?"

"Work on my case, maybe?" Rodney snarled.

"Rodney!" Mrs. K scolded.

"Is there a problem?" I asked sweetly.

"The police are putting pressure on Rodney," Mrs. K put in. "They can't find Angela, and they think he knows something about her disappearance."

"It was that drug dealer," Rodney complained. "He probably killed her. The cops should be looking for him, not bothering me."

"You haven't been in contact with Angela?"

Rodney glared. "No," he snapped. "Whose side are you on, anyway?"

"Your aunt's," I said evenly. "I thought I made that clear before, when you were taken in for questioning."

Rodney scowled.

I wondered if he'd been the one to scratch up my car, instead of Diego.

Not likely, I decided. He was transportationally challenged, and it would have been awkward to pull off with Mrs. K sitting nearby in her Buick.

"She's dead, the poor girl," Mrs. K said fitfully, paying no apparent attention to the current of dislike flowing back and forth between Rodney and me. "I saw it in the cards."

Rodney rolled his eyes.

I'd had some experience with Mrs. K and her weird talents, and I tended to take her seriously. Before I could respond to the remark, however, the office door opened again, and Diego Sanchez swaggered in, grinning.

"She's in a Dumpster," Mrs. K mused on, taking no notice of the newcomer.

Rodney, on the other hand, had *definitely* noticed. He went pale, and sort of sank in on himself, as if he was trying to disappear.

"Small world," said Diego, laying a hand on Rodney's shoulder.

TWENTY-EIGHT

Some of the pieces fell into place.

Shanda had said Sanchez managed the Headbanger Club. Rodney had told Sonterra and me that Angela, his friend from the halfway house, hung out there sometimes. Hence, Rodney's obvious fear. There was a connection between Shanda's ex-I-hoped-boyfriend and the missing Angela.

In light of that, and what I already knew about Diego's history, I wasn't anxious to be alone with him, but Rodney had broken out in a cold sweat, and he was as white as a blank page on my desk calendar. I honestly thought he was on the verge of a heart attack and, besides, if hostilities broke out, I didn't want Mrs. K caught in the crossfire.

"Gosh," I said, hoping to give Rodney and

Mrs. K an out. "Look at the time! I'm afraid your appointment is over."

Mrs. K looked befuddled.

Rodney got to his feet, avoiding Sanchez's keen black gaze, and pulled his aunt to her feet, half dragging her toward the door. The color had drained out of her face, leaving her rouge to stand alone, and I knew she was picking up some nasty nuances.

"Clare," she pleaded, trying in vain to struggle free of Rodney's desperate grasp. "This man—I'm not sure we should leave you—"

"Just go," I said.

Rodney opened the door, and the two of them were back on the sidewalk.

Sanchez watched them leave, with an expression of evil delight. I calculated the logistics of getting my .38 out of my purse and firing it with my left hand—and concluded my chances were similar to those of an ice cube in the desert.

"What do you want?" I asked bluntly. Sometimes, bravado is all I have to work with.

My visitor lowered himself into the chair

Rodney had just vacated. "You look scared," he said.

"Appearances can be deceiving," I replied.

He laughed. "Yes," he agreed, and I noticed, now that I'd had time to look him over at close range, that he wasn't the stereotype of a lowlife that I'd expected. He carried himself with a certain grudging pride, and he resembled Antonio Banderas, in a rough-cut, watered-down sort of way.

"Why are you here?" I persisted.

"To thank you, of course. For getting Shanda off the hook."

"Shanda," I said carefully, "is not 'off the hook.' One slip, I assure you, and Judge Ryan will hang her out to dry."

Diego raised an eyebrow. "And you think I'm that slip?"

"The real deal," I said. "If you're so grateful, why did you mess up my car?"

"That's a nice ride," Diego said, admitting nothing. "According to Shanda, you have money. Why do you want to work in a place like this?"

"I'm sorry if it doesn't meet your lofty standards, Mr. Sanchez."

"You need a strong man in your life," he

reflected sagely. "Soften you up a little. You're too beautiful to be dealing with the criminal element."

Just then, I wished a certain "strong man" would screech up to the curb in his SUV, but it wasn't likely to happen, so I had to soldier on. "Are you threatening me, Mr. Sanchez?"

He did a parody of wounded chagrin, but those black eyes of his told the story. He was the devil incarnate, and he didn't give a damn who knew it. I might have asked myself what Shanda could have seen in him, but unfortunately, I knew. Danger.

"Be nice to Shanda," he said, "and I'll be nice to you."

"If you care about Shanda—and about Maya—you'll stay away from them."

"Maya is my daughter, *Ms.* Westbrook. My flesh and blood. If Shanda takes a fall, I'll be there to catch my little girl before she hits the ground."

"The same way you've 'been there' with child support payments?" I challenged, red in the face.

Diego stood, leaned against my desk, his hands braced against the edge. He leaned in, and I could feel his breath on my skin.

"Don't underestimate me, Ms. Westbrook," he crooned.

"Don't underestimate *me*, Mr. Sanchez."

"Oh, believe me, I don't." He reached out, with one index finger, and traced the line of my jaw, lingering a moment in the hollow of my throat.

I recoiled instantly, but the feel of his flesh against mine lingered, like a trail of slime. "Get out," I said.

"Before you call the cops?" he drawled.

It was then that my unlikely rescuer wandered in. Dr. Thomlinson came through the door, with a file in one hand.

"Am I interrupting something?" he asked.

Sanchez smiled, gave me a cocky nod, and left, jostling the doctor a little as he passed.

"Who was that?" Thomlinson asked, watching as Diego paused at the front window to give a little salute of farewell.

I suppressed a shudder. "His name is Diego Sanchez," I said. If I turned up dead, I wanted someone to know who belonged on the suspect list.

"You seem frightened. Are you all right?"

"I'll be okay," I said. I wanted to call

Sonterra on his cell phone, but not with Thomlinson there, solicitous as he was.

I glanced at the clock. Five-thirty. Sonterra was probably already in transit. "How can I help you, Doctor?"

He was understandably distracted, still staring after the vanished Sanchez. "Oh," he said, and clasped the file more tightly in his hands. "I found some interesting information. About Peter Bailey, I mean. It seems he had an interest in dolls, after all."

TWENTY-NINE

Until that moment, I would have thought nothing could take my mind off Diego's visit, but Dr. Thomlinson had done exactly that.

I blinked. "What? Let me see that file."

Thomlinson handed it over, after a moment's hesitation, and sat down.

I opened the folder and focused on the contents—photocopies of a lot of disturbing doll pictures. A chill spiraled down my spine.

"Where did you get these?"

"They were among Peter's things, at the halfway house. A staff member found them stuffed under his mattress when they were clearing out his room."

I examined the pictures, one by one. They were eerily similar to the ones Peter had shown me, but they were subtly different, too. The others had been in black and white; these were in living color.

The dolls were posed in ordinary occupations—four of them in the midst of a flowering garden, seated around a little tea table set with silver and china to scale. One reclined in a bathtub, with its dark hair pinned up. Another at a desk, hands resting on the keyboard of a toy computer.

All of them stared blankly into the camera.

I shivered.

"Pretty creepy," Dr. Thomlinson said, quite unnecessarily.

I closed the folder. "May I keep these?" They were copies. I wondered where the originals were.

"Be my guest," Thomlinson answered, slapping his palms to his thighs with a hearty sigh, then rising. He glanced at the window again, frowned. "Perhaps I shouldn't leave you alone," he said. "It's getting dark. May I walk you to your car?"

I tried to smile. "Someone is picking me up in a few minutes," I said. "I'll be fine."

He paused at the door, gaze fixed on my

cast. "I was sorry to hear about your accident," he said. "I hope you're feeling better."

The arm was throbbing. Time for a pain pill. "Thank you," I said, wishing he'd go. I wanted a few minutes alone. Between the doll photos and the encounter with Diego, I was thinking about my .38 again. After today, I decided, I would keep it in my desk drawer while I was at the office.

Dr. Thomlinson left.

I got up and locked the door behind him.

Sonterra showed up at 6:05, with Emma and the dogs.

I met him on the sidewalk.

"You don't look good, Counselor," he said, studying my face. "What's wrong?"

I told him about Diego Sanchez's visit, the way Rodney had reacted to his arrival, and my private theory about the missing Angela; the new crop of doll photos could wait. One crisis at a time.

He did the jaw-grinding thing. "I'll run a make on him. Check with the DEA."

Emma smiled and waved from the backseat, obviously delighted to be making a trip to Sonterra's cabin. In her mind, it was probably a family outing.

"I don't want Emma to know about Sanchez," I said.

"We can agree on that much, at least," Sonterra replied. He took my left arm and squired me to the passenger side, opening the door and helping me into the seat. He even did up my seat belt.

Waldo, meanwhile, stuck his head over the seat and licked my face. Bernice yipped with joy. Judging by her expression, Emma might have joined in the celebration, if she'd been a dog.

"Let's roll," she said exuberantly.

Her happiness made me happy, for all my misgivings. I reached back, and she gave me her hand. We squeezed.

Sonterra got behind the wheel, fastened his seat belt, and checked the flow of traffic before pulling out.

"This is so *normal*," Emma piped.

Sonterra grinned. "Yeah," he agreed.

"Tony says you won in court today," my niece said. "Way to go, Clare."

"I am woman," I replied.

"And I am hungry," Emma said.

Sonterra laughed. "Not to worry, Gomer. We'll stop for supper. How does the Horny Toad sound?"

"It sounds good, Goober," Emma answered cheerfully.

It took forty-five minutes to get out of the city and pull into the parking lot at the Toad, in Cave Creek.

The restaurant was crowded, which was usual, given that it was Friday night and the tourist season was already under way. The snowbirds start showing up in September.

We waited fifteen more minutes for a table, and by the time we sat down, my blood sugar had plunged and I couldn't make sense of the menu.

Sonterra ordered for me. A cheeseburger with everything.

"You need a pain pill," he said, when Emma went out to his SUV to look in on Bernice and Waldo, who had been left with food, water, and a partially open window, so they would not lack for fresh air.

"Not without something in my stomach," I answered.

Emma returned just as our meals were being delivered. I took a bite of my cheeseburger, then popped a pill and washed it down with iced tea. Only when all this was done did I notice that she looked troubled.

Sonterra was quicker on the draw. "What's the matter, Gomer?" he asked.

"There's a doll in the car," she said, mystified. "It's hanging by its neck from the rearview mirror."

THIRTY

I went on instant red alert, pushing my plate away.

Sonterra pushed it back. "Stay here," he told Emma and me, getting to his feet. "And eat your supper."

I swallowed, nodded.

Emma dropped into her chair, regarded her own plate of fried chicken, mashed potatoes and gravy, and the accompanying vegetable with wary resolution, and picked up her fork. Sonterra left the table, and his rapidly cooling BLT.

"It's that guy, isn't it?" Emma asked softly. "The one who killed Mrs. Witherspoon and Peter Bailey. He's stalking us."

I made myself take a second bite of my cheeseburger. My legendary appetite was gone, but I knew I would need my strength. "Probably," I admitted.

Emma's gaze strayed to the window nearest our table, even though she couldn't have seen the parking lot from where we sat. The windows in the Toad are frosted, interspersed with panes of colored glass, and mostly opaque. "He's watching us. *Following* us."

"That would be the definition of stalking," I agreed, wishing more than ever that Emma had stayed in Europe. Since that was futile, I soon gave it up. Emma *wasn't* in Europe, she was with us, in Cave Creek. Better to acknowledge reality, and deal with it.

"Are you scared?"

I nodded. Truth time. "More for you than myself."

I noticed that Emma held her knife and fork in the European style, and made a delicate affair of cutting up a chicken breast. "Funny," she said, with a small, faltering smile. "For me, it's just the opposite. I'd rather die myself than see anything happen to you."

My heart clenched, and a ball of emotion closed off my throat. I put my cheeseburger down, and resisted, in vain, the tears that sprang to my eyes. "I guess we're all selfish in that way," I said, when I could get the words out.

"Selfish?" Emma asked, clearly puzzled, as well as unnerved.

"Sure," I answered. "If we die, we avoid the pain of dealing with the loss of somebody we love."

"Unless," Emma argued, for she is, after all, blood of my blood and bone of my bone, "the death itself is painful."

Sonterra returned, looking grim, and just putting his cell phone back into his pocket. He spoke to the hostess and the bartender, both of whom shook their heads, before rejoining us. I wanted to see the doll but, not surprisingly, he hadn't brought it to the supper table.

"No luck?" I asked, though the answer to that question was obvious from his manner and the set of his jaw.

He shook his head, picked up his sandwich. I suspected that, like me, he was eating for fuel, not enjoyment.

"I think we should take Emma straight to the airport. Send her somewhere far away," I said. It was fear talking, I knew that, but I wanted her gone. At a safe distance.

"No!" Emma burst out, stiffening in her seat across the table from Sonterra and me.

Sonterra agreed with a nod, and finished chewing before he stated his case. "I want you both close by—where I can see you. If we separate, he wins."

I pushed my plate away again.

Sonterra nudged it back.

I finished my supper.

We paid the check and left the restaurant. The dogs greeted us with happy barks, and Emma sneaked them a few scraps of chicken skin.

"Where's the doll?" I asked, as Sonterra started up the engine. I was the only one who hadn't seen it.

"Glove compartment," Sonterra said. "Don't handle it. There might be finger-prints."

I opened the small door, peered inside. We both knew there wouldn't be finger-prints—the doll man was too smart for that. He would have worn gloves.

"Why didn't the car alarm go off?" I asked, inspecting the latest offering. This one was a cheap version of Barbie, naked except for its little noose, fashioned of plain brown twine. "You locked the doors, didn't you?"

Sonterra pulled out onto Cave Creek Road, heading west, toward Highway 17 North. "Of course I locked the doors. Either he has a key, or he jimmied the wiring somehow."

The lot was jammed with cars, diners coming and going. "That would have attracted attention," I said. "Wouldn't it?"

"Not if he smiled and acted as if he was having engine trouble. People don't think twice about things like that."

I sighed. Sonterra was right. Even if the car alarm *had* gone off, we might not have heard it in the restaurant, and passersby would be understandably reluctant to risk their lives just to prevent another SUV from being stolen. Some, though, might have called the police from inside the Toad, using their cell phone, or reported what they'd seen to the hostess or bartender.

"The dogs seem calm enough," I mused.

"They're getting used to this guy," Sonterra replied.

Now *there* was a comforting thought.

"Check with the department," I said.

"Somebody might have seen something. Called it in."

"One step ahead of you, Counselor," Sonterra answered. "No reports."

"Give me a rundown on what's happened so far," Emma said, from the backseat. "Maybe I'll pick up on something you guys missed."

"The internet let you down, did it?" I asked, referring to the sources that had apparently kept her up to date on the Perils of Clare while she was overseas. Just about the last thing I wanted to do was fill Emma's impressionable head with images of dead bodies and dolls engaged in creepy activities.

Sonterra reacted differently. He spilled the whole story, while I stared at him in angry disbelief.

"Serial killer," Emma decreed, when he was finished. By that time, we were on the 17, rolling north. "Let's go over the suspects."

"What suspects?" I asked, and was immediately ashamed by the note of petulance in my voice.

"Peter Bailey?" Emma suggested.

"Dead," I reminded her. "He might have

been viable in the beginning, but being a corpse would seriously limit his range of motion."

"Diego Sanchez?" Sonterra reflected.

"Who's that?" Emma wanted to know.

We both ignored the question.

"He's definitely bad news," I said, "but I don't think he's our man. I can't see him playing with dolls."

Sonterra didn't comment. His brow was furrowed; he was thinking.

"What if it isn't a man?" Emma threw out.

"I spoke to him on the telephone. Definitely male."

"Unless she altered her voice, or she's gay or something," Emma speculated.

Sonterra grinned. "Any women trying to beat my time lately?" he asked.

I slugged him in the arm, but not very hard. He'd lightened the mood a little, and I appreciated that.

Emma seemed to be enjoying the puzzle. "It could be some chick who's in love with Tony."

I thought of Leanne Reece, the woman who had called Sonterra's house that morning, a couple of weeks before. I recalled that she was the sister of a murder victim, and she and Sonterra had gotten to know each other during the investigation. Maybe she wasn't in love with Super Cop, but she was certainly interested—Sonterra had virtually admitted that—perhaps even to the point of obsession. She could have done every-thing—except overpower a full-grown man, like Peter Bailey.

It's got to do with your boyfriend, Bailey had said, during an early encounter, when he was warning me about bad people and black helicopters. The thought stuck in my mind like a fishbone in a cat's throat.

"How about the computer nerd?" Emma asked, moving on.

"David Valardi," I said thoughtfully. Then it struck me that Sonterra hadn't mentioned this particular candidate while running through the course of events so far, and I turned in the seat to look back at her. "How did you know about him?"

Emma had the good grace to blush a lit-tle. "You might as well know," she sighed. "I was tapping into your computers the whole time I was in Europe. All I had to do was link my laptop to your network. You should be more careful with your passwords, Clare."

"Why, you little—"

"Genius," Sonterra put in. "Tell me more about this Valardi character."

"He's charged with creating the Barabbas virus," I said, subsiding a little, but still very annoyed with Emma. No wonder she'd known my every move—she'd been sifting through my private files, from thousands of miles away, and probably reading my emails as well. "You saw those doll pictures, didn't you, Emma?"

She was quiet for a few beats. "Yeah," she confessed. "Am I grounded?"

"Yes," I said. "For running away from school. I'll have to think up something a lot worse for this, though. Emma, how could you prowl around in my hard drive like that?"

"I knew you wouldn't tell me what was going on." She paused, probably regrouping. "There's some skill involved in breaking into other people's computers, you know. How about a little appreciation for that?"

"Appreciation? Give me a break. David Valardi has that skill, and chances are it's going to land him in prison." I gave her another look. "You are seriously over the line, Emma Westbrook. I don't read your diary."

She bit her lower lip. "You want me to say

I'm sorry," she said. "I could, but I wouldn't be telling the truth."

I sighed. Out of the corner of my eye, I saw Sonterra grin.

"Valardi," he prompted.

I told him what I knew.

"Guys like that usually don't commit physical crimes," Sonterra concluded, when I was through. "They're introverts. Behind-the-scenes types."

"Could be Rodney," Emma said, evidently undaunted by my displeasure with her long-distance sleuthing methods.

"He's a coward," I said dismissively.

"He's an ex-con," Sonterra pointed out.

Only later, much later, would I realize that, for all our exhaustive speculation, we had missed someone.

Hindsight, as they say, is 20/20.

Thirty-One

It was dark when we reached the cabin, and Sonterra insisted on going in alone to scout the place out before Emma, the dogs, and I were allowed to get out of the car.

We watched as the lights came on, one by one, upstairs and down, and finally Sonterra appeared on the porch, giving the thumbs-up sign.

Bernice and Waldo yelped with delight when they were set free, sniffing around, squatting in the grass. We all waited out the canine process, then trooped inside.

Sonterra got a blaze going in the living-room fireplace.

I put on a pot of coffee.

"Where do I sleep?" Emma asked joyously.

"Inside a steel vault," I said, "if I had my way."

"Fortunately," Sonterra replied lightly, "you don't."

Emma chose an upstairs bedroom, and the dogs followed her. Most likely, she wanted to give Sonterra and me time alone—I knew she was hoping we would fall madly in love and pledge ourselves one to the other for all of eternity.

"Don't sweat it, Counselor," Sonterra said, when she was out of earshot. "We'll sleep upstairs, too. She'll be safe."

"There you go, reading my mind again."

"When it comes to Emma, it's not too hard." With that, Sonterra made sure all the doors and windows were secured for the night, and then ambled back into the kitchen. He poured coffee for me, then for himself.

"How's the arm?" he asked tenderly, when I sank into a chair at the table and cupped both hands around my steaming mug of high-octane java.

"Better," I said. The pill I'd taken at the Toad was still covering the waterfront. No need to mention that I would probably wake up in the night, if past experience was any indication, feeling as though someone had just driven an iron spike through flesh and bone. No matter how carefully I apportioned my narcotics, they had a tendency to wear off at the worst possible time—the pharmaceutical version of Murphy's Law, I supposed.

I opened a packet of sweetener and stirred the contents into my coffee. "Do you think he followed us?"

"Maybe," Sonterra said, turning his chair around to sit astraddle of the seat, Old-West style. "He might be content with leaving the doll on the rearview mirror, though. These perverts like to enjoy the little scares, and anticipate the big ones."

I shuddered. "What must Melanie have thought—felt—when she saw him, and knew he was going to kill her?"

Sonterra reached out, took my hand. "Don't dwell on that, Clare—it's useless. Anyway, she might have been asleep. Never known what hit her."

"In the afternoon?"

"According to forensics, she'd taken medication. Probably for a migraine. You have a choice here, Counselor: you can believe she suffered, or you can believe she never felt anything beyond the first plunge of the knife. Your life will be easier if you take the latter."

"What if it isn't true?"

"What does that matter now?"

We were playing our version of Twenty Questions. Trouble was, it wouldn't stop at twenty. There were still too many answers floating around out there, unconnected.

Sonterra sipped his coffee, then got up and went to the refrigerator to peruse what was left from the last visit. Obviously, his BLT had worn off.

He settled on a hunk of cheddar cheese, silently offering me some, and shrugging when I shook my head. He whacked off a few slices, put the package back in the fridge, and sat down again, munching reflectively.

I hugged myself. "What did you hope to accomplish by bringing us here?"

He smiled. "You heard Emma, when we left your office. This is so 'normal.' And normality is the best way to cope with fear."

"You're afraid?"

Sonterra considered the question. "Cautious, yes," he answered, at some length.

"But scared? No. I won't give him that, no matter what happens."

I tilted my head to one side. "You figure you have a choice?"

"We *always* have a choice, Counselor. As the philosophers say, we can't control a lot of what happens to us, but we can control how we respond."

"I wonder if Melanie thought that, when she looked into the face of her killer, and knew she was about to die."

"Maybe. It's a funny thing about death. When you actually come face-to-face with it, this calm comes over you." Coming from anyone else, this might have been so much theoretical fluff. Coming from Sonterra, who had looked down the barrel of more than one gun during his illustrious career, it had validity.

"Are you saying you never get scared?"

He shook his head. "I'm human. Sometimes I lay awake at night, wondering what I'd do if something happened to you, or to Emma."

This was dangerous emotional territory. If Sonterra feared for Emma and me, it might mean he loved us. I wasn't sure how to deal with that.

"Have you told Emma you're joining the FBI?"

He looked away. "Not yet."

After that, there didn't seem to be much to say.

I wrapped my cast in a plastic garbage bag, secured with rubber bands from the bottom of my purse, and took a shower. When Sonterra joined me under the spray, I didn't protest.

I slept soundly through the night, and when I woke up, I was alone in bed. Conversation wafted up the stairs, and I heard the rattling of pots and pans.

Good, I thought. *We aren't going to eat at the E. coli Café.*

I dressed as quickly as I could, given the cast, and hurried to the kitchen.

Emma, wearing jeans and a sweatshirt with a da Vinci drawing on the front, sat at the table, consuming one of Sonterra's famous canned food concoctions.

"Tony's going to show me the pioneer cemetery," she said, with delight. "You'd better hurry up and eat, if you want to go with us."

Sonterra scooped some odd but savory-looking grub onto a plate and set it on the table in front of me. "N-O-R-M-A-L," he reminded me, prompted, no doubt, by the look of concern on my face.

"Did you know a whole family of settlers got wiped out in the ravine, by a flash flood?" Emma enthused, munching. "Some hikers bought it there, too."

I glanced at Sonterra. While I understood the reasoning behind telling her all that—understanding the inherent dangers of such a place was the best protection he could offer—I didn't like the idea of Emma standing on the crumbling edge of that gorge.

He poured me a cup of coffee. "Who's up for a Monopoly tournament later on?" he asked. "Winner gets to pick the movies we rent and decide what we have for supper."

And so it began, that rare and welcome treasure, a "normal" day.

Emma loved the cemetery and the ravine, and she won the Monopoly tournament hands down. Which is how we ended up eating pizza for lunch and dinner, and watching *Slumber Party Massacre, Ace Ventura, Pet Detective,* and *I Know What You Did Last Summer* on Sonterra's DVD player.

Not a word from the doll man.

By ten o'clock, Emma had chosen a book from Sonterra's paperback collection and disappeared upstairs, the dogs at her heels.

He and I were sitting side by side on the couch, our feet on the coffee table, when his cell phone rang.

"Shit," I said, expecting bad news. The last time we were at the cabin, after all, the doll man had nearly killed Eddie Columbia.

Sonterra answered immediately, and in his customary brusque fashion.

I watched his face as he listened. It told me precisely nothing.

"Pick up Diego Sanchez," he said, and listened again. "Yes, I *know* how common the name is. They're not all drug dealers, for Christ's sake. And run Rodney Gerring in, while you're at it."

I sat up straight, making a hurry-up gesture with my good hand.

Sonterra took his time. "Right," he muttered. "Yes, Sanchez has a rap sheet." Another silence. "Yeah, that's probably him."

After about a year, he said good-bye to the caller and snapped the phone shut.

"Well?" I demanded.

"That was Eddie. They found Angela Kerrigan's body in a Dumpster behind a supermarket in Apache Junction," Sonterra told me somberly. "She was stabbed to death."

Instantly, I recalled Mrs. K's prediction, the day before, in my office, and I shivered. "Diego," I murmured, and my mind leaped to Shanda, Mrs. Rawlings, and, finally, little Maya.

I immediately jumped up, found my purse, and began pawing through it for my day-timer.

"What is it?" Sonterra asked, watching me from the couch and frowning.

"Sanchez," I said, flipping one-handed through the pages. "He's the father of Shanda's baby. She and Maya live with Shanda's mother."

Sonterra was off the couch like a shot. Apparently, he'd jumped to the same conclusion I had: Sanchez knew the police would be coming after him when Angela's body was found and by now the word was out. Breaking news in all media. He needed a way to keep the law at bay—and Shanda and Maya would make perfect hostages.

THIRTY-TWO

"Call Shanda," Sonterra said urgently. "Tell her to get the hell out of Dodge, right now!"

"I can't," I wailed. "The Rawlingses don't have a phone!" I thrust the day-timer at him, open to the page where I'd recorded Shanda's street address and apartment number, soon after hiring her.

Sonterra punched in a number on his cell phone, marking the place in my day-timer with his thumb. "Eddie," he said, dispensing with the preliminaries. "Sanchez's girlfriend might be in danger. Send a squad car to pick her up, along with her daughter and mother." He read off the pertinent information. "Thanks. Call me back, will you?"

Emma appeared on the stair landing, flanked by the dogs.

"What's happening?" she asked, paperback book dangling from one hand.

"Nothing," I said.

Sonterra spared me an impatient glance. "Rodney's friend Angela turned up in a Dumpster," he told her bluntly.

Emma went a shade paler. "Is she dead?"

"Yeah, Gomer," Sonterra said quietly.

I elbowed him, with my cast arm, just in case he was about to launch into the gory details.

She sighed. "I suppose this means we have to go back to Phoenix."

Rodney was about to be brought in for another round of questioning and, like it or not, I was his lawyer. Besides, I wanted to see for myself that Shanda, Maya, and Mrs. Rawlings were all right.

"Sorry," Sonterra replied.

"So much for normal," Emma said, with resignation, and went upstairs again, this time to gather her things.

Half an hour later, we were back in Sonterra's SUV, heading for the city.

Eddie called to say there was no one at home at Shanda's, and no sign of a struggle.

I was not reassured, and neither was

Sonterra, if the look on his face when he conveyed the news was any indication.

I called Mrs. K, partly to distract myself, and partly because it was the next logical step.

"The police are here, Clare!" she cried, as soon as I identified myself. "They're arresting Rodney!"

"I'm on my way, Mrs. K. Try to stay calm."

"How can I stay calm? He didn't kill Angela Kerrigan, Clare. You *know* he didn't!"

"It's routine," I reminded her, taking long, slow, deep breaths. "Whenever a body is found, the police question everybody with a connection. Ask one of the officers where they're taking him."

Mrs. K made a fretful sound, set down the phone, and came back on the line a couple of minutes later. "Madison Street Station," she said.

I didn't look at Sonterra. "Put one of them on."

Another long wait. Then a questioning, "This is Eddie Columbia?"

I sighed with relief. "Eddie, it's Clare. I'm Rodney's attorney, as you probably remember, and I don't want him questioned before I get there."

There was a distinct note of restraint in Eddie's reply. "Right," he said.

"Have you found Shanda Rawlings?"

He hesitated. "No. Half the Phoenix Police Department is out looking for her right now."

"What about Diego Sanchez?"

Hard-won patience. "Clare, I can't discuss that with you, and you know it. Is Sonterra with you?"

I bristled, even though I understood the rules of police procedure as well as anybody. Nevertheless, it galled me that everything had to come through Sonterra. "Yes," I snapped, "he is. It isn't as if I don't have a stake in this, Eddie. Shanda works for me. She's my friend."

"Okay," Eddie said, noncommittal.

I shoved the phone at Sonterra, and he listened to the update.

"Nothing new," he told me, when the conversation with his partner ended.

Emma laid a hand on my shoulder, from her position in the backseat. "Is Mrs. K all right?" she asked worriedly.

"She's in three kinds of panic," I said, tempted to put my foot on top of Sonterra's, and thus the gas pedal. "She could have a heart attack, or a stroke or something."

Sonterra glowered at me. "Get a grip," he said. "You're scaring the kid." That was rich, coming from him. Mr. Tell-It-Like-It-Is.

Emma squeezed my shoulder. "I guess Waldo and Bernice and I will have to go to the jail with you," she said, trying to sound resigned. "You can't leave us alone, and Loretta and Kip are spending the weekend at the ranch."

She had me there.

At quarter after ten, we arrived at Madison Street.

Mrs. K was sitting in the waiting room, and she jumped to her feet when she saw us.

Emma hugged her. "It's cool, Mrs. K," she said. "We'll sit with you." The "we" being, I guessed, herself and the dogs.

"I thought you were in Europe," Mrs. K murmured, squinting as though Emma might be an apparition.

"Didn't we all?" I put in.

Sonterra went to the desk, got a fix on Rodney's location, and gestured to me briefly before heading for the elevators.

I embraced Mrs. K quickly, told Emma to

behave, and hurried after him. It would have been just like Sonterra to leave me in the lobby. I stuck to his heels, and we found Rodney in an interrogation room.

"I didn't do it," he said.

I pulled up a chair beside him, facing Eddie and a couple of detectives I didn't know across the battered table. "I know," I answered.

"Can we start now?" one of the detectives asked, with sarcastic indulgence. "If it's all right with the little lady?"

THIRTY-THREE

"Stow it, McCullough," Sonterra said, before I had a chance to get my teeth into the "little lady" remark.

McCullough, a long-faced veteran with pouches under his hound-dog eyes, smiled. "I hear you're gonna be a Feeb," he told Sonterra.

The desultory reference to Sonterra's upcoming career change set the tone for the rest of the interview. Lots of cops resented federal agents, whatever their acronym, FBI or otherwise; with the power of Uncle Sam behind them, they could override local investigations if they chose. While many officers appreciated the help, others viewed it as arrogance, and simple interference.

McCullough was evidently of the latter persuasion.

"Word gets around fast," Sonterra replied.

Unless you happen to be the person closest to the prospective Feeb, I thought, with a sting of sorrow. Then, determinedly, I put my private emotions aside. I had a job to do.

"Are you charging my client with a crime, or just harassing him?" I demanded, fixing McCullough and his partner with a steely glare.

"Lawyers," McCullough muttered.

"*Lady* lawyers," confirmed his buddy, who was even older and apparently more jaded than McCullough.

"Get over it," I said. "I'm a lawyer, and I'm female. Now, can we get down to business?"

McCullough gave Sonterra a pitying look. Evidently, our relationship was common knowledge, too.

"Where were you last night, Mr. Gerring?" asked the hound-dog.

The questioning proceeded from there. It went on for hours, covering the same ground over and over again. It was grueling, exhaustive, and got us all absolutely nowhere.

"I want to stay here," Rodney said, as dawn broke through the barred, reinforced windows high on the eastern wall of the interrogation room. "In protective custody."

I was surprised, but not amazed. Jail was not the safest place in the world, but I had seen Rodney's fear of Diego Sanchez firsthand, in my office. It was the kind of terror that made a three-hundred-pound oaf sweat, turn pale, and lose control of his bodily functions.

"Who says it's 'protective'?" McCullough's partner asked. "Maybe we're busting you for real. On a murder rap."

I turned my gaze on the portly partner. "Where's your evidence, Officer—" I peered at the badge and ID hanging around his thick neck. "—Robbins. You don't have enough evidence to hold my client. Simply knowing the victim is not a crime."

McCullough sighed heavily and sat back in his chair. "Get him out of here," he told me. "He's stinking up the room."

Rodney pounded a fist on the table, bouncing everybody's Styrofoam coffee cups. It was the first sign of spirit I'd seen in him since my arrival. "Sanchez was Angela's connection, all right? He knows I know that. He's going to kill me if I leave here!"

I put a hand on Rodney's arm. I did *not* look to Sonterra for backup, though I was sorely tempted. "Mr. Gerring has a point," I said evenly. "If he's injured or killed, the responsibility will be partly yours. And you can bet your next doughnut, Officer McCullough, that I will clamp your balls in a vise if that happens." Okay, so it wasn't a very ladylike thing to say. You have to play hardball with these guys; it's the only game they know.

McCullough gave up a small smile, glanced in Sonterra's direction again. Maybe he thought Sonterra ought to put the little woman in line, or maybe he just felt sorry for him. It could have been both.

"All right," he said. "We'll put the pretty boy here in a holding cell. Twenty-four hours is all the hospitality he gets, then he's either out, or he's a long-term guest."

Robbins stood up, hauled Rodney to his feet, and put him in cuffs. He was off to the holding cell.

McCullough leaned forward in his chair.

"Are you always a bitch, Ms. Westbrook?" he drawled.

Sonterra took a step toward us, and I put up a hand to stop him.

"Are you always a prick, Officer Mc-Cullough?"

He laughed and sat back in his chair, folding his arms. Amazingly, I got the impression he was beginning to like me. "Most of the time. It serves a purpose."

"So does being a bitch."

I stood up to leave, and Sonterra followed without a word.

Emma, Mrs. K, and the dogs were sound asleep in the waiting room when we got downstairs.

Mrs. K stirred, blinking, and sat upright. "*Where* is Rodney?"

"In protective custody," I said gently. "He's afraid of Diego Sanchez."

Emma yawned, stretched her arms. "I don't know how you stand this job," she told Sonterra brightly. "It's boring as hell."

"I wish," Sonterra said, wearily wry. "Mrs. K, you shouldn't be alone right now. How about coming home with us?"

Home, as in, his place. I let the reference pass.

Mrs. K shook her head. "If there were any threat to my safety, I'd know it," she said, with utter confidence. "It's Rodney I'm worried about. I don't seem to get anything when I try to read his future." She looked at me. "Is my nephew safe here, Clare?"

I couldn't lie to her. Number one, it wouldn't have been fair. Number two, she would have sensed deception anyway. "Yes and no. He's probably out of Sanchez's reach, but jails are—well—jails. Full of dangerous people."

"At least let me drive you home," Sonterra said. Waldo was on his feet, licking Sonterra's hand.

"I have my Buick," Mrs. K replied, with another shake of the head. She squinted a little in the daylight pouring through the lobby windows. "I wouldn't mind a hot breakfast, though."

"Me, either," Emma agreed.

"Done," Sonterra said. "I'm buying."

We all hied ourselves to the nearest twenty-four-hour restaurant, Mrs. K in her Buick, the rest of us in Sonterra's SUV. I ordered biscuits and gravy, and ate every bite.

After the meal, Sonterra took Emma, the dogs, and me back to his house.

We'd been up all night, and we were whipped, but I knew Sonterra didn't intend to crash. Neither did I.

"What now?" I asked, in his kitchen, while Emma took a shower in an upstairs bathroom. The dogs were probably curled up on the bath mat, supervising.

"I'm going to hook up with Eddie, find out what's happening with the search for Sanchez," Sonterra said. "Maybe Shanda has turned up."

"Check with Father Mike Dennehy, at St. Sebastian's," I said. Throughout the night, my mind had been occupied with McCullough's endless questions. Now that I'd taken some carbohydrates onboard, the fog was clearing. "He's her friend. She might have gone to him, if she was scared."

With one finger, Sonterra smoothed a strand of hair back from my forehead. "I'll find out," he promised gruffly. "Get some sleep, Clare. You're exhausted. The world will go on turning without your help."

I grinned. "You're sure of that?"

He kissed me. "Positive. Lock the door behind me and put the chain on."

"Yes, sir." I kissed him back. "Can I use your computer?" I wanted to run through the list of websites David Valardi had given me, see where he'd been, in his cyber travels.

"Like it would stop you if I said no," Sonterra scoffed.

I batted my lashes. "Are you always such a prick?" I teased.

He touched my nose. "Are you always such a bitch?"

THIRTY-FOUR

I went back to the Valardi case after Sonterra and I spoke, but I had a hard time concentrating. David had visited a lot of websites, everything from Monster.com—evidently, he'd been *looking* for a real job—to the singularly strange home pages of various certain grandiose nutcases who fancied themselves the successor to Bill Gates.

Hello, I thought. *You live in your mother's basement. Chances are, the next Microsoft will not be launched from the family Ping-Pong table. Which is probably buried in laundry anyway.*

I opened my day-timer, found David's home number, and called.

"Betty's House of Dolls," a female voice answered.

I was so stunned that, for a moment, I couldn't say a word, let alone identify myself.

"Hello?" the woman, presumably Betty, pressed impatiently. She had a smoker's voice, rough and throaty.

"My name is Clare Westbrook, and I'm David Valardi's attorney," I said, recovering a little. Maybe it was a wrong number. A really wild coincidence. "Is he there?"

"David!" Betty shrieked, not bothering to cover the mouthpiece. I winced. "Telephone! It's the freebie lawyer!"

"Mrs. Valardi," I said carefully, while we waited for David to come to the phone, "do you run a doll shop?"

"'Mrs. Valardi,'" she scoffed. "That was three husbands ago. And, yes, I sell dolls." A note of hopeful avarice slipped into her voice. "You a collector?"

"Er—yes," I lied. "What kind of dolls do you carry?" I half expected her to say naked ones, decorated with duct tape and little nooses. After all, I'd gone a long time without sleep.

"I've got a little of everything," she said.

David arrived. Betty mumbled something to him, and then he came on the line.

"Hello, Clare," he said. "What's up?"

Your number, Buddy, I thought, *if you turn out to be the doll man. And right now, you're looking pretty good for it.*

He had to know how his mother answered the telephone, and that I would be correspondingly intrigued. Unless he *wasn't* the doll man. I've run into stranger coincidences in my time, but they're rare.

"I was just going through the list of websites you gave me," I said, using a businesslike tone on the off chance that he didn't know I'd caught on to his doll proximity. Unlikely, given the fact that Shanda and I had shown him one of the emails, and he'd traced it to Mrs. K's computer. Or *pretended* to trace it. "So far, there's nothing incriminating."

He sighed. "Good," he said.

"I need the names, David. BoogerBrain and Flasher and Who's-it."

"HumpDoggy," Valardi told me helpfully.

"Right," I said, and rested my forehead in my left palm.

He surprised me. "I've got their names

and addresses," he said, sounding pleased. "I wrote them down. Hold on a second."

He was gone before I could ask to talk to his mother again, so I bided my time. In the background, I heard pots and pans clanking, the TV news playing, and Betty complaining about something. I tapped the fingers of my good hand on the surface of Sonterra's desk and wished I could hop into my car, drive to Betty's House of Dolls, and get a firsthand look at the situation.

My car was still at the office, where I'd left it when Sonterra, Emma, and the dogs collected me for the trip to the cabin. Even if I'd had ready access to it, I couldn't have left Emma alone.

David returned, huffing with exertion— down those basement stairs to his computer lair, then back up again, no doubt— and read me the information.

I wrote it all down, promised Valardi I would be in touch, and said good-bye.

I considered calling Sonterra with the new development, but decided against it. He was on his way to St. Sebastian's to speak with Father Mike, and that was equally important. Even he couldn't do two things at once.

What to do? Call the police?

I pictured Detective McCullough, and the smug expression that would cross his face if I were stupid enough to tell him what I suspected. *Running a doll shop isn't a crime*, he would say, throwing a version of my own words back in my face.

I knew, of course, that I could have contacted someone else, but to me, in that nerve-jangled moment, McCullough represented all cops—with the exception of Sonterra.

I decided to wait. I'm not very good at waiting.

I was building lunch—grilled cheese sandwiches—when Emma came downstairs and followed her nose to the kitchen. The dogs pawed at the patio door, and she let them out, yawning expansively.

"Where's Tony?" she asked, when they were back inside, plopping into a chair.

I wedged a spatula under one of the sandwiches, slapped it onto a plate, short-order-cook style, and set it down in front of her. "Working." I'd been listening for his call, expecting a report on the chat with Father Mike, and a chance to tell him about Betty's House of Dolls, but so far, nothing.

"You look terrible, Clare," my niece observed, lifting the top of the sandwich to inspect the cheese beneath, as she has done since she was old enough to eat solid food.

"Gee, thanks."

"You should get some rest."

I served up my own sandwich and sat down across from Emma. "Later," I said. I was exhausted, but I couldn't have slept, not with all the possibilities stewing in my brain. I decided to bounce some of them off my niece, since she knew the worst of it anyway.

Maybe she'd have some insights.

She listened intently to my Betty's House of Dolls theory.

"Awesome," she said, when I finished.

I frowned. "Awesome? This guy might have murdered three people, and I'm next on his list. How, may I ask, is that 'awesome'?"

She waved a hand. "I don't mean that. You just talked to me like you think I'm a person or something."

"Of course I think you're a person!"

"No, you don't. You think I'm a baby."

I didn't point out that a baby is, by definition, a person. It would have been splitting hairs, and far be it from me. "I *think* you're thirteen years old. You're the center of my universe. If I don't tell you things, it's because I want to keep you safe."

"That's a load of crap. The last part, I mean, about keeping me safe. I'm not stupid, Clare—and besides, I'm almost *fourteen*."

"Oh, that makes all the difference."

She flushed with indignation. "You can't protect me. Nobody can really protect anybody—maybe not even themselves. When you don't tell me stuff, I'm in the dark. More vulnerable than I would be if I knew what was really going on." She paused for a breath, and a mouthful of grilled cheese. "And I don't want to be the center of your universe. It's too much responsibility."

I pretended to pull an arrow from my chest.

She softened. "It's a pretty strong coincidence that David Valardi lives in a house full of dolls," she observed.

"Yeah. I think so."

"Did you tell Tony?"

"I will, when he calls."

"Why can't you call him?"

"Questions, questions. He's *working*, Emma. He doesn't need me bugging him."

"He's a homicide cop. This *is* his work."

"He's doing something else right now."

Emma finished off her sandwich, ruminating all the while. "I think we should check the place out ourselves, then. Valardi probably knows you're on to him. He might be heading for the hills even as we speak."

The phone rang.

I moved to answer, but Emma got there first.

Her face lit up. "Hi, Goober," she said. "Clare found the doll man."

THIRTY-FIVE

"What does she mean, 'Clare found the doll man'?" Sonterra wanted to know, as soon as I wrested the receiver from Emma and said hello.

I told him about the call to David, and what I'd learned about his mother's vocation as a purveyor of small plastic people.

He let out a low whistle of exclamation. "Interesting," he said.

"What did Father Mike have to say?"

Sonterra hesitated. I didn't like that.

"Sonterra," I prompted.

"He didn't show up at St. Sebastian's this morning," Sonterra said. "I got his address and stopped by his house. Nobody home."

My stomach threatened to throw back the

grilled cheese sandwich I'd just eaten. "What if Sanchez has him?"

"He's probably with Shanda, Clare," Sonterra said reasonably, but without much conviction.

"You've got to find him," I whispered.

Emma moved to stand behind me, kneading my rigid shoulders with her hands. I fought the relaxing sensation; I needed to stay alert.

"We will, Clare. We will."

"I wish I had your confidence."

"So do I. Half the cops in Maricopa County are out looking for him and the Rawlingses right now," Sonterra said. "The other half are turning over rocks, hoping Sanchez will crawl out from under one of them. We're doing everything we can, Clare."

"Are you going to check out Betty's House of Dolls?"

"No," Sonterra replied. "I'm doing an interagency thing with McCullough and Robbins—they're following up for now. Technically, that's on their turf anyway. I'm coming home, taking a shower, wolfing down some food, and crashing for the night. I've been up for twenty-four hours, and my brain is mush."

"McCullough and Robbins?" I protested. "Is that the best you can do?"

"They're good cops."

"They're officious bastards."

"No argument there, Counselor, but the two aren't mutually exclusive. They're still good cops."

"Sonterra, this is what they call a hot lead. David Valardi has the computer skills, and access to the dolls."

"Circumstantial," Sonterra said. "I couldn't get a warrant, and you know that—Counselor. Besides, a lot of places sell dolls. And even if the ones we found came right off Valardi's mother's shelves, it wouldn't necessarily implicate him. Could be one of the customers. McCullough and Robbins will get a feel for the setup and we'll go from there."

"You're not taking this very seriously, Sonterra."

He swore softly. I pictured him shoving a hand through his hair in frustration. "I'm *handling* it, Clare. For now, will you just let that be good enough? Even if Valardi is the

asshole-of-interest, he's not going anywhere."

"How can you be so sure of that? He
could be on a bus to St. Louis by now!"

"He lives with his mother," Sonterra said
quietly. "He's never had an apartment of his
own, or held a job for more than a few
weeks. Proactive, he ain't."

"Sometimes," I said, "you *really* piss me
off."

"My reason for living. Thaw out a steak,
will you? I'll grill it when I get home. I could
eat a bear."

I was a long time answering. "Sure. I'll
thaw out your damned steak."

He laughed. "Thanks."

Emma, having picked up that much from
my end of the conversation, left off the mas-
sage to hurry to the freezer.

By the time Sonterra rolled in half an hour
later, she had a chunk of top sirloin marinat-
ing in bottled sauce, a potato in the microwave, waiting to be zapped, and was in
the process of chopping salad greens.

"Where did I go wrong?" I teased, releasing the chain so Sonterra could come in
through the door connecting the kitchen

with the garage. I hadn't raised my niece to cater to a man.

Emma grinned, set the microwave, and put the steak under the broiler.

Sonterra put his arms around me and kissed the top of my head, then went upstairs for a shower.

When he came back down, wearing clean jeans and a T-shirt, his dark hair tousled and damp, I almost served up the steak myself.

"We'll check out the doll shop together," he told me. "Tomorrow."

"Can I go, too?" Emma asked excitedly. By then, she'd exchanged her pajamas for day clothes. With a few hours of sleep behind her, she was raring to go.

"No way," Sonterra said, sitting down to his meal. "You're going to school."

Emma's eyes narrowed. "Oh, right. Just when things get really exciting, you guys shut out the kid!"

THIRTY-SIX

A man of his word, Sonterra polished off a substantial meal, lovingly prepared by Emma, and went straight to bed.

I might have joined him, but I didn't trust my niece not to call a cab while I was upstairs dozing, or even hijack Sonterra's SUV, and head for Betty's House of Dolls.

For that reason, I stretched out in the living room, on the couch. I snoozed, but not deeply, and I was aware when Emma turned the TV on low, to watch cop shows on one of the cable networks, and when she took the dogs into the backyard to play. The telephone rang a couple of times, and I listened while Emma spoke, in whispers, to Loretta—back from the ranch in Tucson—and then one of her friends from school.

Around sunset, I stirred to use the bathroom, and Emma served me a bowl of chicken noodle soup with all the solicitude of Florence Nightingale tending one of her wounded soldiers.

"You'll wake me if Shanda Rawlings calls?" I asked, managing the spoon with my still-awkward left hand. I was getting better at using it, but I still felt like a bird with a broken wing. It gave me a new appreciation for all southpaws, bravely functioning in a right-handed world.

Emma smiled from her seat on a nearby hassock. "Yeah, Clare. I'll keep you in the loop."

On the television screen, a couple of cops wrestled a redneck out of his hiding place, beneath a dog bed. The obligatory trailer loomed in the background.

"Why don't you watch something peaceful, like cartoons?" I fretted, and sucked up a noodle. Privately, I was fretting about Shanda. Was she okay?

Emma rolled her eyes. "Sure," she said. "Cartoons. After that, maybe *Sesame Street,* or *Clifford, the Big Red Dog.*"

"You like dogs," I pointed out, sleep-fuddled. Bernice cuddled in her lap, and Waldo sat beside her, receptive to a gentle ruffling of his golden ears.

"I like cops," she replied. "I want to be one."

That brought me up from the dregs of slumber. "You'll get over it," I said. "Three months ago, you wanted to be a lawyer, and three months before that, a rock star."

She grinned. "How old were you when you decided to get a law degree?" she inquired innocently.

I remembered the exact moment. Tracy and I were in Family Court, with one of a long line of social workers, and an attorney walked confidently up the center aisle, briefcase in hand, high heels clicking on the hard floor. She spoke, and the judge paid attention. Things happened. Things *changed*.

"I was seven," I admitted.

"And you never had second thoughts?"

I smiled. I'd been maneuvered, and I knew it, but I admired Emma's style. "For a while, I considered becoming a nurse, and then an astronaut, but the die was pretty much cast."

Emma spread her hands. "I rest my case."

"Smug brat," I said affectionately.

She laughed. "In four years, I'll be out of high school. I'm going straight into the Academy."

"Wrong," I said, setting my empty bowl on the coffee table. "You're graduating from college first."

"I won't change my mind."

"Maybe not," I agreed, lying back on my pillows. "But you're still going to get a degree."

"What kind of degree?"

"Any kind."

"Lie back and sleep," Emma said.

Right about then, the most recent dose of codeine kicked in. Or maybe it was some kind of kid-hypnosis. In any case, I closed my eyes and fell asleep in a couple of seconds.

I dreamed of Emma, all grown up, and carrying a badge.

Sonterra shook me awake the next morning. Freshly showered and dressed for the street, he grinned down at me.

"She's back among the living," he told Emma, who stood nearby, looking distinctly uncomfortable and dressed for school.

"Gomer's about to hit the books," Sonterra announced. "I'll drop her off."

I sat up, blinking. I was still struggling with a desire to keep Emma in my sight at all times, but I knew Sonterra's take on the situation was right—keep things as normal as possible. She needed to get on with her life.

"If you think you're leaving me here to watch cable TV, Sonterra," I challenged, "you are misguided."

He grinned. "Get a shower and make yourself some breakfast. I'll pick you up in forty-five minutes."

"You'd better," I warned.

"You're going to the doll place without me," Emma accused, her gaze swinging from me to Sonterra and back to me again.

"Nothing much gets by you," Sonterra remarked easily. "Let's go, Gome. Time's a-wasting, and we're burning daylight."

I wondered, going by Emma's expression, if she was reconsidering her dear-old-dad fantasies about Sonterra.

"I promise we'll tell you every single detail," I said. I understood her need to be in the center of things. She came by that honestly, after all.

"Do you double-swear?" she demanded.

I raised my hand. "Double-swear," I said.

She studied me closely for a long moment. "All right," she conceded. "But I don't have to like it."

I hid a smile. "No," I agreed. "You don't."

Forty-five minutes later, Sonterra came back to collect me. I was dressed and ready, with a serving of cold cereal in my stomach.

Sonterra took in my jeans, black turtleneck, and lightweight tweed jacket, the sleeve of which just barely accommodated my cast. "Lookin' good," he said, with a slight growl in his voice.

We were alone. The last few days had been especially stressful.

Our departure for the doll shop was a slightly delayed one.

THIRTY-SEVEN

Betty's House of Dolls was in a downscale Phoenix neighborhood, housed in the converted garage of a split-level ranch house. It wasn't Betty who greeted Sonterra and me when we arrived; David Valardi came trundling down the front walk, looking disturbed.

"There were two cops here last night," he said. "Asking questions about my mother's dolls."

I took a moment to make sure my face was composed. "This is my friend, Tony Sonterra," I said. "Tony, David Valardi."

The two men shook hands, sizing each other up.

"I called your cell phone, and all I got was

voice mail," David said. His thick neck was red with annoyance.

"I'm here now," I pointed out quietly.

"If you didn't get my call—"

"I checked my messages this morning," I lied. The truth was, between getting a good night's sleep, taking codeine, and making hot love with Sonterra in his living room, I hadn't exactly had my mind on business.

"Do they think I'm the guy who sent you that stupid picture?" David wanted to know.

I put a hand on his hairy arm. "Relax," I said, neatly avoiding the question. "Tell me about last night."

David did relax, a little. "Come inside. I'll get us some sodas."

"I'd like to see the dolls," I ventured.

David, turning away to lead us up the walk to the front door, stopped and gave me a suspicious look. "Why?"

"I have a niece," I said.

"Oh," David replied. "Okay. That's the way into the shop." He pointed, unnecessarily, at the well-marked entrance to the altered garage. "I'll get the sodas."

"Thanks," Sonterra said, speaking for the first time since we got out of the car. He put a hand to the small of my back and steered

me across the gravel space that would have
been a lawn in any other state but Arizona.
"Nice save," he added, when David was out
of earshot. "You didn't listen to your messages, as far as I know, and Emma is too
old for dolls."

"Trust you to state the obvious," I replied.

The shop was a jumble of low-grade mer-
chandise, and Betty was behind the
counter. She looked pretty much as I'd
imagined she would: loose cotton smock,
overpermed hair, tobacco-stained teeth.
Sometimes I think I'm psychic, like Mrs. K.

I nodded to her, looked around to find
hundreds of little painted or glass eyes staring back at me, and suppressed a shiver.
"I'm Clare Westbrook," I said, reaching
across the counter to hand her my card,
freshly plucked from the supply in my left
jacket pocket. "David's attorney."

She assessed Sonterra, and I wondered,
given the depth of her scrutiny, if she'd
made him for a cop. When she looked at me
again, she seemed disappointed. Maybe
business was slow.

"I'm looking for something for my niece,"
I said.

Betty brightened and came out from behind the counter just as David entered by an inside door, two cans of soda pressed against his side by an elbow, another in his hand.

"Mom," he began, "this is—"

She cut him off with a wave. "I know," she said. She had a potential customer on the hook, and was apparently unconcerned that her son was in enough trouble to need a lawyer.

I checked out the stock. There was a wide selection, starting with cheap plastic "fashion" dolls, progressing to china children with ringlets and pouty mouths, representatives of other lands, and characters from well-known fairy tales.

The fact that there was a mob of them, and the way they stared, made my forearms prickle.

Sonterra accepted a cola from David and popped the top. I turned mine down, but politely. None of the dolls I'd seen so far had appeared in any of the photos Peter Bailey had given me, nor did I recognize the one buried in Sonterra's flowerpot at the cabin, or the one who'd been lynched from his rearview mirror, but there were a number of viable candidates. A change of costume, a different hairstyle, and you had a duct-tape scene, or an eerie tea party in the woods.

"How old is your niece?" Betty asked helpfully.

"Five," I said, not making eye contact with Sonterra.

She lifted a blond doll in a pinafore down from a high shelf. "This is Alice Blue," she said fondly, stroking the toy's gleaming synthetic locks. "Closeout. I could let you have her for $49.95."

"I'll take her," I said, and kept looking. I wasn't in the market, but I was sifting the atmosphere for vibes.

David spoke up. He'd been all that while working up his nerve, I suspected. "About those cops last night," he began.

"Put a sock in it," Betty said.

I risked a glance at Sonterra. He was swilling cola and checking out a display of teddy bears in little dresses. Never too early to shop for those interdepartmental Christmas gifts. I would have suggested the panda in the pink tutu for McCullough.

David stepped in my direction. He looked conflicted, and defiant. He did not meet his mother's acid glare.

"They were asking a lot of questions," he

said, in a stage whisper, as though that would keep Betty from overhearing. "They wanted to look at the dolls, and they didn't buy anything. It's because of that email you got that day at your office, isn't it?"

I took a Little Red Riding Hood off the shelf and handed it to Betty, to keep her at bay. Instead, she hovered.

"Yes," I said.

"They think *I* sent that picture?" David asked anxiously. A light seemed to go on in his head. "Maybe you think that, too."

I shook my head. My gut said no. The vibes weren't there. "No, David," I said honestly, feeling a little deflated. "I don't." Sonterra had been right all along; resentful as he was, Valardi was a mama's boy. His criminal activities, if he had any, were confined to the computer.

Sonterra set two of the bears on the counter, effectively drawing Betty back to the register. While he paid for his purchases, he chatted her up. How was business? Did she deal with a lot of collectors? Sell dolls over the internet?

That gave me a few minutes to quiz David. "Does your mother keep a list of clients?" I asked casually.

He wasn't buying the casual routine. His eyebrows were lowered, and a vein in his neck was pulsing. "Why?"

"Because I want to know if I'd recognize any of the names," I said.

"But you really don't think I'm the one who sent that picture?"

If he was the doll man, he might have slipped, and said "pictures"—plural, instead of singular. That, of course, would indicate that he knew there had been other incidents.

"I know you didn't."

He leaned in a little, smelling of sweat and some kind of cheesy snack. "She keeps her customer list in a database. I'll have to email it to you as an attachment," he whispered. "When Mom's not around."

"Thanks," I whispered back. He'd snagged my attention again. "You have my email address?" Trick question. The doll man had it, too. I didn't give it out all that often.

"No," he said.

I reached into my blazer pocket and pulled out another card. Scrawled the necessary information.

Betty cheerfully rang up my purchases, and we left.

"What's with the teddy bears?" I asked, on the way back to Sonterra's car.

"I have a couple of nieces myself," he answered. "So, what did you make of the setup?"

"Wild-goose chase," I said, with a sigh. "Sorry."

He opened the passenger door for me and stashed our stuff in the back while I was buckling up.

"Where to?" he asked, getting behind the wheel and starting the engine. I was a little surprised that he didn't offer a comment on my assessment of the situation at Betty's.

"Don't you have to work?"

"I *am* working," he replied. "You're the one who's off the clock."

"You could drop me at my office," I suggested.

"So you can pick up your Escalade and run all over town playing Stephanie Plum?" he fired back, with a grin. "Not a chance."

"Lots of one-armed people drive, Sonterra," I said.

"Not you," he replied.

"Then let's go by Shanda's apartment."

He sighed. It was another useless trip, in his opinion, but he was willing to play along. "What's the address?"

I dug out my day-timer and gave him the street and number.

"After that, I'd like to look for Father Mike."

I was assuming, of course, that there would *be* an "after that."

THIRTY-EIGHT

The Rawlings apartment was in a sixplex constructed of cement blocks, like most of the buildings in Phoenix, but without the obligatory layer of stucco. The paint job looked original—sun-faded yellow, with touches of spray-painted, multinational graffiti to break the monotony. A scuffed plastic tricycle lay forlornly on its side in front of number 4.

I saw the curtains jiggle at the same moment Sonterra did.

He eased me behind him before I had a chance to dig in my heels, and pushed back the side of his jacket, uncovering the service revolver he carried in a shoulder holster.

"Police," he said clearly. "Open up."

I heard the chain being released, the dead bolt grinding.

Mrs. Rawlings stood just beyond the threshold, her face rigid. "Shanda isn't home," she said. I looked into her eyes, and saw a plea there.

I reached into my purse, closed the fingers of my operative hand around the butt of my .38.

The whole desert seemed to sink into a strange stillness. I couldn't hear the midday traffic out on the street. I couldn't hear anything, except my own heartbeat.

Sonterra said something; it didn't register.

He reached back, trying to shove me to one side, and in that moment, Mrs. Rawlings came hurtling toward us, shoved hard from behind.

I got a glimpse of Sanchez, eyes glittering like those of a rabid wolf, and felt Sonterra go for his revolver. It all happened in slow motion.

Then came the shot.

Sonterra went down.

I raised my .38 and fired blindly into the doorway.

Sanchez's face exploded in a splash of crimson gore.

Mrs. Rawlings screamed, then screamed again.

I dropped, still in slow motion, to my knees. Maybe thirty seconds had passed since Sonterra knocked on the door.

"Sonterra?" I whispered.

He was facedown in a pool of blood. He didn't move, or speak.

I set the .38 aside, scrambled for my cell phone, dropped it on the concrete walk, retrieved it. Dialed 911 with my thumb.

"A police officer has been shot," I heard myself say, from somewhere just beyond my body. I reeled off the address, with Mrs. Rawlings still shrieking in the background, and grappled Sonterra over onto his back. He'd been shot in the chest, but I couldn't tell where. There was too much blood.

I put my ear to his breast bone. He was breathing, and there was a heartbeat, though it was barely discernible.

Sirens chirped in the distance.

Mrs. Rawlings continued to scream.

"Sonterra," I said, cupping his blood-spattered, graying face in my hand. "Help is coming. Hold on, okay?"

His lashes fluttered.

The sirens drew nearer.

"They're coming," I told Sonterra. I lay down beside him on the concrete, and held him as best I could, with my right arm in a cast. "They're coming."

He let out his breath, a long, rattling sound, and didn't draw another one.

I got to my knees, bent over him, pried open his mouth, made sure his tongue wasn't lodged in the back of his throat, and started CPR.

I heard running footsteps, felt strong hands drag me away from Sonterra. I struggled so ferociously that I had to be restrained.

EMTs crouched on either side of Sonterra. One of them put an oxygen mask over his face, while another fired up a pair of portable paddles.

I shrieked and fought to be free.

"Ms. Westbrook? Clare?" The voice was familiar, but I didn't look around to see who it belonged to. I watched as Sonterra took the first jolt of electricity. His body convulsed violently.

I screamed.

The man who'd been holding me stepped in front of me, blocking my view of Sonterra.

Atienzo, one of the cops who'd come to

my office the night of the drive-by shooting. I tried to claw my way past him.

"They're doing everything they can, Clare," he said gently, holding me by the shoulders. "You won't help him by getting in their way."

"Pulse!" one of the EMTs barked.

I went into another frenzy.

"He's breathing," someone else said.

My knees buckled. Atienzo let me fall, but he eased the way down.

"Jesus," I wailed, "Jesus, Jesus—"

There were cops everywhere. I focused on Atienzo, who was on his knees, too, and facing me. His hands still gripped my shoulders.

"What happened, Clare?" he asked, giving me a little shake.

"Sanchez—Sanchez shot him." The earth seemed to pick up speed, spin faster, and then faster still. I was covered in Sonterra's blood. Mrs. Rawlings had stopped screaming. What had happened to Mrs. Rawlings?

I swayed, and Atienzo steadied me.

"Are you hurt?" he rasped.

The universe came back into skewed focus. The contents of my stomach boiled into the back of my throat, scalded my tongue. "I—I don't think so—" I peered past Atienzo's shoulder, saw the EMTs shift Sonterra onto a collapsible gurney.

I tried to get to my feet, follow, but Atienzo's grasp was inescapable.

Through a forest of cop legs, I saw Sanchez's body—the hollow-point from my .38 had hurtled him backward, into the apartment's tiny entryway. I knew he was dead—I'd seen his features disintegrate— and I was glad. God help me, I was glad. I would have spit on him if my mouth hadn't been dry.

"Diego Sanchez?" Atienzo asked, following my gaze.

I nodded. "I shot him."

Atienzo helped me to my feet. Made sure I could stand on my own before he let me go. I heard another siren: the ambulance, taking Sonterra away.

My knees went weak again.

Again, Atienzo held me upright.

That was when I spotted the second gurney. Mrs. Rawlings was lying on it, unconscious. An EMT hooked up an IV as I watched, and then she, too, was whisked away.

I put my hand over my mouth. It smelled of gunpowder, and blood.

"Was she hit?" I whispered.

"Heart attack," Atienzo said.

McCullough and Robbins appeared out of the conglomeration of blue uniforms. "You all right, Ms. Westbrook?" McCullough asked. At a nod from him, Atienzo stepped aside. McCullough took my arm.

"Sonterra's been shot."

"You don't look so good yourself," McCullough observed, with surprising gentleness. "Officer Atienzo here will take you to the hospital. Have you checked out. Is there anybody we can call?"

After all I'd been through, it was McCullough's kindness that almost brought me down. Tears stung my eyes, and I nearly doubled over.

"Loretta," I said. "Loretta Matthews." I recited the number as though it were a prayer.

"Atienzo," McCullough murmured, taking out his cell phone. "Take her wherever they took Detective Sonterra. Make sure she's seen right away."

"My niece—tell Loretta to pick her up at her school, in Cave Creek—" Dear God, when Emma found out Tony had been shot, she was going to be wild with worry. I had to trust Loretta to take care of her.

I heard McCullough making the call, relaying the message, and then I was handed over again, led through a pulsing maze, seated in the back of a squad car. Culver drove, and Atienzo sat with me, gripping my hand.

"Don't they want to question me?" I asked. I felt drunk, disconnected from the rest of the world. Pain screamed through my broken arm, reasserting itself now that some of the shock was wearing off.

"Time for that later," Atienzo said grimly.

A picture of Shanda took shape in my mind. In my imagination, she was holding Maya in her arms, and both of them looked scared. "Was there anyone else in the apartment?"

"No," Culver answered, from behind the wall dividing the front seat of the squad car from the back.

"I think I might throw up," I warned.

"You wouldn't be the first," Atienzo replied. "Culver, hand back a bottle of water, will you?"

Culver complied. Atienzo unscrewed the lid and gave the bottle to me.

"Sip it slowly," he warned.

I sipped, then guzzled.

Then threw up.

The squad car whipped from lane to lane, the siren whooped. Atienzo produced a roll of paper towels and did his best to clean me up. He made some progress with the vomit, but the blood saturated my hair and clothes, seeping into the very pores of my skin.

The ambulances Sonterra and Mrs. Rawlings had ridden in were in the bay in front of the emergency room when we arrived, the back doors wide open, the red lights still flashing.

I waited, numb, while Culver shut off the ignition, got out of the car, and opened the door on my side.

I took a stumbling step toward the entrance.

Sonterra was in there somewhere, maybe alive, and maybe dead.

I had to get to him.

THIRTY-NINE

I didn't want to be examined. I didn't even want the blood washed away. I wanted to go to Sonterra, take his hand, will him to hold on to life with whatever strength he had left. I wanted to guide him, breath by breath, heartbeat by heartbeat, out of the shadow lands and into the light.

An efficient emergency room doctor informed me that he'd been taken straight to surgery. Mrs. Rawlings was being stabilized.

Nurses, interns, and orderlies cut away my clothes, swabbed off enough of the mess to make sure I hadn't been shot, and took a blood sample. An IV needle was thrust into my left arm. The deepest regions of my brain rebelled—I was defenseless now, as surely as if my hands had been bound at the wrists.

I lay shivering in a hospital gown when Loretta rushed in, alone, and I was fiercely, incomprehensibly afraid.

"Sonterra—" I began, but the name caught on a sob.

Loretta grasped my hand. "I know," she said. "I know."

"Where—where's Emma?"

"The police sent a car for her. She'll be here soon. *Breathe*, Clare. Your face looks like a death mask." Her gaze ranged from one end of my pitiful, trembling frame to the other. "Are you hurt?"

Was I hurt? Good question. I hadn't taken a bullet, or even a blow, but I was injured, all right. I was mortally wounded, at the very core of my soul.

"If Sonterra dies—"

"He *won't*," Loretta said firmly. As if she had any say in the matter. Last time I looked, the universe was not consulting Loretta, or anyone else, before it unleashed some new and murderous mayhem into the world.

I felt compelled to describe what had happened, over and over. Maybe I was try-

ing to make sense of it, maybe I was just fix-
ating. I was born and raised, after all, in
Dysfunction Junction. "Sanchez was there,
in the apartment, with Mrs. Rawlings," I rat-
tled on. "She tried to warn us, I think—but
he was holding a gun on her."

Loretta squeezed my hand. "Don't dwell
on it, Clare."

I couldn't help it. The experience was so
real that it should have had its own zip
code. Horrific images not only lingered,
they whipped through my mind like a kalei-
doscope on fast-forward. "I saw him—
Sanchez, I mean—and then there was a
shot. Sonterra fell. I emptied my .38 into
Diego's face."

"Good work," Loretta said, but tears were
slipping down her cheeks.

The doctor reappeared.

"Is she hurt?" Loretta asked. She was determined to get an answer out of somebody.

The lady doctor, a diminutive Jane
Seymour type, shook her head. "We're ad-
mitting you for observation, Ms. Westbrook.
Given your pregnancy—"

"My what?" I broke in, trying to sit up.

Loretta and Dr. Jane pushed me back
down, one on either side.

"It showed up in the lab work," the doctor said. She looked uncertain, realizing I hadn't known I was pregnant.

"I take birth control pills," I protested.

"They don't always work," Dr. Jane replied.

I closed my eyes, waiting for the examining room to stop spinning around me.

"Son of a gun," Loretta enthused, beaming through her tears.

I was overwhelmed. Too much input. The processing plant was jammed, a woodchipper trying to grind up an oak.

Sonterra was in surgery, and I was carrying his baby. Talk about life being the things that happen when you're making other plans.

A scuffle ensued beyond the curtains of my little alcove, and Emma burst in. The look on her face made my heart turn over inside my chest.

"They wouldn't tell me anything!" she cried, rushing to my side.

I put my arm out, and she fell to my chest, sobbing.

Dr. Jane slipped out, and Loretta withdrew a little.

"Tony's been shot," I said. "He's in surgery right now."

"I knew it was something like that!" Emma wailed.

I held her as best I could, given the cast and the IV needle. "We have to be strong," I said. How we were supposed to accomplish such a feat, I didn't know.

Emma lifted her head to look into my face. "Your hair is all bloody. Did you get shot, too?"

"No," I said gently.

"Was it the doll man?"

"It was Diego Sanchez. He's dead, Emma. I killed him."

She sniffled. "Good," she said, and visibly braced herself, perhaps expecting a bolt from heaven.

I stroked her hair.

"You have to be all right," she informed me.

"I will be," I said. If Sonterra didn't make it, I would want to collapse, fold in on myself, stay in a cocoon of grief forever, but I didn't have that option, and I knew it, even then. I had Emma to think about. And the baby who had defied staggering biological odds to take root in my womb.

Dr. Jane returned, accompanied by two orderlies wheeling a gurney. "We're admitting Ms. Westbrook," she said, gently but firmly, addressing Loretta and Emma. "You can see her again as soon as she's settled in her room."

"Admitting her?" Emma croaked.

Loretta put an arm around her, led her away. "For observation," I heard her say.

I was taken to a private room, given a shot of something that knocked me out almost instantly.

When I opened my eyes, a strange woman was standing over me, frowning.

"Who are you?" I asked.

"Leanne Reece," she said, still frowning. She was looking me over, assessing me, in an odd way. Taking my measure. From her expression, I'd say I didn't quite add up in her mind.

Leanne Reece, I thought. Sonterra's one-woman fan club.

"Because of you," she went on. "It happened because of you."

I tried to sit up. Did they let just anybody wander in and out of hospital rooms? Out of the corner of my eye, I spotted a bouquet of flowers on the bedside table—and the centerpiece was a doll.

"Did you bring that?" I demanded.

She tracked my gaze, shook her head. "You need to get out of Tony's life," she said. "You almost got him killed."

A nurse bustled in. "I'm sorry," she told Leanne. "No visitors."

Leanne shrugged away when the angel of mercy tried to take her arm and escort her to the door. "I'm going," she said, and blew out like a gust of steam.

"Who brought those flowers?" I asked the nurse, using the little remote I found at my side to raise myself into a semi-upright position.

The nurse blinked. "I don't know," she said. She smiled. "They're pretty, though."

My brain was still in overdrive, careening from one concrete wall to another. "Tony Sonterra," I said. "He was brought in with a gunshot wound. How is he?"

She was up on that much. "He's critical."

"I want to talk to his doctor." I was startled when I heard those calm words come out of my mouth. I would have sworn I screamed them.

She patted my hand. "In a little while," she promised.

In a sudden burst of frustration and grief, I reached out, swept the floral arrangement off the table, watched with stubborn satisfaction as it shattered on the floor.

The nurse looked puzzled, then compassionate. "Try to relax, Ms. Westbrook," she said, bending to gather fragments and blossoms. "This kind of stress isn't good for the baby."

I subsided a little. I hadn't wanted or planned this pregnancy, but the child was mine, and Sonterra's, and I would do anything to protect it. I laid my hands to my abdomen in an unspoken covenant.

"Your niece and your friend are outside," the nurse said. "Would you like them to come in?"

"Yes," I said, wondering how and when to tell Emma about the baby. I might never get the chance to tell Sonterra.

"Kip was here," Emma said, the moment she and Loretta entered the room. "I gave him my key. He's going to pick up Waldo and Bernice from Tony's place and take them home."

Unconsciously, I'd been worried about

the dogs; I knew that by the little rush of relief I felt. Kip, Loretta's husband, to the rescue.

I searched Loretta's face, silently asking if
she'd told Emma about my pregnancy. In
that weird way of best friends, she read my
thoughts and shook her head.

"Why are they keeping you here if you're
not sick?" Emma wanted to know. She was
looking down at the debris of the flower
arrangement; apparently, the nurse hadn't
picked up all the pieces.

"What's this?" she asked, before I could
answer. She bent, came up with the doll.
Her face darkened.

Nurse Helpful had vanished, only to return, too late, with a broom and dustpan.

"That *bastard*," Emma said, when I didn't
explain. "How did he know you were here?"

"Police scanner, probably," Loretta put in.

Just then, an older version of Sonterra
appeared in the doorway. The man was
graying at the temples, but he had the same
dark hair, brown eyes, and powerful build. If
Sonterra lived, he would look very much like
this someday.

"Hello, Clare," the visitor said, hesitating
on the threshold.

"Come in," I told him.

Emma stood aside, and Sonterra's father came to stand beside my bed. He bent to kiss my forehead.

"The police told me what happened," he said. "Are you all right?"

"I'm fine. How is Tony?"

He smiled, but his eyes glittered with a thin film of tears. "He is strong, my Antonio. With all his aunts praying for him, he has no choice but to survive."

"I'm so sorry." I heard Leanne Reece's voice echoing in my mind, saw her face, contorted with rage. *Because of you. This happened because of you.*

Mr. Sonterra touched my face with the backs of his work-worn fingers. He was a man who had worked with his hands for most of his life, building the landscape business now run by his eldest son. "Clare," he said, evidently seeing something in my face. "Be careful not to blame yourself. Tonio, he is a policeman. It is dangerous work. He knew that when he took the job."

I wanted to tell him about the baby, about his grandchild, but it wasn't the time. He was keeping a vigil for his son.

"Ryan—" I began, thinking of Sonterra's stepson.

"He will be told," Mr. Sonterra soothed.

"Have you seen him? Tony, I mean?"

"Yes. He is unconscious, Clare. But he is *alive*. He is holding on, and we must hold on, too."

We. I have never been so grateful for a single word.

"I have to go," Mr. Sonterra said. "You rest. Stay strong. That is the best thing you can do for Tonio right now."

I nodded, unable to speak.

He left. When I could see past the tears again, I noticed that Loretta was clutching the doll in both hands. As if she wanted to strangle it.

"I'm telling the police about this—this *thing*," she said.

"Damn straight," Emma agreed staunchly.

I closed my eyes, and was instantly sucked down into the deepest shadows of my soul, where the monsters lived.

FORTY

Next thing I knew, it was morning. With the help of another nurse, I took a very hot shower, scrubbing off the last of Sonterra's blood. Loretta and Emma were waiting when I came out of the bathroom, my freshly scoured body wrapped in a hospital robe.

"We brought your stuff," Emma said, holding up a small carry-on bag. "They're letting you out."

"How is Sonterra?" I asked. The question of that hour and many, many hours to come.

"Holding his own," Loretta said carefully.

"I want to see him."

"Me, too," Emma added.

They helped me into my clothes; I seemed to be all thumbs.

I checked out at the nurses' station, and was given instructions to rest and see my personal physician right away. Nobody mentioned the pregnancy, for which I was grateful. I would tell Emma in good time, but Sonterra should hear about the child first.

I didn't ask permission to visit the patient. I knew he was in the Intensive Care Unit.

I took the elevator up three floors, accompanied by Loretta and Emma.

Mr. Sonterra was in the waiting room, looking haggard, and his wife, Alberta, Tony's stepmother, was there, too. Evidently, the rest of the family was occupied elsewhere.

"I have to see him," I said.

"Yes," Mr. Sonterra agreed. He took my elbow and squired me to the appropriate desk.

I was in.

Leaving Loretta and Emma behind, I stepped into Sonterra's room. It was a place of cables, wires, and bleeping machines. He was at the center of all that, pale as death, his eyes closed. A ventilator forced rhythmic puffs of air in and out of his lungs.

I made my way to his bedside. Touched his face.

I'd seen a lot of bedside speeches on television, and read about them in books, but the reality of being there, watching Sonterra struggle to stay alive, tied my tongue into knots. Tears blurred my vision. I bent and kissed him softly on the top of his head.

One of his hands was free of tubes. I took it, pressed it gently against my abdomen, where our baby nestled.

He didn't stir.

I stayed with him until a nurse came in. Five minutes was the limit.

Loretta and Emma were waiting outside, and I tried to speak, but couldn't. Simultaneously, they each took one of my arms. Nobody said anything; there were no words anyway. For me, it was enough that they were there, taking me in, holding me up.

Loretta drove Emma and me back to her house. We were halfway there before I found my voice.

"Mrs. Rawlings—?"

"She's alive, Clare," Loretta said. "The police are looking for her daughter and the little girl."

I leaned my head back and closed my eyes. *Shanda, Maya,* I pleaded silently. *Where are you?*

I was settled into Loretta's guest suite, with her and Emma in almost constant attendance, when McCullough and Robbins showed up. Eddie Columbia brought up the rear.

"It's okay," I said, when Loretta hovered.

She took Emma and half-dragged her out of the room, closing the door, shutting me in with my welcome inquisitors.

McCullough drew up a chair, next to my bed, while Eddie loomed on the other side, watchful and protective. In this context, he was the next best thing to Sonterra, and I was glad of his presence.

"From the first, Ms. Westbrook," McCullough said, pen and pad in hand. "Exactly what happened yesterday?"

I started at the top, and told him everything I remembered.

"We haven't found Miss Rawlings and her daughter," McCullough told me, when I'd finished. "Father Michael Dennehy is still missing, too. I'd be lying to you if I said we didn't suspect foul play."

I closed my eyes. *No*, I thought, but I knew there was a chance—a good one— that Sanchez had killed them all, maybe the same way he'd killed poor Angela Kerrigan.

At best, they were stashed somewhere, maybe injured, maybe bound and gagged, and certainly terrified. Why he'd kept Mrs. Rawlings alive was anybody's guess— maybe he simply hadn't had time to murder her before Sonterra and I showed up.

Eddie cleared his throat. "Loretta says you got a flower arrangement in the hospital, Clare. With a doll inside."

I opened my eyes. Nodded. "Like yours," I said.

McCullough and Robbins tracked the conversation. They were up to speed on the doll man's activities, but I could see they hadn't heard about the latest episode.

"Not Diego Sanchez," Eddie reflected. With his partner in critical condition from a gunshot wound, he could be forgiven for saying what all of us already knew.

McCullough rose from his chair, and Robbins followed suit.

"Back to the battle," McCullough said, with wry resignation. He squeezed out a smile. "You take care, Ms. Westbrook."

I merely nodded. Just then, I was keeping my head above water. It was all I could manage.

"Am I in trouble for shooting Sanchez?" I

asked at length and as an afterthought. It wasn't the first time I'd shot a man to death, and they certainly knew that.

"In my opinion," McCullough answered gruffly, "you should be given a citation."

I felt only moderately better when he and Robbins left.

Eddie took the chair McCullough had just left. "Are you really okay?" he asked.

I took a moment to swallow a throatful of painful tears. "As 'okay' as can be expected," I said. "Have you seen Tony?"

Eddie nodded. "I looked in on him a little while ago." He smiled sadly. "His aunts are gathered in the waiting room, burning candles and saying prayers."

"I hope God is listening," I replied.

"Me, too," Eddie said. He took my hand, squeezed it, and then left me alone with my thoughts—which were not very good company.

FORTY-ONE

I woke up early the next morning, before the sun had risen, with a sort of grim energy running through my veins. I showered, dressed, and put on jeans and a T-shirt from an armload of stuff Loretta and Emma had retrieved from Sonterra's.

Emma was still asleep when I looked in on her. Waldo and Bernice, standing guard, raised their heads curiously at my entrance. I would have to trust Loretta and Kip to look after them all.

I put a finger to my lips and backed out.

No sign of Loretta or Kip in the main part of the house, and Rosa, the maid, hadn't come to work yet.

I got my purse and my freshly charged cell phone—my .38 was still in police cus-

tody, because of the Sanchez shooting—
and crept out of the house. Loretta's Lexus
gleamed in the driveway, but I draw the line
at grand theft auto. I called a cab from the
curb and paced while I waited.

Twenty minutes passed, by my watch,
before the taxi appeared.

I climbed into the back and told the driver
to take me to the hospital where both
Sonterra and Mrs. Rawlings were patients.

Sonterra's condition was unchanged. He
was still alive, though, and that, for the moment, was good enough. I spent the allowed five minutes at his bedside, willing
him to recover, greeted his devoted aunts,
who were keeping watch in the waiting
room, and went in search of Shanda's
mother.

She was sitting up in bed, staring at the
opposite wall, paying no mind to the muted
TV, where a newscaster mouthed some
fast-breaking story.

"Hello, Mrs. Rawlings," I said quietly, from
the doorway, not wanting to startle her.

She turned her head. "Clare," she said. I
couldn't make out her expression, since the
room was still partly in shadow and her bed-

side lamp was off. She stretched out a hand. "Come in."

I made my way to her side. "How are you?"

"Worried half out of my mind," she said. "How are you?"

"About the same." I let go of her hand long enough to pull up a chair. Then we locked fingers again, our palms pressed together.

"I know the police have probably hammered you with questions," I said, "but—"

A tear slipped down her cheek. She wiped it away with the back of one hand. "Your friend, the policeman. Is he all right?"

"He's still with us," I said.

"That monster, Sanchez," she whispered. "He's hurt my babies. I know he has. My babies, and so many other people. May he sizzle in hell!"

"What was he doing at your apartment, Mrs. Rawlings?"

She sniffled. "I wanted to be there, in case Shanda and the baby came back. He—Diego—must have followed me."

"You didn't see Shanda and Maya, then? Before that, I mean?"

She shook her head. "I went to stay with

a friend. Father Mike was going to take Shanda and Maya to some shelter, or that was what I thought. Then he disappeared, too."

"Have you heard from her since then?"

"Not a word." She turned an imploring gaze on me. "She'd come to me, if she could. It's been on the news, what happened. She'd come."

I bit my lower lip. Nodded reluctantly.

"Or she would have called you. But she hasn't, has she?"

I had been checking my messages regularly. Nothing from Shanda.

"No," I admitted.

"You've got to find her," Mrs. Rawlings said. "If she's alive, she needs help."

"The police—"

"The police," Mrs. Rawlings scoffed. "You and I both know they're getting nowhere."

The truth was, I'd already made up my mind to find Shanda. I knew what Sonterra would say, if he was conscious. I knew what Loretta would say, too, and Eddie Columbia. Hell, I even knew what *I* would say, if all this was happening to somebody else.

I had a broken right arm. I was pregnant.

I had no business taking the law into my own hands. But there are times when expediency has to come before prudence.

"I'll find her, Mrs. Rawlings," I said, having no idea how I would go about doing so.

"Thank you," she replied, and broke down.

I kissed her moist cheek and left the room.

Once I was outside the hospital, I summoned another cab. I was at my office within ten minutes. The place was quiet and, as far as I could tell, undisturbed.

My cell phone rang.

With a sigh, I answered.

"Where the hell are you?" Loretta erupted. "Emma's frantic!"

"On a mission," I replied. Now that I'd made up my mind to take action, I was more sanguine.

"Clare Westbrook," my best friend sputtered, "you get back here, right this minute!"

I smiled. Except for Sonterra's complete recovery, there was nothing I wanted more than to be back at Loretta's, with her and Emma and the dogs. But I had some things to do first.

"Keep an eye on Emma," I said. "She might bolt if she gets the chance."

"Clare, will you listen to reason for once in your life? You've got that baby to think about!"

"Trust me, I'm thinking about the baby."

"Then come back here. Now."

"I've got to find Shanda and *her* baby."

"You think you can do what the police haven't been able to manage?"

"I've got to try." I would start by checking the messages on the office voice mail, in case Shanda had tried to get in touch with me there. Under duress, she might not have remembered my cell number. If she'd called Sonterra's, she would have gotten voice mail, and I had neglected to ask him for the code.

I had neglected to ask him so many things.

"You're at your office, aren't you? I'm coming down—"

"Stay with Emma," I said. "Keeping her safe is priority number one."

"Who's going to keep *you* safe?"

"I am," I answered. "And don't try to get here, Loretta, because I'll be gone before you're out of your driveway."

With that, I hung up.

There were several messages on the office voice mail, mostly from concerned clients, David Valardi among them. I endured them all, waiting, praying for a lead. A place to start the search for Shanda and Maya.

The fifth caller made me stand up straight and catch my breath.

"Clare, this is Father Mike. It's imperative that I speak with you. Please call me at this number."

I scrambled to write it down, momentarily forgetting the "dial eight-eight to return this call" option. With the mechanical operator's coaching, I pressed the appropriate key twice and waited with my heart jammed into my throat. One ring, two. No answer. After seven, I disconnected in frustration.

The bell over the office door jingled, and Dr. Thomlinson stepped over the threshold.

"I thought I saw you come in," he said.

I was in no mood for a neighborly chat. Urgency sang through my veins. I thought I could hear the clock on the office wall marking the swift passage of Shanda's life, as well as Sonterra's, tick by tock.

"What do you want?" I asked impatiently,

jerking open the desk drawer and rummaging for the keys to my Escalade, which was still parked behind the office. Or, at least, I hoped it was. In that neighborhood, anything could have happened.

"I just had a call from Father Michael Dennehy," Thomlinson said, sounding mystified. "We're associated through the halfway house, you know. He asked me to bring you to him. He's with the girl and the baby."

My mouth dropped open. "Just give me the address," I said.

He smiled gently. "You're in no condition to drive," he scolded.

My knees were weak, and my heart was racing. So much for serenity born of decision.

For a smart woman, I can be such a sucker.

FORTY-TWO

Dr. Thomlinson's Cadillac was parked behind the storefront, within a few feet of my Escalade. I had second thoughts, that spiky feeling in the pit of my stomach again, and started toward my own vehicle.

Thomlinson caught hold of my elbow, just above the cast. "I can't allow you to drive," he said soothingly. "You would be a hazard to yourself and others."

He was a doctor. What he said made sense. Still, I hesitated.

He tugged me in the direction of his Cadillac, unlocked the doors with the remote on his key chain.

I allowed myself to be settled solicitously in the car. At least I fastened my own seat belt.

He rounded the car, got behind the wheel, and immediately locked the doors again. I had a sudden and violent urge to wrench open the door, but managing that and the seat belt with one hand was far beyond my present abilities.

"Why would Father Mike call you?" I asked.

"Because he couldn't reach you," Dr. Thomlinson replied. "He left a message at your office and you didn't call him back."

That was true. I'd just heard that message, and according to the robot operator's voice, it had been left around the time Sonterra was shot. I'd been a little busy since then.

"I didn't know you were acquainted with him."

"The social services community is a small one, Clare."

We were pulling out of the alley, onto a side street. Cars and SUVs whipped past, traveling in both directions. So many people around, and all of them isolated from each other, locked in their little metal boxes, oblivious.

I shifted uneasily. One-armed, a threat to myself and society or not, I longed to be in my own car, at the controls. I put that down to private neurosis. "Where are they? Shanda and the baby and Father Mike, I mean?"

"In a safe place," Thomlinson said. He didn't look at me. "Don't worry, I'll take you there."

"I think we should call the police," I said. I reached for my purse, lying on the floorboard at my feet.

Dr. Thomlinson got hold of it first, and tossed it into the backseat with a wild swing of his arm.

That was when I knew for sure that I was in trouble. Again.

"We won't need the police," he said.

At last, my visceral doubts solidified into genuine alarm. "Stop this car and let me out! Now!"

He favored me with a benevolent smile. "You must know I can't do that. Things have gone too far." He paused, squinting a little, savoring some thought. "Open the glove compartment, Clare. There's a gift inside."

I would sooner have opened a box of snakes.

Thomlinson leaned over, pushed the button, and revealed the contents, maps, registration slip, the usual glove compartment stuff, but none of that mattered.

It was the doll he wanted me to see. One of those eleven-inch jobs, with no clothes and a blindfold fashioned of rubber bands. I flung it away as if it were on fire.

"You," I breathed, and twisted to try the door handle again, jerking at it frantically, and to no purpose at all. He'd engaged the car's child-lock system. *He* controlled the buttons—and my destiny.

"Don't make me hurt you, Clare," he crooned.

I waved wildly at the old man in the Chevy truck rolling alongside us. He smiled and waved back. No help from that sector.

"Why? Why the dolls, and the killing? Why?"

He didn't answer. His knuckles were white where they gripped the steering wheel. I thought fleetingly of Peter Bailey's very first visit to my office, and realized he'd been trying, in his convoluted, schizoid way, to warn me. *About his doctor.*

"You don't know where Shanda and Father Mike are, do you?" I rasped. In a strange sort of way, I was relieved. "It was just a trick to get me into your car."

Duh, said the voice of my deeper mind.

"Maybe I do," he said. "And maybe I don't."

It has something to do with your boyfriend, I heard Bailey say.

"This isn't about me at all," I said. "It's about Sonterra!"

Thomlinson's profile hardened, and he grasped the wheel even more tightly. He clearly wanted to crush something. I hoped it wouldn't be my windpipe.

"How did Peter know about your fixation with dolls?"

"It's not a fixation," Thomlinson said indignantly. "My mother collected them. They're all I have left of her."

I drew deep, slow breaths, trying to clear my head. "Okay," I said carefully. "How did he know about the collection?"

"We had sessions at my house. Role-playing is used in therapy, Clare."

"You killed Melanie Witherspoon—and Jack, too. Why?"

He smiled, apparently reminiscing. "Jack was a colleague of mine, did you know that?"

Careful, Clare, I thought. *Don't push too far, or too fast.* "No," I said. "I didn't."

He sighed. "It was careless of me, going there. I assumed, you see, that you and the Witherspoons were closer than you were. I thought they knew about the dolls you'd been receiving, and I wanted so badly to know what your reaction was. I tried to present the question artfully, but I could tell they were suspicious, and I'd started them thinking just by bringing up your name. I knew I had to get rid of them, before they had a chance to talk to you. I went for Melanie first. Jack tried to stop me, of course, but with his bad heart, he was no match for me. I subdued him easily. Melanie nearly escaped, but I caught her. I dragged her into the bedroom. I decided then and there that she would make a good object lesson to you, so I killed her, and took a photograph with my new cell phone. Isn't technology wonderful?"

We were already leaving the city limits, traveling down a badly paved suburban road in the old part of Phoenix, lined on either side by towering palm trees. I tried the door again.

"What does any of this have to do with Tony Sonterra?"

The bottom of the Caddy hit a rut, and a

great, metallic shudder went through the car. Instinctively, I laid a hand to my abdomen. To my baby.

"He broke her heart." The words were spoken with quiet, despondent hatred. "It only seemed right to break his. But I wanted him to suffer a while first."

I frowned. "Whose heart?"

"My sister's," Thomlinson said. "Leanne has been through so much. When her twin died, she counted on *Detective* Sonterra to get at the truth, see that justice was served. She fell in love with him. Gave him her heart. He threw it back in her face—because of you."

Leanne. I'd ascribed my uneasiness about her to my own insecurities about men in general and Sonterra in particular. But not even my paranoia could have brought me to connect her to the doll man.

"Her twin," I reflected, at last making the mental shift from panic to laser-focused thinking. "Her brother. But wasn't he your brother, too?"

"Leanne is my stepsister. And Lance was a bad seed. A demon. He deserved to die."

Another revelation. "You killed him, didn't you?"

"I *released* him. There's a difference, Clare."

We rounded a bend, and a large stucco house came into view, well kept and yet somehow derelict, as if it were rotting from within. There were palm and cottonwood trees on all sides, crowding in. Instead of generating oxygen, they seemed to suck it in.

"Why Eddie Columbia? Why did you go after him?"

"He was Detective Sonterra's partner. His best friend. Reason enough to wipe him out." Thomlinson put on the brakes, shifted into park, shut off the engine, and flipped the lock switch. "Get out of the car," he said.

No problem there. I unsnapped my seat belt, opened the door, and hit the ground running.

I almost made it to the trees before Thomlinson caught up to me, struck me hard in the back of the head. Darkness closed in from all sides, and I dropped to my knees, then my face.

I woke up in what appeared to be a wine cellar, my hands bound behind my back with duct tape. I was lying face-to-face with another woman. I wasn't the only captive, then.

I waited for my vision to clear a little, studied my companion more closely. Dark hair, caked with blood. Scared brown eyes.

Oh, Christ. I must be hallucinating! I was looking at myself.

The other Clare was bound, too. Her lips moved, but no sound came out.

I blinked, and when I opened my eyes again, she was gone.

It was the blow to the head, I assured myself. *You are NOT going crazy, Clare. You don't have time for luxuries like that.*

Undiluted agony ignited in my right arm as I regained full consciousness, and I was acutely aware of my baby. My child and Sonterra's. I had countless reasons for wanting to live, but just then, a tiny fetus was my whole focus. The will to survive surged through me, primitive and all-powerful. I struggled against my bonds, but it was useless.

A door creaked open, and a shadow fell over me.

"I want to show you something," Thomlinson said, and, reaching down to grasp my left arm, he jerked me to my feet.

My head spun. "You're insane," I said. Perhaps not the best choice of words, but they were out of my mouth before I could weigh them.

In reply he thrust me toward a set of narrow steps. Light spilled from the doorway at the top, and I instinctively gravitated to it.

The cellar door opened onto a hallway, which led into a great room of some kind. I have never seen so many dolls—the walls were lined with them, on floor-to-ceiling shelves. They stared at us from every surface—the long mantelpiece, the tabletops, even the floor. They were a silent, breathless mob, waiting to witness another death.

It wasn't the dolls he wanted me to see, as it turned out.

Shanda sat wide-eyed in a chair near the fireplace, Maya in her lap, and the priest lay unconscious on the floor. At least, I hoped to God he was unconscious, and not dead. There was blood congealing on his scalp, staining his white, wispy hair.

"Clare," Shanda said. "Oh, Clare."

I looked at Thomlinson. "Untie my hands, you freaking maniac," I said. Diplomacy tends to desert me in situations like that.

Unfortunately, I've been in enough of them to notice a pattern.

The doctor shrugged. "They're not much good anyway," he said, "with one of them in a cast." I think he took pleasure in ripping that duct tape off—he made it hurt, and I couldn't help wincing.

Maya started to cry.

"It's okay, baby," Shanda said, bouncing her a little. In all that time, she hadn't taken her eyes off me. I saw the plea there, hopeless but determined.

I scanned the room for a weapon. No guns, no knives. Reassuring, in a way. Very bad news in another.

I crouched beside Father Mike, felt for a pulse. It was strong—so strong that I dared hope he might be playing possum. "What did you hit him with?"

"The fireplace poker," Thomlinson said mildly. His expression turned disapproving as he looked down at the priest. "I've always admired him, but it turns out he's evil."

"In what way?" I asked. I was stalling. The aforementioned fireplace poker would do as well as anything—except my vanished .38, which I longed for with a poignant and useless intensity—and I prepared myself to ease toward it.

"He tried to overcome me. Imagine it. A man of the cloth—turning to violence." Thomlinson sounded genuinely disenchanted. Apparently, the inherent contradictions eluded him. Or perhaps he simply felt that his own savage behavior had been justified, forced upon him by the unruly nature of others.

"Imagine," I said, getting to my feet. I took half a step toward the hearth, pretending an interest in the dolls lining the mantel. "If only people were like dolls," I mused. "They would stay where you put them, and never give you any back talk."

"Get away from that fireplace," Thomlinson said.

I stepped back as casually as I could, trying to look surprised. Even innocent.

"You think you understand me, don't you?" The doctor picked up a ballerina doll from a tabletop—he was perhaps six feet from me at that point—and touched its tiny pink satin dancing shoes. "You think you're so smart."

Just then, the huge double doors opened

on the other side of the room, and there was Leanne.

"Thurgood," she said, gazing at her brother, "this has gone far enough. It's over."

"*Thurgood?*" I echoed.

Thomlinson flushed. "What are you doing here?"

I bit my lip. Out of the corner of my eye, I saw Shanda shift Maya off her lap, shunt her around back of the chair. Father Mike didn't stir.

"Listen to your sister, Thurgood," I said. "You're in over your head. The game's up."

"For you, it is," Thurgood said. "Get out of here, Leanne. I don't want you to see this."

"See what?" Leanne demanded, striding into the room. "You're not going to hurt these people, especially the child." Her gaze fell on Father Mike. "What the *hell* is going on?"

"I'll kill you too if I have to," Thomlinson warned, with a note of regret. He pulled a pistol out of his jacket, to show he was in earnest, and pointed it directly at Leanne.

That was the moment Father Mike chose to act. He leaped to his feet, with surprising agility given that he was overweight and well into his sixties, grabbed the fireplace poker, and flung it in my direction.

"Catch!" he yelled.

The poker bounced off my cast and clattered to the floor.

When I bent to pick it up, a bullet ripped through the space my torso had just occupied, and pinged off the far wall.

I grasped the poker and came up swinging.

Leanne screamed.

The poker struck Thurgood Thomlinson across the mouth with a sickening thud, and the gun went off again as he dropped heavily to his knees, tearing a chunk out of the floor.

Shanda grabbed the pistol out of his hand, then held it gingerly, but with deadly aim.

"I ought to blow your brains out," she informed him. "But I won't because it wouldn't be good for Pretty Baby."

Father Mike took the gun from Shanda as Thomlinson—and three or four of his teeth—fell forward onto the expensive Oriental rug.

Leanne came at me in a rage. "Look what you've done to him!"

I turned to face her. I still had the poker in my left hand, and though my palm was slippery with sweat, there was nothing wrong with my grip. "Stop right there," I said fiercely. I had Sonterra's child inside me, my child. I would have killed Leanne Reece or anyone else to protect it.

She froze.

"A phone," Father Mike fretted, moving the pistol from hand to hand. "*Where* is the phone?"

Leanne stood her ground for a few moments, then dropped into a chair and put her head in her hands. I wondered how much she'd known about her brother's activities. If she'd been a part of them. She'd seemed surprised and, on the other hand, *not* surprised.

The police could decide.

"Give me the gun," I said to Father Mike. "I'll keep track of Thomlinson while you find the telephone."

He handed it over, with some reluctance. Patted Shanda on the shoulder. Left the room. Little Maya, perhaps the wisest of us all, stayed behind the chair.

I kicked the twisted strands of duct tape

that had bound my own hands toward Shanda. "Tie him up," I said.

Shaking, she complied. "My mama—I heard on the news—"

"She's all right, Shanda. And she'll be a lot *more* all right when she sees you and Maya are okay."

Thomlinson groaned, tried to turn over. Shanda planted a streetwise knee in the small of his back.

"Don't you even *think* about it, you dirt-bag," she growled, and tightened the tape around his wrists.

Shanda was a good assistant. I hoped I wouldn't lose her to a career in law enforce-ment; she showed a definite propensity for subduing the suspect.

"Don't hurt him," Leanne begged.

"Give me a break," Shanda replied.

Father Mike returned. "The police are on their way," he told us.

Leanne put her face back in her hands.

We all waited, listening for sirens. But even the police aren't *that* fast.

"How long have you been here?" I asked Shanda. She was still on the floor, keeping Thomlinson pinned with her knee.

"Days," Shanda said. "I took Maya and

beat feet for the church, looking for Father Mike, after Diego came at me. The scumsucker here happened to be at St. Sebastian's, making confession, if you can believe it. He said he'd drive us to the halfway house, that he had business there anyhow. Instead, he brought us here."

"Did you try to get away?"

"He knocked Father Mike around with the butt of a pistol," Shanda told me. "And I had Pretty Baby to think about. I did what I was told."

I nodded. Under the circumstances, she'd made the only possible decision.

Indirectly, Thomlinson was responsible for what had happened to Sonterra. I resisted an urge to kick him hard in the ribs.

"What about you?" I asked Leanne. I was going to wait for the police to clear up that part, but they were taking too long. "Did you know what he was up to?"

She looked up, her face bloodless. Her eyes were haunted. "No," she whispered.

Maybe madness ran in the family, I thought. Her brother was certainly a candidate for a rubber room, and their mother must have been a few bricks short of a patio, too, gathering this army of dolls around her.

I believed her, as far as the abduction was concerned, anyway. It wasn't intuition; it was the fact that she'd seemed disturbed to find us all there. Father Mike, lying face-down on the floor, had been a major clue that all was not well.

I wasn't surprised when Atienzo and Culver were the first officers on the scene, closely followed by McCullough and Robbins and a slew of EMTs.

"Are you guys assigned to me or something?" I asked, when Father Mike led them into the great room.

Nobody answered my question.

Culver actually smiled a little when he spotted Shanda holding Thomlinson down. "We'll take it from here," he told her. Atienzo took the gun from my hand and handed it to a crime scene technician.

Thomlinson had regained consciousness, at least partially. Culver and Atienzo hoisted him to his feet.

"The doll man, I presume," McCullough said, taking in the hundreds of silent witnesses lining the walls.

"That's him, all right," I replied. I paused.

In the excitement of staying alive, I'd almost forgotten about someone else who was fighting the same battle. "Any word about Sonterra?"

McCullough smiled a little. "In and out of consciousness," he said. "Off the respirator. They're moving him to a private room. Good thing he doesn't know what you've been up to—he'd probably lapse back into a coma."

I had been so strong in the crunch. Now, I felt like folding up, though this time, it was from relief.

"You can put down that poker now," Robbins told me, watching as an EMT gathered up Thomlinson's scattered teeth.

I had forgotten the weapon; now, I realized my fingers were locked around it. My knuckles ached. I dropped the poker.

"You know," McCullough observed, "if you ever get tired of chasing ambulances, you'd make a halfway decent cop."

"Thanks," I said, because I knew it was a compliment, and probably the only one I would ever get from Mr. Hard-boiled Detective.

"Who's that?" Atienzo asked, gesturing toward Leanne, who was still sitting on the edge of her chair, staring numbly into space.

"Thomlinson's sister, Leanne Reece."

"Involved?" McCullough inquired, looking her over.

"I'm not sure," I said. The back of my head was starting to throb, where Thomlinson had struck me earlier, when I tried to run for the woods. I reached back, felt the wound, and winced.

"Take her in for questioning," McCullough said. "Even if she's clean, she might be able to give us some insight into the strange world of Dr. Death."

"Can we leave now?" I asked. "Shanda needs to see her mother, and I want to look in on Sonterra."

McCullough and Robbins consulted each other in undertones, and Robbins answered. "We'll call you a cab. Right now, we can't spare a squad car."

I could have kissed him. Leanne and Thurgood weren't the only ones with a pile of questions to wade through—Shanda, Father Mike, and I would all have our fair share. But we were being given a grace period to tie up loose ends.

Atienzo called for the cab, and it arrived within fifteen minutes.

Father Mike was seen in the emergency

room, while Shanda and I headed for the elevators. The back of my head was a mess, but any medical attention I needed would have to wait.

Only when the doors closed, and we were alone, except for Maya, did Shanda burst into tears. "Thank you for coming to find us, Clare," she said.

I touched her arm. "You know about Diego, don't you?" I asked cautiously. If she wasn't aware that I'd been the one to fire the shots that killed him, she had to be told. And her opinion of me could easily change.

Shanda nodded. "I'm so sorry he shot Detective Sonterra."

"Me, too," I said. "And I'm sorry it all came down the way it did, Shanda."

The elevator stopped on Mrs. Rawlings's floor, and Shanda, carrying Maya, stepped out. "I understand about what happened at the apartment, Clare," she said. "You had to do what you did. Diego would have gunned you down."

I couldn't speak. You never get over killing another human being, even one like Diego Sanchez.

Shanda turned and hurried away, eager to be reunited with her mother.

The doors whisked shut again, and I was on my way up to the Intensive Care Unit. It couldn't have taken more than twenty seconds, but it seemed more like a year. I was trying to prepare myself for the visit to Sonterra.

McCullough had said he was "in and out," and that he was being moved to a regular hospital room. I wondered how much to tell him, if indeed I found him awake.

That Dr. Thurgood Thomlinson was the doll man, and he was in police custody? Yes. That would ease Sonterra's mind considerably. In his cognizant moments, he was probably fretting about my being in danger.

The baby? I would play that one by ear.

I reached the proper floor, and the doors opened.

A woman was standing directly in front of me. She was wearing my clothes—and my face. Staring straight ahead, into the elevator, as though she had something heavy on her mind.

I shut my eyes, opened them again.

She was gone.

FORTY-THREE

I rubbed my forehead. I'd just seen myself, for the second time in the same morning. Maybe my head injury was serious after all. And maybe it was hormones, or the residual effects of stark terror.

I would think about it later. For now, Sonterra was all my brain had room to accommodate.

"Clare?"

Sonterra's father stood a few yards away, watching me closely. "What's happened to you? Is that blood in your hair?"

I had neither the strength nor the patience to explain. "Tell me about Tony," I babbled. "Is he really awake? Detective McCullough said—"

Mr. Sonterra came to my side, put an arm

around my waist, leaned back to inspect my head. "Yes, Clare—Tonio is awake. He is in a great deal of pain, but he will recover. That is the important thing."

"I need to see him."

"Yes," Mr. Sonterra said distractedly, "but first—this wound of yours—" He looked around, caught a nurse's eye, and called to her. "This young woman is injured," he said.

She took one look at me and rushed for a wheelchair.

I grasped Mr. Sonterra's warm hand. "Don't let them take me away before I see Tony," I pleaded. *"Please."*

Mr. Sonterra bent down to look into my face, and he spoke softly. "How do you think Tonio will feel if he sees you bleeding?" he asked reasonably.

I started to cry. He handed me a clean cotton hankie from the pocket of his khaki trousers.

"There, now," he said. "It will only be a little while. You don't want to upset him, do you?"

Sonterra was going to be plenty upset, once he found out about the things that had happened since he was shot. With luck, he would learn the truth in increments. Say, one piece every hundred years.

I shook my head, sniffling.

The nurse wheeled me back to the elevator. The emergency room was full, and McCullough and Robbins were there, waiting while a medical team gave Dr. Thomlinson a once-over. Leanne was nowhere in sight, nor was Father Mike.

At a word from McCullough, I was taken directly to an examining room.

I had to have X-rays, and then stitches. The hardest thing, though, was not jumping to my feet and running to find Sonterra. Every cell in my body was magnetized, and he was the positive pole.

"Have you had any unusual symptoms?" an intern asked, scribbling in my already voluminous chart.

I supposed he would regard seeing myself as unusual, but I wasn't about to broach that subject. I'd be in the psychiatric ward for who knew how long if I did.

"I'm really all right," I insisted. "May I go now?"

The intern sighed. "Yes," he said.

I swung my legs off the examining table and made a run for it.

FORTY-FOUR

I probably could have tracked Sonterra by the smoke from the candles his bevy of Catholic aunts were burning in the fifth floor waiting room, though McCullough had given me his new location downstairs, while I was jumping up and down beside the elevator.

Mr. Sonterra snagged me as I zoomed past.

"Here," he said, and handed me a baseball cap with the name of his landscaping service emblazoned on the front.

I was puzzled, not to mention impatient, and it took a few moments for his reasoning to penetrate my abused skull. He didn't want his son to get a glimpse of the line of stitches parting my hair.

I tugged on the cap. "Thanks," I said.

He smiled and gestured for me to get going.

I didn't need much urging.

Sonterra was sitting up in bed, his bare chest wrapped in bandages. He looked ghastly, pale and surly and very agitated. A nurse was trying to give him a bath.

When he saw me, something sparked in his dark eyes. The old fight. I never thought I'd say this, but I was glad to see it.

"Lying down on the job," I said.

The nurse looked at him, looked at me, set aside the basin and sponge, and left the room.

"Remind me not to follow up on any more of your leads, Counselor," Sonterra said, but he held out his hand.

I hurried to his bedside, and he pulled me close for a moment.

"The doll man is in custody," I said, after a few gulps of Sonterra-scented air. "It was Dr. Thomlinson, the shrink from the clinic next door to my office."

Sonterra held me away, but not far, and studied my face, frowning. "What's with the hat?"

"Bad hair day," I said.

He narrowed his eyes. "How did they find him?"

"McCullough and Robbins will fill you in on the details," I hedged, and, remarkably, he let me get away with it. Maybe he sensed the truth, but he hadn't been out of his coma all that long, after all, so I figured his noggin was still addled.

He pulled me close again, kissed the top of my baseball cap. My stitches stung. "Thank God," he said, in a raspy voice. "When I first came to, I figured Sanchez must have shot you, too. Jesus, that put a lot of things into perspective."

I let myself cling to him for a little while. I'd just faced death. I was entitled. "I'm okay," I said, and despite the stitches, the hallucinations, and everything else, it was true. I was standing on my own two feet, and I was breathing, and I had a secret tucked beneath my heart.

I ruined all this bravery by starting to cry.

"Hey," Sonterra protested huskily.

I drew back, looked at him. Wondered if I should tell him about the baby right then, or wait.

"What?" He frowned. "Sanchez didn't get away, did he?"

"He definitely didn't get away. I blew up his face with my .38."

"That's my girl," Sonterra said, and patted me where no other man would *dare* pat me. "You okay with that?"

I sighed. "Sort of."

He traced my jawline with the tip of an index finger. "It's done," he said. "Never look back, Babe."

I swallowed, nodded. "Know something?"

He waited.

"I love you," I said.

He grinned. "Call the doctor," he teased. "I'm hearing things."

"I'm serious," I said.

He kissed me. Considering that I'd wondered if I'd ever feel the touch of his mouth on mine again, it was an earthshaking experience. "I love you, too, Counselor," he replied.

"Does this mean you're not going to join the FBI?"

"Hell, no," he answered. "Are you going to give up your law practice?"

I laughed. "Hell, no," I shot back.

"Square one," he said, but his eyes were twinkling.

Someone cleared their throat. Both Sonterra and I looked toward the doorway.

McCullough and Robbins were just entering.

I glanced at my watch. "Look at the time," I said. "Gotta go."

Sonterra held on to my wrist when I would have split for the waiting room, where the clan was gathered. If the fire marshal hadn't run them off, that is.

"Your lady is quite the little hero," McCullough told Sonterra.

Sonterra's grip tightened. "Is that so?"

I tugged.

Sonterra held on.

"Oops," McCullough said, but he looked smug.

"Clare," Sonterra growled. "Look at me."

I looked. I didn't have a whole lot of choice, after all.

"What happened?"

I told him.

"Shit," Sonterra barked, when I was through. Then he pulled off the baseball cap and, taking hold of my chin, turned my head so he could see the stitches. " 'Bad hair day'?" he grumbled.

"The worst," I replied.

By degrees, he loosened his grasp on my arm.

"I'll be back later," I said, and split, giving McCullough a scalding glance as I passed.

Loretta and Emma were in the corridor when I stepped out of Sonterra's room. The door closed silently behind me.

I straightened my shoulders. "I'm not hurt," I insisted.

Emma flung herself into my arms, hanging on for dear life. I held on just as tightly.

"You're all over the news," Loretta said.

"Is Tony all right?" Emma wanted to know.

"Yes," I answered, kissing her forehead. "He's a little touchy right now, though."

And he loves me. He told me so.

I wasn't ready to share that part just yet.

"You actually captured the doll man?" Emma sniffled.

"Not single-handedly," I said. "I had help from Father Mike and Shanda."

"He was the one who kidnapped them?"

"Yes."

Loretta took my left arm and Emma's right, and marched us toward the elevators. "You can tell us in the car," she said.

"I need to talk to Sonterra first."

"That can wait," Loretta said.

I gave in.

When we got to Loretta's place, I zonked out and slept for fourteen hours.

Mrs. K was just coming out of Sonterra's room when I went back the next morning, with Loretta and Emma, who were now, it seemed, my constant companions.

"Rodney is a free man," Mrs. K informed me, with a beaming smile. "Off the hook."

Loretta and Emma went into Sonterra's room.

"That's good," I said.

My friend studied my face closely, and frowned.

"What's the trouble, Clare? Tony's going to be all right—you know that, don't you?"

I took her arm, pulled her aside. Here was a person I could tell about the other Clare. Someone who wouldn't immediately decide I was crazy.

At least, I *hoped* she wouldn't.

"Something happened, after I was hit on the head," I told her in a whisper.

Her frown deepened. "What?"

I searched my mind for words that would

make the experience sound a little less weird, and came up dry. It *was* weird—no getting around that. "I saw myself."

She tensed. "What do you mean, you saw yourself?"

"The first time, I was lying on the floor of Dr. Thomlinson's cellar. I *saw* myself. As if I was looking into a mirror. I was tied up. She was tied up. She—I—looked really scared."

"Understandable, given the circumstances," Mrs. K mused, but she seemed troubled. "You said 'the first time.' Did it happen again?"

I nodded. "Just as I was getting off the elevator yesterday, on my way to look in on Sonterra. I met myself."

Mrs. K put a hand to her mouth. At least it wasn't to my forehead.

She was pale. Thinking she might drop to the floor, I took her arm and escorted her to a chair in the waiting room, now void of Sonterras. Having achieved their purpose, the aunts had snuffed out their candles and gone home.

"Am I headed for the loony bin?" I pressed.

"You're the sanest person I know," Mrs. K

said, but she picked up an old copy of *Time* and fanned herself with it.

"But I *did* sustain a head wound."

"Has this ever happened before?"

I sifted back through my colorful history. Some of the mental files didn't open right away. "No," I said. I *had* glimpsed my late sister once, but that was a whole different situation.

She took my good hand, squeezed it. "This is going to sound really strange," she warned.

"I think we're already knee-deep in 'strange,' Mrs. K."

"In certain traditions, Clare, seeing yourself is a warning. The phenomenon is called 'autogenic hallucination.' It's usually related to migraines, but a stroke or a hard blow to the head can bring it on, too. And sometimes it just occurs spontaneously."

My heart sank. "Oh, crap. Now I'm going to start seeing things?"

"If it happens once," she paused, shrugged dismissively. "Twice, even, not necessarily a big deal. But three times—that would mean your subconscious mind was definitely trying to get your attention."

I was bewitched, bothered, and bewildered. "And that's a warning? What kind of warning?"

"That you are in very grave danger."

If anybody else said that to me, I would discount it, hands down, but I knew enough about Mrs. K's track record in spooky matters to take her seriously. "Not again," I groaned.

She smiled. "Don't worry, dear. I don't see your death happening in the near future. You just concentrate on loving Detective Sonterra, and carrying the baby of yours to term."

I narrowed my eyes. "Did Loretta tell you I'm pregnant?" I'd sworn my best friend to secrecy. If she'd been spreading the news before I had a chance to break it to Sonterra, and then Emma, I'd wring her neck.

Mrs. K's smile widened, and the light came back into her eyes. "Of course not," she said. "I saw it—a little golden light, nestled in your tummy."

I smiled back at her. "Of course you did," I said.

Mrs. K let go of my hand and got to her feet. "Well, I'd better be off. I'm dropping Rodney at the bus station—he's moving to

Tucson—and then I've got an assignment at a Chinese restaurant in Mesa. I've put on five pounds since I took this job."

I stood, too. "Rodney's leaving?"

"Now that his name's been cleared, he wants to start over. I don't mind telling you, it will be nice to live alone again."

Will wonders never cease? I would have thought getting rid of Rodney would require an exorcist. "Take care," I said, and kissed her on one powdery cheek.

She looked straight into my eyes, and her expression was serious again. "If you see yourself again, will you tell me?"

That much I could promise, because I wasn't going to have that experience again. It was connected to getting my brains scrambled, that's all.

"You'll be the first to know," I said.

She nodded, and left. I watched her until she disappeared behind the elevator doors.

When I stepped into Sonterra's room, he and Loretta and Emma were conferring about something.

"What's going on here?" I demanded, with mock suspicion. "I think I smell a plot."

Loretta and Emma grinned.

"Meet you downstairs," Loretta said.

Just like that, they were gone.

Sonterra crooked a finger. "Come over here," he said.

"If you're going to give me a hard time about getting involved in the doll man bust—" I warned, staying right where I was.

"It's not about that," Sonterra replied. He looked so innocent. I should have suspected something.

I moved to his bedside. "What?"

"I love you."

I grinned. "Yeah. You mentioned that."

"I know you, inside and out."

"You'd like to think so."

He pulled me onto the mattress, and I lay next to him. "You're keeping a secret," he said.

I sat up. "Did Loretta—?"

"Loretta has nothing to do with it. It's a look that comes into your eyes when you're up to something. Give, Counselor."

I turned to look into his face. "Okay, I'll tell you. We're going to have a baby."

He stared at me. A smile took shape in his eyes, made it to his mouth. He gave a low, throaty whoop of joy. "Yes!"

I was a little surprised. I was also delighted. "I wasn't sure how you'd take the news."

He kissed me. "I've had some time to think, being cooped up in this place," he said. "One thing about almost dying, it puts things in perspective."

We were quiet for a while. I don't know about him, but I was having a party inside my chest.

Finally, I broke the silence. "I want to know what you and Loretta and Emma were talking about when I came in."

He shifted, reached for something on the bedside stand, presented it to me. "This isn't the most romantic setting," he said.

It was a box. A small, black velvet box.

My breath caught in my throat.

"Sonterra—"

With a motion of his thumb, he raised the small lid. A diamond ring glittered inside. "It was my mother's," he said. "I had Dad bring it in."

I stared at the exquisite setting, speechless.

Sonterra gave me a nudge.

"Will you marry me, Counselor?"